JENNA
TAKES
THE
FALL

JENNA TAKES THE FALL

A NOVEL

BY

A. R. TAYLOR

SHE WRITES PRESS

Published 2020
Printed in the United States of America
ISBN: 978-1-63152-793-7
ISBN: 978-1-63152-794-4
Library of Congress Control Number: 2020903828

For information, address:
She Writes Press
1569 Solano Ave #546
Berkeley, CA 94707

She Writes Press is a division of SparkPoint Studio, LLC.

Book design by Stacey Aaronson

In memory of Joyce Engelson, so gifted, smart, and kind.
She knew everybody's secrets.

A Friday in Late August, Manhattan, 1999

I don't like being fifty, and I don't like thinking about death.
—HOWARD STERN, The Howard Stern Show,
WXRK radio, 1998

He should be shot with shit 'til he's dead and dirty.
—MARGARET GRACE MCCANN,
Jenna McCann's grandmother

PROLOGUE

Vincent Hull lay on the floor, his gray pants and white boxers around his knees, right arm splayed out in front of him. His left arm curled under his body, as if protecting his privates. Everything about him was obscene, especially the fleshy buttocks exposed to the air. Jenna pulled off her jacket and bent down to where he lay on the left side of his face. She could see only one eye, that one unblinking. His famously long, almost shoulder-length, white hair looked slightly damp, as the poor man stared straight ahead at eternity.

Jenna sank backwards down into a chair next to the leather couch. Rigor mortis—she'd heard of it, possibly seen it on television, but didn't really know what it entailed. Would he be stiff like that? Probably not yet. She looked at her watch; over an hour since Vincent Macklin Hull's publicity person, Tasha, had telephoned her. She loosened one button on her blouse, undoing another. Clean, she was altogether clean and, of course, stone cold sober. She picked up one of the heavy cocktail glasses, pouring herself a stiff shot of vodka, careful to leave her lipstick on the rim. For a moment, she and the dead man communed in a sort of silent prayer. She touched his back, she touched his head and smoothed his hair. He was cool under her touch. This awful change between the living, breathing man he had once been to this lifeless pile of bones on the floor, it was horrible, much worse than seeing her grandmother in repose. She didn't want to put herself beneath him, as had been her instructions. Why not just sit right here and tell her story to paramedics? Perhaps, though, that would raise even more questions, since what she was doing there would look suspicious. She poured herself another, shorter vodka shot and drank it quickly.

Beside the man now, she took off one of her shoes, then pulled the bottom of her blouse out from her waist, but she could put her task off no longer, as she knew time was part of her assignment. She tried to lift his arm, but it was too heavy and flopped back down again. Should she roll him over? Could she? He was maybe six foot four and at least two hundred pounds. For a moment, across her eyes flashed the many photos she had seen of him in life, at charity dinners, holding little children's hands, clasping the rich and the famous with a grin. How would this particular image play if it were made public? But presumably, only the authorities would see it, thank god. She shoved him a bit, but he lay still. Finally she got at his head, her two legs akimbo above it and began to slide herself down under him. It was difficult, and only as she managed to get him to about her knees did she see liquid dripping out of his mouth.

As she pulled him up, that spit trickled down onto her breast. She grimaced and looked away from the pale face that loomed above her and continued wriggling. Her instructions had been to get his DNA all over her. The fact that there would be no semen, at least not in her, didn't seem to be a problem as long as she smeared something else of his over her. But maybe there was—maybe he was still wet from his longings. He might have expired in the very act and then withdrawn. Horrible thought. Still, she continued to wriggle, legs wide apart now, skirt hiking up so that her thighs rubbed against the dead man's pants.

His head hung heavy and kept banging against her as she moved. She could smell, what? Liquor still on his breath, something metallic, and for a moment she thought she would gag.

But now she felt something else, his naked body. Though his arm and face were cold, he was hot still in the center, his penis against her leg, erect, heavy. Was this from just recent sex or from that thing called "angel lust," when men die violently and end up hard as a rock? She turned her head and retched onto the floor. Most of the vodka came up, and then she began to cry. What the hell was she doing? She should get up and have another few drinks, start over with all this, but she could go no further. She did not want to feel this fifty-nine-year old dead body any closer to her or deeper into her.

She snaked her arm back to grab the telephone off the coffee table and pulled it down to her side. With great difficulty she punched in 911, but then hung up immediately. She had to have a script, some speech in mind that would sound authentic, and it wasn't too hard to imagine what that might be. She decided to turn her face directly toward Hull and look into his eyes. They were still dark but fixed, a blank. Did they now look upon God or some nasty Hell? She began to cry, and then she howled and she screamed, amping up the hysteria, grabbing the phone again, wailing now in earnest. When the 911 operator answered, she shrieked into phone, "He's dead, he's dead! Help, come quickly! It must be a heart attack." When she had calmed down enough to give the address and the name of the dead party, the operator asked to have it repeated twice. "Yes, it's Vincent Hull. Come now!"

She shoved the phone away and lay quietly now underneath the man, his face so well known to her.

PART ONE

Early June, 1999

Even presidents have private lives. It is time to stop the pursuit of personal destruction and the prying into private lives and get on with our national life.

—WILLIAM JEFFERSON CLINTON, statement from the White House following his Grand Jury testimony, August, 1998

I want this room as shiny as two dogs' balls under a bed.

—MARGARET GRACE MCCANN

ONE

Vincent Macklin Hull had been having an affair for close to a year with someone he should not have been. This struck him vividly, and he had been trying to sort his way out of it. Up until now, most of his romantic involvements had been short-lived adventures that he kept hidden in the most compulsive, meticulous way. For the absurd scandals of his fellows, he felt only contempt, and ruining his life for a woman did not figure in his playbook at all. This latest involvement, however, actually demanded his attention; it was getting out of hand. He didn't know if he loved her or just occupied himself with overheated fantasy, but he spent more and more time with his mistress. Alas—time—there just wasn't enough of it, nor of space, either psychic or real. He wanted to craft it, to remold it to his liking, but time fought back at him and resisted.

About his wife, he felt not so much guilty as annoyed. In the past, Sabine Hull had ignored various lapses, swimming along as she did in their mutually prosperous sea. During their fifteen-year marriage, Vince had provided her with four homes, each crafted in a restrained but opulent way: the townhouse in Manhattan, a weekend house in Water Mill on Mecox Bay, their Hawaiian island getaway on Lanai, to which they rarely went, and a ranch in Jackson Hole, Wyoming, their "hunting lodge *nouveau*," as Sabine called it. Unfortunately, his current dalliance could prove expensive, and a huge cloud of absolute impossibility hovered over his head, as in not allowing himself to think about how bad things could get. Because of his age and wealth, he had counted on the benefactor role to smooth over any marital lapses on his part; he thought his wife would love him for all he'd given her, and she had for a time, but lately he had grown anxious. He could feel the molecules vibrating asymmetrically, as if a whole new world of energy pulled them apart.

Sabine came from a middle-class family with its roots in Villefranche on the Côte d'Azur, and when Vince Hull first met her sixteen years ago, she had been comely and funny. And younger, only twenty-seven at the time. In the early days, he had needed her, because he wanted to stonewall his own forty-three years. He had enjoyed her French coolness, her unflappable gentility, her European maturity, and with her swaggering bob of short dark hair, often in motion, she seemed always about to applaud some imaginary triumph; but now, at fifty-nine, he just felt older than the world. She too had changed.

Of late, she protested her treatment because Vincent didn't sleep with her much any more, and he was longer and longer away from whatever house she occupied. For him this posed problems, as he wanted to be near his two daughters, but he did not want to make love to his wife, and so between the time issue and the love issue came a blockage of a most confusing sort. About her he had moved from passion to clarity to tolerance, poised for anything that might slip out of her voluble French mouth. She talked. A lot. She loved to talk, she had a ball talking, as if she could consume the world with words, and Vincent finally decided the French needed three words for every English one. Inevitably he had retired to a listening attitude, not wanting to have to respond. In the larger scheme of things, and this he knew, Hull was the kind of man who would have been bored with an uncomplicated, unchallenging personal life. Vincent Macklin Hull came from a long line of seriously competent bastards. His celebrated grandfather Malcolm Erskine Hull, an engineer from Edinburgh, had discovered and worked copper mines in Chile, subsequently inventing several very useful drill bits, but in his spare time he cursed humans and kicked dogs. Vincent's father, Myron Hull, had grown the business to include an array of drilling companies, along with pipeline manufacturers, all the while acquiring pipeline rights across several other Latin American countries, and while the family empire continued to expand depending on the whims and character of these men, it came to include serious money losers in the United States, among them three tabloid newspapers, two radio stations, a publishing company of scientific journals, even an amusement park, all to give work to a host of dull-witted relatives.

The first family home was in Chicago, currently occupied by his 102-year-old aunt, along with five caregivers. His father, two uncles, and yet another aunt had long ago owned lavish residences in New York, the hub of the Hull empire. All dead now, they still whispered in his ear random curses in the night. In 1962 Vince's father announced to his beleaguered family, "I want to control the lines of talk, so I can control the national conversation," and that had led him first to acquire *NewsLink*, a rival then to *Time* and *Newsweek*, but with more gossip and bigger, more vivid photographs. In his later years, he bought into telecom, his single most spectacular bet, but he remained an uncouth, loutish roustabout, despite his many donations to the world of culture. He badgered Vince relentlessly and got drunk on Saturday nights, often raising a hand against both son and wife.

As an only child, Vince hid himself away when the family battles raged, then tried to enlist the help of neighbors. In the worst incident, his father tried to strangle his mother, at least that's how he heard it from the safety of his own bedroom. The twelve-year-old had opened the door to find his mother cowering on the floor, his father clasping her neck in one hand and holding a drink in the other. They had both stared up at him, momentarily lifted out of their battle, and he had backed out, terrified about what to do next. He had run to the kitchen, finding refuge in the broom closet.

Vincent was only too glad to see the mean old man go, and when he finally did "cark it," his son was grateful right down to his soul, if he had a soul, relieved at the vast fortune the man had passed down, though it was a legacy accompanied by harrowing burdens. All through his youth, Vince had had both great regard for himself and a fair amount of self-loathing, yet for the failings of others he had no tolerance whatsoever, and this bled into his relationships at work. Still, as his current life stood, he could indulge any and all of his feelings from behind the protective wall of inherited money, only emerging to talk to his two girls' schoolteachers or to his very sociable wife's friends. When he got too upset, he went to the gun range downtown on 20th Street, or he bought things.

On this day in early June, he wanted to get home quickly to check out a present he had just given himself, a very big present. Pausing for a moment outside his townhouse at the corner of Fifth Avenue and 71st Street, one of the largest single-family residences in Manhattan, he hoped to find no member of his family at home, only the help, wanting privacy with his purchase. Sure enough, as he entered the foyer—and what a foyer, of carved stone and marble, inconspicuous little television screens scanning the four levels of the house—there stood a Mark Rothko painting from a series done in 1969. It leaned against a table across from the carpeted winding staircase that led up to the living room, and, wrapped in plastic and masking tape, it had the homey aspect of an ordinary package.

Vince was tempted to snip the tape apart but then thought better of it. Instead, he sat down on the last step of the stairs and simply stared at it. Through the filmy covering he glimpsed the feathery black wash that bled down onto the turbid, much larger gray rectangle that lay beneath. One of a group of works that seemed to explore successive levels of despair, Rothko must have painted it with the calm, sure knowledge that peace would be upon him whenever he too merged into the darkness, as he did one year later when he committed suicide. Vince wanted to savor the complexities of the object and its maker before he could even think of getting the housekeeper to deal with the plastic, but he couldn't think very long because his eleven-year-old daughter burst through the front door, heaving her backpack onto a chair, grabbing her friend, as the two prepared to raid the kitchen.

"Daddy," Amelia cried and ran to kiss him. The friend hung back, intimidated by the house and the truly enormous object propped up on the floor. "What's that?" his daughter demanded.

"A new painting. Do you think you'll like it?"

"How should I know? I can't see it. Want us to pull off all that stuff around it?" The two girls giggled, then held hands, threatening to jump on it maybe, while Vincent still observed them from his seat on the steps.

"Absolutely not. It's a present I'm waiting to open."

"You're silly." She kissed him on the top of his head. "It's not Christmas."

"I want every day to be Christmas."

"It's summer. Can't you tell? I'm going to sleep-away camp or maybe France, so you have to unwrap it before I go."

"Of course I will." The girls scampered off, leaving a trail of noise and laughter. Vince could hear their chatter as the refrigerator door opened, and in that moment he felt comforted. Despite the contempt he felt for all the toadies and sycophants in his life, such feelings conflicted with his very real neediness. He told himself that he craved privacy, but actually he wanted to be surrounded with people. He needed noise, action, family, phone calls, plans, purchases—the works.

By dinnertime two maids and a house manager had unwrapped the painting, but still it remained lounging against the table in the foyer. When she came home, Sabine Hull stopped in her tracks to look at the thing, displayed in all its glory. The size and the opaque bleakness of it, at least to her way of thinking, had her stunned. It was dull, it was dark, it was depressing. Where would they put it? There weren't any more blank walls, even given how many walls they had.

In point of fact, the Hull mansion housed a priceless art collection, American and European works from the seventeenth and eighteenth centuries, but Vince now preferred the moderns. In his younger days, he had wanted some validation by buying well-known, accepted names, but later on he bought whatever he wanted, and he wanted the greatness of experimentation, the lustful energy that cried out for incomprehension or annoyance, or some major emotion. The safety of chaste and charming pictures no longer attracted him, and this was surely his most important purchase as well as his most expensive.

At dinner Amelia and her friend, now revealed as

"Thea," huddled next to each other whispering and giggling, while Vince's older daughter, Claire, a quiet, exotic blonde with almond-shaped blue eyes and a lot of hair, three years older than her sister, kept listening distractedly for the phone in the hall. "Why do you listen for your calls all the time, Claire? I don't encourage people to call me at home."

"You don't encourage people at all, Dad."

"I talk to people constantly." His older daughter looked away, while her mother sipped her wine and picked up another piece of bread, buttering it carefully as she framed her words.

"What does this painting mean, Vincenzo?" She had started to use this mysterious nickname just recently, and to him it sounded demeaning, as if he were an Italian lounge singer. "Why did you buy it?"

"It's magnificent. One year later the painter killed himself."

"Charming." She stuck her fork into another chunk of the beef stew before her. "It's completely blank, just dark colors. Anyone could do that. I don't see how it has any value whatsoever."

Neither of the girls listened to what she said, and as her husband threw back his head, savoring a finely roasted potato, neither apparently did Vince, but after dinner he insisted his wife come with him to observe his magnificent purchase. As they stood before it, he put his arm around her shoulder, and she responded by touching his hand.

Vince said nothing but pointed to the center of the painting. "See how the dark and the light blur together, so beautiful, Japanese almost, a nightmare or a point of rest."

"Yes, I do see that," she said and held onto his arm. "Who's the new girl?"

"Which girl?" No, he shouldn't have said this.

"A girl from the office called today."

"Probably just one more of these floater-types. Let's see if she can figure anything out. They come, they go, and my executive assistant just keeps telling me to fire them." But he wasn't sure what to say, as he didn't know which girl she referred to and was not prepared to learn more. Out of nowhere, suddenly, Vince murmured, "I need you," and pulled her into his arms. She opened her beautiful mouth and kissed him, caught up in his embrace.

TWO

Today, on this muggy day in June, after a remarkable few weeks of floating incompetently through reception, advertising, subscriptions (the biggest demotion of all), then upwards into research, Jenna McCann occupied her desk at the center of an astonishing suite of offices, one of the most incredible in this opulent New York world. "Office"— the word did not do justice to Vincent Hull's domain. How she had gotten here mystified no one more than herself. In her tiny hometown of Burton, Ohio, she was regarded as smart but clueless, mouthy, erratic, up for anything the wind blew her way, but lovely too, with mounds of light brown hair, beautiful white shoulders, sexy calves. She looked like a well-fed woman, curious but naïve, openly waiting, even asking for something to happen to her. After the death of her last living relative, her grandmother Margaret Grace McCann, her art history professor at Ohio University had interceded with someone who worked at a New York art gallery, who in turn was familiar with the fact that Vincent Hull lost assistants the way a fisherman loses bait. So, why not suggest this rootless twenty-something who had had one or two menial jobs, in possession of a fairly useless degree, not actively evil to anyone's knowledge; why not recommend her for a job at Hull's somewhat tacky magazine, *NewsLink*, and give her a shot at the big wide world? Up until now she had had very few helping hands.

Each day Jenna's new job began the same way—opening up a bag full of colorful, misspelled cards, notes, and ragged clippings meant to insult or castigate her boss, Vincent Hull. These letter writers were the people who rarely could penetrate Hull's private email address, although if they did, an IT guy dealt with them. No, these were the Luddites with pen and pencil, with old typewriters, even pinking shears, sometimes using cut-out letters like writers of ransom notes, and boy did they rave. Today's batch contained worse, much worse, as she held up a thick piece of white paper onto which had been drawn a man dangling from a rope, with a swastika upon his chest. Misshapen legs, arms, and a large male member stuck out from the torso. "Eww," she shouted over to Hull's other assistant, his real one, the executive one, Jorge Garza, a nattily dressed fiftyish man with graying black hair, thick glasses, and a perpetual air of stern and deep thought. So far she knew nothing much about him except that he collected labels off the bottles of wine that he and his family drank, a family that consisted of his mother and a disabled brother.

Jorge came over to her desk to get a better look. "Shows a certain flair, I think, in the hatred department. What did you reply?"

"Dear Mr. —hmm, he only calls himself Sam. Dear Mr. Sam, Vincent Hull appreciates very much your interest in *NewsLink* and your views on its politics. He is committed to maintaining an open dialogue with his readers, and letters like yours keep that conversation open. Please do continue to let us know what you think."

"Send it up to Security."

"Okay, you're right, but I'm just wondering what a little kindness might do for this guy."

Jorge frowned. "We don't do kindness here, but at least you spelled everything correctly."

"I really can't lie to save my soul."

"Don't worry, that's a skill you'll learn." He certainly did not want to tell her how the most recent letter-writing girl had gotten fired when Hull actually read one of her replies and then stood before this very same desk shouting at top volume, "You can't even fucking use a comma correctly. Your sentences just go on and on, typos, grammar errors. I sound unbelievably stupid. You sent this crap out under my signature? If I put a gun to your head, could you figure out the fucking spell-check key?" He had shouted into her ear and then actually picked up a pencil and poked her in the forehead with the sharp end. The woman had fainted on the spot, and only the resultant several weeks of heavy lawyering could get Hull out of the whole expensive business.

"*Luxe, calme et volupté,*" Jorge whispered into Jenna's ear now. "You and I need to create that here because nobody else is going to do it; no one else cares, so it's up to us. Luxury, peace, and—" but he didn't want to say "exquisite pleasure" so instead, he said—"beauty, that's what we're going for. Some French poet, I forget his name, once described a room that way."

"Baudelaire."

"Holy god, at last someone who knows something! We've been a brain-free zone for quite a while."

"Ohio University, major in art history, minor in French. I owe it all to them, but of course I do miss my last job at the internet start-up in Cuyahoga Falls. They were into porn."

"Maybe you could've gotten stock and become a billionaire."

"Not a fucking chance. Oops, no swearing around here, right?"

"Not by you and me, anyway." As things stood now,

Jorge didn't want to burst her bubble about how thrilling this promotion from Ohio porn might seem. In fact, he wanted to clue her in on several upcoming difficulties, but didn't quite know how to start. When Jenna's phone bank lit up, he retreated to his desk across from hers on the opposite side of the foyer. Several feet behind them lurked Hull's inner sanctum, an office that resembled a large living room, several times larger than the apartment Jenna shared with two roommates in Gramercy Park. To its left was the kitchen and behind that the executive dining room, a small but companionable space. To the right of Hull's office, behind a perpetually closed door, resided a much smaller, "secret" office, entirely off limits except to those invited in.

The mystified girl stared down at the buttons on the telephone console before her, all of which, all twenty of them, appeared to link them to the known universe as it stood today. One was labeled "Janitor," one "Executive Editor," and another knob sported the word "Washington" ominously pasted beside it. Could "Washington" mean the President of the United States? This phone button? "Hey, I could scramble jets through NORAD. Let me think of people I can bomb."

"Now, now, these are early days. Power must be used wisely." Jorge folded a piece of copy paper into an airplane and lobbed it her way. No matter what the new girl said, she said it with a lilt, a bit of joy at the end of each sentence, and he began to feel better about his life.

A button lit up, and she punched one of the flashing lights on the magic machine, receiving only bits and pieces of someone shouting through a cell phone as if through shards of glass. "Yes, yes? Who's there?" she cried, into the digital void apparently, because now she heard no sound at all. "Okay, if that was Mr. Hull, I'm totally

fucked. Geez, sorry, my grandmother used to say I had no
governor on my mouth, but I'll work on it."

"Don't worry, probably not him. He's been AWOL
lately." Jorge actually hoped the great one himself had
finally decided to show up. Since late April, Hull had
rarely come in to work. He could often not be found; instead he allowed Jorge to do every single thing for him.
Not that this executive assistant hadn't already had that
function, but now the situation had deteriorated. Habitually his boss's feet rarely touched pavement. Cars, bills,
appointments, phone calls, taxes, gifts, children, dogs,
doctors—Jorge had handled it all. If someone had ever
asked him, he would have said, "I live his life." And that
he did. It was an odd sort of ventriloquism, but the man
who takes up ownership of a big chunk of the world
needs a stand-in, a dummy with a mouth talking but saying exactly what the ventriloquist wants that world to
hear. At the present time, though, Jorge could no longer
even find out what his lines were supposed to be. Constant accessibility: once upon a time his boss's mantra,
but for several months he'd gotten only the occasional
email, followed perhaps by a late-night phone call. If only
people knew that almost everything in Vincent Hull's life
originated with a bean-counting-type guy from Queens
who lived with his agoraphobic brother and a mother
with multiple health complaints. In another life he would
have figured as the designated priest in the family.

Jenna's phone bank lit up again. A gravelly male voice
announced, "I'm coming in," then hung up. Say what?
Jenna held the phone out in front of herself and stared
into its silent microphone.

"Okay, Jorge, that had to be him."

"Deep voice, authoritative, like an SUV crushing
dirt?" Jenna nodded, but Jorge looked grim, staring down

at his watch. "Jesus, I wonder what's going on? It's so late in the day, almost five. Go check out his office and straighten things up in there. Maybe dust a bit."

"I'll make it 'shiny as two dogs' balls under a bed.' That's what my granny always said." In shock, Jorge could find absolutely no reply.

Jenna ran into the kitchen, got two towels, and then went back through the foyer into Hull's office, only the third time she had actually entered that room. To her art-history-trained eye, her so-far invisible boss inhabited an art museum. Chinese scroll paintings unspooled along mahogany walls, onyx statues with grimaces on their faces backed up against the four corners of a room that sported a marble desk the size of three dining tables. Colors were muted, deep green and brown, down even to the Persian rugs, all sumptuous, oozing importance and the luxury of a thousand choices. Outside of the Cleveland Museum, Jenna had never seen anything like this before, and it reemphasized the importance of the people who owned it, certainly of the man whose assistant she now was, no matter how temporarily. As she surveyed her surroundings and then the panoramic view from the windows, she could almost feel the rich man's cultivation of his contemplative self. The phone didn't even ring here; it lit up silently, to her eyes like a tiny bomb. Staring down at the flickering buttons, some coming on, others dying out, she hoped she had time to fix things up, though why was something of a mystery, as, according to Jorge, nothing ever got moved or touched except by Mr. Hull's wishes.

Jenna swept over almost every art object with the soft towels, including the fat, laughing Buddhas, lining them up evenly on the shelves. Books that had crept out of place got pushed back. She glanced at a few titles and saw they all related to current events, mostly written by notables who had signed the first page. A little too intimate for her, this private contact; as if she were touching a part of the man himself. When she got to Hull's desk, she found an antique silver frame that had fallen face down, and when she propped it up again saw a slender, dark-haired woman hugging two young girls in parkas, snow-capped mountains behind them. The family, no doubt, and she stopped a moment to see them better because they looked so happy. She closed the heavy office door behind her.

Before she could run out to primp, a skinny man with red spiky hair brushed straight skyward popped his head around the doorway. "Want some shrimp amandine?" It was only five thirty in the afternoon, but perhaps dinner started early in these parts.

"Hmm, I don't know if I should." Jenna was hungry and anxious, but she wanted to please Hull's personal chef, mainly to score freebies she could take home. No gift too small in this, the dark-hearted city, so she took the plate and walked back to her desk, Chef Martin trailing behind.

Jorge smiled over at her. "You've got to watch Martin. He'll have us all fat."

"That is not true. My food is pure, no chemicals, no bad stuff, you will lose weight on it, I guarantee." Martin retied his apron and straightened his bowtie while he spoke. His voice had a foreign ring to it, but Jenna couldn't place the accent.

She rushed through the delicious concoction to finish before the great man arrived, and indeed within moments after wiping her mouth and putting on more lipstick, she heard heavy footsteps coming toward them. Jorge made a sweeping hand gesture that signaled, *Sit up straight.* Down through the hall, they heard people greeting Mr.

Hull, subdued though these greetings were, and she couldn't pick up any reply from him at all. Hurriedly she wiped her mouth again, but not before a very tall man strode through the door.

He didn't look at her, didn't look at Jorge either, and she only glimpsed an impressive profile. He went straight for his office, waving a hand in the air like the conductor of an orchestra. All Jenna had really seen was the back of him, his black leather jacket and his blue jeans.

She looked over at Jorge uncertainly, who mouthed, "Just wait." Nervously she wiped her mouth again, afraid of stray amandine, and for a whole hour she fretted; no sound from Hull's office, only the ominous little gleam of the phone lights. What should she do? Jorge always worked feverishly, but he barely looked up. At last Hull buzzed her —she knew at least that much about the system, and she picked up. "Come in here, please," the man said in a low, slightly less harsh voice than the one she had heard before.

"Right away, sir." To herself she made a face and then unaccountably threw her fingers up around her eyes like a pair of googly glasses, all the while shaking her head at Jorge, who laughed. Just then Vincent Hull popped his head out of the doorway, surveyed her for a moment, and waved her in.

The powerfully built, tall man bent down over a package covered with customs stamps and bound with canvas straps, which he was trying to wrestle open. Jenna thought maybe she should help him but was too frightened to advance, worse yet to retreat, and so she waited. The silence had just about gotten to her when Hull looked up and fixed his dark brown eyes upon her, what the Irish call "speaking eyes." His face was square, with a prominent nose and a high forehead, and his white hair curled slightly around his ears. This was the only soft feature on a big man who looked more like a well-dressed lumberjack than someone who ran a significant chunk of the New York world. He surveyed her and cleared his throat. "Do you like food?"

"I eat it," she said, a little too loudly, clasping her hands together to stop herself from fidgeting.

"Some women don't eat. Watch them at parties, they're figuring how not to actually ingest anything." He grabbed a box cutter from a drawer in the desk and began slashing at the carton.

"Oh, that wouldn't be my problem, as you can see."

Now he smiled, and it was a broad grin that made her sure his laugh would be even better. He sat himself down cross-legged in front of the box and began to root around with his hands. Out fell heaps of white Styrofoam popcorn. "Jorge tells me you're handling the letters well."

"I don't know, I mean they're pretty disgusting. Umm, could I help you with that, sir?"

"No." He pulled out the black walnut stock of a hunting rifle from the rubble of plastic and ran his hand along it. "This is part of a custom made Mauser 98," he said, and she watched silently as he assembled the pieces, several engraved with silver tracery. "What's the matter? Not used to guns in Manhattan? Or just guns period?"

"Not used to Manhattan with a gun in it."

He pointed the amazing firearm toward the floor-to-ceiling window before them. "I could drop anyone or anything with this, and from a long distance."

"'When you're dead, you're dead, as dead as Kelsey's nuts.' That's what my granny used to say. Nobody cares which gun shot you." Hull let out a harsh laugh in Jenna's direction and hugged the weapon to his wide chest. She forced herself to shut up. No chattering, another new mantra.

Certainly, she had never seen the makings of a gun quite like this, but she had seen guns. From her stepfather she knew deer rifles firsthand. He would spend hours cleaning his latest firearm from the Galco Army store, spreading all the components down onto the kitchen table, then working away with baby diapers and oil, while a grainy, bitter smell filled the house. This in order to take potshots at the rabbits and gophers out in the yard, one of whom he nicknamed Billy. He became obsessed with this one particularly elusive bunny, but he never hit anything whatsoever, though Jenna had lived in fear that he might.

"But you're used to food, as you said." Vincent Hull wiped his hand on his jeans and then stared at her again with those dusky eyes, and she knew he saw before him a non-New York kind of person. Plumper than her predecessors no doubt, with freckled skin, her hair bunched together imperfectly in a black barrette, today she wore a floaty yellow dress adorned with random daisies. It hugged her breasts, and Jenna could read the man's blunt assessment, but didn't move away from his concentrated look. After what seemed like forever, Hull cleared his throat. "I want you to take charge of the executive dining room. Jorge doesn't have time, and it's not rocket science, it's food and people sitting at a table. You check in with Martin every morning, Jorge will give you the list of guests, and then you call and confirm each one. He'll show you the menu. If there's anything that looks disgusting, that's where it'll get tricky. You'll have to handle that yourself."

"That's true." Any controlled or witty language deserted her.

"He's not an easy man." Jenna stood there watching as he continued to work on the stock of the gun, massaging it with a soft cloth. "Besides, there's not that much for you to do, and I'm not here as often as I should be."

"That's what I was told." She was afraid to say too much, though felt certain that she already had, like a fool.

"Jorge told you that?"

"Was he not supposed to?"

Now Hull just stared at her. "Okay, check with Martin tomorrow and see what's happening. He needs all the help he can get." As she walked out of the room, she felt conscious of how her body moved and that he must be assessing the dimensions of her rear end.

Jenna had been in the great man's office so long that, unusual for him, Jorge had stepped to the door to listen. When she finally reemerged, she almost ran right into him. "I'm sorry," he whispered, but she brushed past him to flee what she considered the single most baffling interview she'd ever had.

"I must be insane, talking that way. I can't believe he asked me to take charge of Martin. That's your job, isn't it?" She plopped down into her desk chair, fooling with her hair compulsively.

"Was my job, dear. I'm so happy. Never try to deal with a chef, just open your mouth and consume. Tell me, though, how did you get here?"

"By subway."

"No, here in this office, at this time. You're from Ohio, no?"

"Right, Burton, Ohio, but I have connections, or my art prof does. He thought I needed a change, and you know, 'a change is as good as a rest.'" Jenna gazed up at him philosophically.

"It is?"

"According to Granny Mac."

"My grandmother never said much except, 'Shut the

friggin' door, you moron,'" but Jorge stopped himself from saying more, horrified at the cultural contrast between Queens and rural Ohio. Of necessity this young woman had to like him, because lately the mood in the Hull realm had turned even darker than usual, intensified, actually brought about by their leader himself, who, after years of being actively engaged, almost hyper-engaged, now occupied some mysterious psychological limbo. He refused to deal with the editors and writers at *NewsLink*, hid out at one of his far-flung residences for weeks at a time—even while his family remained in the city—and when he did come in, threatened bodily harm to his employees and then refused to acknowledge their existence, an unusual mode, since normally he charmed them to death or showered them with money after he had insulted them. It was ghastly, and Jorge had no playbook for this state of affairs. At the very least, he needed help. Jenna was the first decent candidate for a job that was both menial and important, and he could tell right away that gratitude was high on her list of virtues, as after the first interview she had thanked him at least five times and also sent him a handwritten card.

THREE

The next day Hull showed no signs of making an appearance, but Jorge shoved his personal schedule Jenna's way. "Inscribed by the man himself," he announced, as if it were a sacred document. Just a series of dates in big block handwriting. "You must have made a good impression." Jorge patted her on the back. "Usually he communicates with a shout."

"You don't care for him?" She looked up at the neat little man in his black V-neck sweater and his blue-checked shirt, apparently so comfortable in this Hull world. He looked like a professor of something serious, maybe statistics, and she almost waited for the word "stochastic" to fly out of his lips. What was his age, forty, fifty?

"Liking isn't really the issue with somebody like that. He's the man, the one, he owns us, and we're his little pawns. Is he a benevolent king? Uhh—no. Is he rational? Only sometimes. He wants big, and he gets big, but the bad that comes his way comes thick and fast and gets ugly fast too. You'll see."

"I don't know if I want to."

"Wanting isn't allowed around here. Now get cracking. Here's the list of writers invited for lunch, in-house people. Poor schmucks probably think the boss will show up."

Jenna straightened her tight blue skirt assertively and peeked through the door into the kitchen, where she saw the chef turning a wooden spoon around in a saucepan. He started when he heard her, throwing the spoon up vertically and waving it at her like a flag. "It's beautiful.

Those crummy journos don't deserve this. Half of them smoke! They can't taste anything, their lungs are shot, and they can't smell either, but their clothes smell, you betcha." He scooped out a bit of sauce and held it toward her. Something touched her tongue that was thick, buttery, exquisite, with a hint of sherry. "Oh my god, I can't stand it," she moaned.

"Good, you're my taster from now on. You appreciate Martin Riegel. You will be at the head of our unhappy band." Martin had an airy, theatrical form of declamation, and it threw her off momentarily. "How many people are there today?"

She looked down at her list. "I think about ten, though according to Jorge several of them haven't responded."

"I must know, I must know now. Scallops wait for no man and certainly for none of the women around here."

Jenna hit the phones immediately, this time with success, and when, hours later, the participants filed in, she tried to appear cheerful and upbeat, welcoming them like a hostess. To the dismay of a number of them, Hull never did show up, but still they seemed grateful to feed in his lair. Most barely noticed her, but one tousle-haired young man, "Inti," he had announced when he first arrived, had casually asked about the identity of the expected guests. Was "Inti" his name or an object of some kind? In any case, she couldn't remember any of the names, and somehow or other she had misplaced the list. Inti was handsome in a boyish, off-kilter way, blue-eyed with curly black hair, a slightly crooked nose, and an expansive smile, very much at home in this setting, in contrast to a number of the other writers, who seemed harried, on edge. Was there more for her to do? There had been no job description at all, just get them in and out and satisfied.

When the last invitee had trailed away, Jenna sank

down into her chair with relief. "You note that most of them had no idea whether Mr. Hull would appear. Keep them in line, keep them wanting more, it's a life technique. He should write a book on it." So opined Jorge, in a sardonic, post-mortem mood. He perched on the side of her desk, quiet, concerned.

"You really worry about him, don't you?"

"I do. He's worth worrying about, despite all the bad stuff, or maybe because of it."

The next several days produced more lunches and another bag of letters, and Jenna found herself overwhelmed with food and bad handwriting. She saw nothing of Hull but felt him to be a looming presence, both in Jorge's occasional asides and in Martin's fuming and fussing about what the great man might like to eat, should he ever actually eat with them or somewhere near them. She had had a few disasters, as when an assistant ran in and handed her a list to be stealthily given to one of the writers while he was in attendance at lunch. This turned out to be an overdue dry cleaning bill, so Jenna took the heat, nasty heat too, from the angry writer himself. "Are you trying to fucking ruin me?" he hissed into her ear after everyone else had filed out.

"I don't even know you. Why would I be trying to do that? Your assistant gave me the note and said it was important."

"When I am in that room, nothing is important. My mother could eat anthrax, my father could set himself on fire, but it makes no goddamned difference to me. Got that?"

"Of course. I'm sorry." What was wrong with these people? Why should this man tie himself in knots over what happened in the dining room, since Hull hadn't even been there to see the gaffe?

Later, standing at the coffee cart, Jenna puzzled over her new situation, thrust upon her, it seemed, as a result of her professor doing her a good turn. She had hardly had time to recover from her grandmother's demise when now she found herself at the center of something that those who surrounded her gave great importance to, almost like life and death. Yet when she read *NewsLink*, she thought it just a slick summary of the news, lots of photos, almost every one embarrassing to the person caught in the act of whatever, the occasional gossip item with way too many column inches devoted to it, several features, almost all about state senators doing bad things, and quantities of sports. She sank down with her coffee into a chair in the hallway, though many passed her by, almost stepping on her. When the Inti guy again approached, she beamed. At last, someone she kind of knew. "Sort of a deer in head-lights look you have about you, Miss McCann." He sat down next to her. "I'm Inti, remember?"

"Of course I remember. Guess I'm still back in Ohio, thinking about my grandmother."

"How is she?"

"She died six months ago." Inti looked abashed, but she continued. "She was ninety-four, and her helper stopped the clocks at the hour of her death, opened the window to let her spirit escape, and covered the mirrors out of respect, the Irish way. Granny didn't suffer, she just forgot to take a breath. That made me feel better."

"I'm so sorry." He'd just wanted coffee and to chat up a lovely girl, and now this.

"I will never forget how beautiful she looked in her coffin." Amid shuffling feet and chattering all around the coffee cart, Jenna wanted to cry. "'Inti,' what kind of name is that?"

"The Inca sun god. I'm from Olympia, Washington,

home of Evergreen College and innumerable hippies, among them my parents. Besides, they were desperate for sun, but they had to settle for me."

"I never heard that name before."

"No one else ever has either. How about I take you out to dinner Friday night? I'll cheer you up."

"Wonderful." He looked promising, fashionable in a beige linen jacket and navy slacks, and he might be interesting, what with that name. Positively everyone else here wore a black T-shirt and jeans, the men that is. The women writers, of whom there weren't many, wore dark pants with a tailored blouse and a black jacket. They never said much, always just seemed to rush around in consternation. Besides, anything was better than another strained evening with her two roommates, one a skinny, eccentric person named Vera, who claimed to be in interior design. Jenna understood that to be retail, as in selling strange lamps and couches in Soho. The other girl, Allyson, a chunky, athletic blonde, worked at Chase Manhattan bank and, according to her, shuffled millions of dollars about daily. Smoking endless numbers of cigarettes while holding a beer, she then shot the butts through the little opening in the cans. She was carrying on an affair with a sportswriter at *The New York Post* and spent hours on the phone with him explaining herself, brew and cigs in hand.

No news from Vincent Hull that day, so Jenna merely sat, opening up yet more letters, one containing a graying, mashed piece of chocolate, sent as a gift presumably, while Jorge answered phones and seemed to work on endless spreadsheets. So efficient, so competent he appeared, while she wondered how she'd managed this upward climb without having done much of anything. Despite the paltry salary, others considered her something of a higher-up, and after being here only one month. Extraordinary, undeserved, and she pondered her good fortune, swiveling her chair around toward the immense window that let her see down onto Fifth Avenue. The heat flickered in the air and caused ripples across the glass and steel of the buildings. It was a different kind of heat from what she knew in northeastern Ohio—that had been wet, like the sky sweating. Of the many things she hated about where she grew up, the weather loomed as her sworn enemy. Thank god she had gotten out, if only to land in this cauldron of blossoming, proliferating heat. According to her roommates, three more months of this weather, possibly four, loomed, and they moaned that there had been no spring at all.

Jenna looked at her watch: almost five. Jorge was still working. On this night, her roommates had included her in their usual dinner at the neighborhood burger joint, probably because they felt guilty, having given her only a fold-up couch in the living room, but this was Gramercy Park after all, a posh address, no matter the small, dingy apartment. "Hey there, girl," Jorge called over to her. "You've got a new assignment."

"I already know, managing Martin."

"That's an oxymoron if I ever heard one, or possibly just a moron. No, we—and I do mean the imperial we—need you to pick up this special brand of bath oil and take it to the Hull hotel suite at Sixty-first and Park Avenue."

"Why do they have a hotel suite when they already have a townhouse?"

"For guests, for relatives, for anyone they want to please." Cryptically, he raised his eyebrows. "Don't try to figure them out. It's not possible."

Yes, this was why she had graduated college, struggled and gone into debt, and worked now for almost no money—for bath oil. The only compensation, she got to ride in the Hull limousine with Angelo, a round, red-faced Italian, with nine brothers, and he the youngest. "My god, do you have any idea of the odds against that? Statistically, of course, it was impossible, and my mother knew that somehow. A girl had to be forthcoming but never was. She blamed my father, naturally."

"Naturally."

While the gigantic vehicle idled outside, double-parked, Jenna entered an unlikely address on Madison Avenue, a place stuffed with dolls and jewelry, every surface covered with boas and rhinestone chandelier earrings. In among the frills lurked a dark blue bottle of oil from France, Huile d'Automne, so precious it fetched one hundred and fifty dollars an ounce.

After much waiting, honking, and swearing on Angelo's part, they had traveled two large city blocks across town and six uptown in the time it would have practically taken Jenna to drive from Columbus, Ohio, to Akron. Sweat flowed down the side of her blouse, and she would now have no time to make it to dinner with the ghastly roommates, at least some form of company on this lonely island. Worse yet, if Mrs. Hull looked up at all, she would find a scary slob at her door. Hoping at last to jump out and leg it, she stopped herself when Angelo said he was on the clock, and this was all part of his "let's spend the rich people's money" scheme, so they crawled. At long last, limo at the Regency Hotel, the doorman seemed prepared for her. "Don't worry, he knows me," Angelo explained as she clambered out and rushed in.

Jenna had never been in such a place and straightened herself up just to look worthy of the lobby. With key in hand, she ascended to the tenth floor and traversed a hallway lined in plush dark blue carpet. Sliding the plastic card into the slot, she waited a moment before getting up the courage to enter, but when she did, she encountered a setting more like a museum: heavy burgundy curtains, gray velvet furniture, and golden light fixtures. Yellow calla lilies soared out of a glass vase on a round mahogany table.

As she edged forward, uncertain where to find the bathroom, she heard a sound coming from behind one of the closed doors. Someone was there, the maid perhaps. Cautiously, Jenna moved into a large living room area, seeing no one, but then she heard a woman's voice, loud, angry, and moments later, crying. Not sniffling, but wracking sobs. "Oh don't say that, don't say it's hopeless. I love you." Jenna backed up right away into the table and nearly knocked over the flowers. Should she leave the oil right here and flee? But these had not been her instructions, and she was insanely curious, anyway. As she rounded the corner, through another half-open door, she spotted an athletic leg swinging back and forth and a black phone cord draped over a well-manicured foot. The foot stopped swinging, so too the wailing. In the ominous silence, Jenna advanced toward the door, and as she did so, a woman's voice rang out in a distinctly French accent. "Hello? Who's there?"

"Hi, it's just me, Jenna McCann, from the office?" She uttered this last bit as a question.

"You can't come in here." But in another moment the door opened, and Jenna found herself in front of a trim woman possibly in her thirties, whom she recognized from the office photo as Mrs. Hull. She was dressed in yoga pants and a T-shirt as if she had just stopped in from the gym and wore a thick diamond eternity band on her ring finger. Pushing a strand of dark hair behind her ear, she grabbed a Kleenex out of a box on the table and wiped her eyes. "Oh, the oil. Thank you, put it down here," she said, but then she hid her face in the crook of her arm. After waving at Jenna in dismissal, she blew her nose and once again picked up the phone. Jenna could hear only an angry comment as she backed out of the room. "That's the way he always is, *c'est dégoûtant.*"

Jenna hurried along the ornate corridors of the hotel, embarrassed at coming upon so intimate a scene. She wouldn't tell Jorge about the crying. It just seemed too personal, and due to her own tumultuous family times, she had vast experience in keeping secrets. Maybe she could make it in time for a burger, even though her roommates condescended to her so aggressively. At least she would have some company.

"How was the little woman?" Angelo waved her into the enormous vehicle.

"Unhappy, really unhappy."

"Oh dear, we go by the Mafia code around here, *omertà* all the way. Just don't say anything."

"As if anyone I know would be interested."

"Please. There's a world of gossip out there." As soon as he said this, Jenna insisted on jumping out of the car and headed for the subway. This New York life was just too weird, too unreal. Through the grime and heat and late dinner-eaters rushing about, she got herself to Mc-Swiggan's pub near Gramercy Park, heartened to see Vera and Allyson drinking martinis perilously close to a television dangling above their heads. She waved, and several guys in suits looked over, but the noise was too great, and the need for solace so immediate that she sped her way through the crowd, not even looking. "Hey you," Allyson sang out, and at once Jenna felt herself at home. She knew someone, and that someone called out to her. "We waited for you."

Vera too looked up and smiled. Maybe they thought she was important somehow. "How is it in the land of the tycoon?"

"Sadness reigns."

"Come on. Money reigns, and I'd like some." Allyson had her values firmly in hand and would marry her *New York Post* sportswriter if it killed her. Not that he made that much, but something bigger surely loomed in his future—or else. Vera had once told Jenna, "If it doesn't work out, she'll kill him or she'll kill herself."

"I've been promoted, I think." Jenna described her upward trajectory as manager of the chef, adding on a description of the immense size of the dining room for effect.

"Sounds lateral." Allyson smoothed her blond hair back from her round, ample face, as she searched for a cigarette in the cavernous black leather purse she always carried.

"You should be careful." The skinny, ever-vigilant Vera peered at her. "Those people are notorious."

"For what exactly?" Despite her low status, Jenna felt protective of her boss. He fit into a category she had already experienced: people who create awe and anger around them, misunderstood people like her grandmother, who had no more expected to rest with the angels than with the devil, never believing in a spiritual solution to her end.

"He probably just wants to bang you," Allyson shouted through bar noise, breaking into Jenna's reverie. "You're going to have to watch that mouth of yours."

"What do you mean?" But she knew what this annoying girl was suggesting and thought it all too gross. "Don't be ridiculous. He must be, I don't know, fifty years old, sixty even. Besides, he's married."

Vera screwed up her face like an angry monkey. "The more reason."

Allyson laughed but patted Jenna on the arm. "He's fifty-nine. Just enjoy whatever goodies he sends your way. Listen, Vera, how about our summer get-out-of-town plans? Anything yet? I mean, Jesus, we're lurching toward July, and it's unbearable already."

"I'm working something on the North Shore."

"You're all leaving town?" Jenna envisioned herself now stuck in the heat with no one to talk to in an empty apartment.

"Just for the weekends." Allyson inhaled her cigarette and looked at Vera as if she wanted to warn her off the subject. To Jenna this meant they definitely would not invite her to go along. The only promising event that loomed, her date with Inti, was scheduled for this upcoming Friday.

FOUR

Jenna's boss dropped out of sight during the next week, in France, according to Jorge, but at least she didn't have to arrange lunches, and anyway most of the writers had escaped town. The magazine seemed to be on autopilot, and even the hate-filled letters melted away. Jenna continued obsessing about how she herself could flee on these lonely, overheated weekends in an apartment without air-conditioning. "Seriously, Jorge, any bright ideas where I might go for the weekends? I have to go somewhere, or I'll melt."

"I never leave in the summer unless Hull lets me visit one of his vacation homes when he and the family are elsewhere. Wait, wait, here's a thought." He got up, pulled off his suit jacket, shaking the sleeves slightly, and hung it on the back of his chair. His thinking mode, she had learned. "Hull owns so much art, and he's been saying lately that he should have someone do an inventory. That someone should be you, possessed of your little art degree. You could go from house to house. In fact, the maestro called in from the plane this morning to say he's rushing back to host a charity shindig at his house in the city this Friday night. If he doesn't show, at least, presumably, the missus will. You could get drunk and then chat her up about this very project."

"Brilliant," she said, but remembered right away two serious problems. First off, Inti. Could she possibly take him? "Definitely. I'll just work you and a plus one into the guest list." Jorge liked nothing better than to goose others' happiness, and he smiled like a practiced conspirator, typing fervently into his computer. But she had another, more pressing reason not to go, that being the awful stuff she had overheard Mrs. Hull say on the phone at the hotel.

Unfortunately, Jorge was so pleased with himself, she couldn't think how to bring that up or even if she should. "You'll meet all kinds of luminaries, those who hover at these festivities. Our esteemed leader serves on the boards of two progressive schools in the city, and they say if he wanted to, he could get the Democratic nomination for governor, but so far he's expressed zero interest in a political life. Too much to hide." Jorge laid his finger aside his nose.

"Will you be there?"

"*Nein.* I have to make lasagna for my mother."

Despite her fear of the missus, this plan could make her life a lot simpler; still she had to say something. "Jorge, I'm not sure if this really is proper. I didn't want to tell you, but I overheard Mrs. Hull being very upset on the phone to someone."

Jorge stared at her. "That's all?" Jenna nodded. "Get with the program, McCann. You are going to hear a lot of things, and you must ignore all of it, and I do mean *all*."

"Okay, I guess." She would encounter her formally sometime, so why not in the presence of many other guests, with copious liquor about? And, then too, the "take Inti along" idea seemed quite promising: a party, not too much intimacy, no pressure to get to know each other in too steamy a setting like a restaurant with small tables. She didn't tell Jorge that her date was actually a writer at this very magazine, but she called Inti immediately, and after talking up how important this fiesta was to her continued existence in the city's summer heat, he agreed to go, though somewhat reluctantly.

Four days later, on a brutally hot Friday afternoon, Jenna draped herself in a swingy, light green crepe dress that would allow her to flap her arms for air if she had to. With her hair brushed back behind her ears, she tried for a more gamine, less schoolgirl look, and to her eye, it had worked, sort of. Outside the Hulls' astonishing residence, on a scorching hot sidewalk, a scrum of guests at the massive front door flashed their invitations toward a black-suited security man, complete with headset and clipboard. Jenna waited nervously for Inti, who, when he appeared, stood out from the crowd as that relaxed fellow in the blue linen shirt and beige pants, seemingly at home even in New York's concrete oven. He bent down and kissed her quickly on the cheek. "I've heard about this Belle Époque monstrosity, but I've never gotten an invite before."

"It looks like a hotel. I'm not totally sure I should be here either."

"Why not?"

"I'm such an underling, and it's kind of trumped up, me wanting to corner him about doing an art inventory at all his houses."

This was news to Inti, and he immediately did not like it. "Hull certainly has a lot of etchings." Sarcasm wasn't usually his thing, but her remark demanded it. Word around the office played up the boss's personal life, supposedly a gaudy mix of rigorous attention to family, secretive personal involvements, extravagant art purchases, aided and abetted by constant travel, and a high profile in the world of charity.

Inti looked down at Jenna, seeing her upset and wanting to help her out. "Don't worry, he'll love it, a beautiful girl like you who admires him. He'll gobble up yet another slice of adoration." Jenna blossomed at the word "beautiful" but didn't like the insinuation. At the moment, though, she was too nervous to care and right away she took his arm.

Once inside, the two of them stopped to take in the immense staircase and then the ivory-and–deep-green Persian carpet that spooled upwards. Both somewhat cowed, Jenna tried not to stare at the plentiful array of paintings in ornate golden frames, but when she spotted a bank of video cameras recording the household's every move, she blurted out to an overdressed woman in an electric blue suit, "Can you believe this?" The woman turned away.

At the top of the steps, a man in a tuxedo guided them forward into a room with an eighteenth-century desk in the center, more finery and carpets, a large shining metal sculpture, and a table laden with cherries, strawberries, and blueberries in glass dishes, colorful cheeses piled high on cutting boards, ringed with crackers and bread. Jenna looked around for someone, anyone she knew, not that she would know anyone, and finally spotted her boss hunched forward in conversation with his wife, forming their own little unit—the very woman Jenna had last heard sobbing in that hotel suite, a woman she absolutely did not want to speak to until she'd had a lot to drink. Happily the couple seemed oblivious to others, despite circulating clumps of people who tried to break in on their conversation.

Jenna suddenly panicked. Could anyone get lower in the food chain than she? "He thinks well of his writers, doesn't he?" She looked up at her handsome date and hoped she could siphon off some of his cred.

"He does, actually, at least some of them. I'm not in that club. Too junior, too local."

"You look quite comfortable here, actually."

Inti flashed a smile. "Good. I'm going for big-city so-phistication." This loose-limbed, tall man, in his early thirties maybe, gazed down at her with concentration.

Jenna had already appraised his charms. "Believe me, you're entirely there."

Without warning, he pulled her backwards into a corner next to a bust of what appeared to be a Roman general. "I think I should tell you that I'm leaving *News-Link*."

"You can't leave. We just met."

For a moment, Inti seemed disconcerted. "I'm going to The *Rye Register*." Jenna stared at him, guarded and uncertain, as he explained that he couldn't take the at-mosphere anymore. "'If you don't want to come in Satur-day, don't bother to come in Sunday.' That's the mantra. It's too much like a cult."

"Do they know?"

"Not yet. I wanted a look at the great man's house before I abscond. And to get to know you, of course."

"You think he's great?"

"Here's what I really think." Inti lowered his voice. "He's a magnificent asshole."

"Shh, he might hear. . . ." Though she couldn't see the man anywhere nearby.

"Believe me, he's been called everything in this world and couldn't give a rat's ass what I call him. Actually he's a visionary and an asshole. He sees the future of news where few others do. It's a fusion, with new sources cropping up everywhere. Gossip, celebrity, leakers abound, everyone wants to get in on the action. It's all going to be 'Breaking News,' and a lot of it will be no news at all unless it's goosed up considerably. Hull gets it and is planning for this."

"Funny, I've been thinking how odd *NewsLink* is in that way, a mash-up of stuff, and I can't tell what's important and what's not."

He took her arm. "I'm not sure the reader is supposed to know. Let's wander through the crowd, but not anywhere forbidden or we'll get shot."

Inti Weill proceeded to fill her in on his trajectory from Olympia, Washington, to the halls of *NewsLink*. Eight years older than Jenna, he had come to New York with the highest possible expectations, to be a reporter, a longed-for dream since age ten when his father got him a subscription to the *Seattle Post-Intelligencer*. Not for him the comic books and action figures, no, he loved the sportswriters, and the crime beat guys, even the business reporters, all following the path of noble truth, at least in his idealistic mind. These noble truths he had now been following for *NewsLink,* but in the outlying boroughs, specifically the doings of various zoning commissions. Not Inti's dream job, yet he could see the glow of the *New York Times* building glittering in his sights. Now he would have to take what he hoped was a brief detour to one of the upscale burbs. "Rye isn't that far away, and we can still see each other."

Jenna could think of nothing to say because she didn't know the location of Rye, and she barely knew this man. "I'll get us some booze." She hurried toward the bar, intent on scoring dual martinis. She rarely indulged in quite so much alcohol, but this occasion demanded more than an entry level of inebriation.

As the bartender handed her two ice-cold drinks, a tall, remarkably beautiful black woman came over and introduced herself. "Hello there. You're here at last."

"Why at last?" Jenna felt ridiculous holding two martinis, looking like a fully committed alcoholic.

"Mr. Hull loses a lot of assistants. The previous one claimed his 'aggressions against her' had caused some strange illness, so they finally put in for temporary help. I'm Tasha Clark, by the way, from publicity." She patted Jenna on the arm in greeting and then turned to survey the room, in particular Mr. and Mrs. Hull, who remained together talking. After a moment of silence, she lifted her head up as if to peruse the ceiling, and then turned directly toward Jenna. "Here's a piece of advice. Never marry a man that everybody else wants." Abruptly she walked away, pausing to greet guests, apparently knowing all and sundry.

Tasha was obviously a person of fashion. Rangy, full-breasted, possibly in her mid-thirties, she had a mass of thick molasses-colored hair tied at the nape of her neck with a black velvet ribbon. She wore a long, chiffon-like dress of jade green and over it a black silk biker jacket that even an Ohio girl knew cost a fortune, and Jenna envied the bohemian boldness of the look. She herself never could achieve offbeat or even unconventional; usually she felt downright bizarre or irregularly duded up in order to draw attention to herself. She wanted to talk more to the woman, but had to deliver Inti his martini, and just as she found him, silence fell, and their host walked to the center of the room. Tasha stepped forward to join him, along with the four winners of a scholarship program Hull had endowed at an inner-city school. The young people stood awkwardly next to him—he looked like a tree and just that stiff—but he paid them a moving tribute, at once eloquent and simple, free of the usual jargon used when schooling became a subject.

This was the first time Jenna had a chance to look carefully at the man in all his height and presence and mastery of the world. His face glowed when he smiled, but became stern and angular in repose, looking younger though in this party setting. Tasha seemed involved with all this somehow or knew the children, or perhaps her role in publicity placed her there. In any case, they made a fetching group, and Jenna envied their shared purpose. But Mrs. Hull barely looked his way as he delivered his remarks, but rather huddled near a white-haired woman in a navy suit, whispering all the while. At some point in the middle of his speech, Vincent Hull looked over at his wife sharply, and she quieted down.

In a burst of self-confidence after her martini and shortly thereafter a glass of white wine, Jenna put her arm under Inti's and drew the two of them nearer to the circle surrounding Vincent Hull. She tried to move herself into his field of vision but found that difficult, given the shifting tide of admirers. Finally, though, she lurched forward, very near to his arm, and took it upon herself to touch him. He pulled back, startled, apparently, by the intimacy. He scrutinized her a moment, and she lit up, expecting a greeting. No, he turned away, his back like a wall, but not before he grimaced.

Another man slid between them and blocked their view. "Is he mad at you or something?" Inti had seen the move and was as shocked as she.

"I don't know." Jenna didn't understand but could only surmise that Hull didn't want her here, she being a lowly assistant.

"Not possible to figure that guy out." Inti bent down now and whispered in her ear, "Some say he is, in fact, actively evil, because whoever you are, wherever you are, he can print a rumor that will ruin you."

Jenna had the impulse to swing to his defense. "He's got responsibilities, he's a man of the world. If he didn't have enemies, what kind of leader would he be?"

"Spoken like a loyal subject."

"I'm no subject," she said bitterly. But what had Hull meant by snubbing her, or had he meant nothing at all? Jenna had to get away from everybody. Turning uncertainly, she took off down a long hallway, finally stopping at an embroidered bench that faced still more paintings, modern and valuable. At once, she experienced them as too many. It was too much for any person alive to have all this. She moved her eyes along the array and was stopped by a work that looked like something out of a dream, a dusky blackish rectangle floating down and merging with a bigger misshapen block awash in gray and white, surely a Mark Rothko. Normally she didn't care for this level of abstraction. Wasn't it too easy? Couldn't a schoolchild do it, as every museumgoer said to anyone who would listen? Still, she walked over to face the painting head-on. Sadness, darkness, light coming through water, a boundary through which one could not pass, but then that all merged into one. Behind her she heard footsteps, and she jumped back. The striking form of Vincent Hull marched her way.

"What have you been up to while I've been out of town?" He held out a glass of wine to her as he said this.

"Answering your letters, pretending to be you."

"Not very uplifting, I'm afraid. The people who like me send emails." He looked at her intently. "What's wrong?"

"Nothing, I'm just hot in the city." At once she sensed sexual innuendo in her words, but fortunately he turned away, back toward the painting.

"You like this Rothko? He did it in 1969, near when he killed himself."

"I love the feeling, something strange about it, but I've never really understood him." She stopped, out of her depth. She had only seen a few reproductions of his work in her college textbooks.

He stayed quiet a moment, but then he looked back toward the painting. "The poor man wrote something I've been thinking about lately: 'Like the old ideal of God, the abstraction itself in its nakedness is never directly apprehensible to us.'" He moved behind her and put his hands on her shoulders. "Can you see that in it?"

Jenna felt herself blush, flustered at the intimacy of his touch. She struggled to speak. "Perhaps it's his sight dimming, as if there's no hope."

"Ah, you've given me the easy answer."

Refusing to cower before the man, she moved away. "Jorge suggested I do an art inventory for you because it might be helpful."

"Good idea. Maybe you'll learn something, specifically how to appreciate this painting. I recall some art history on your resume, and of course there'll be very few lunches to arrange this summer. We don't want you malingering in the city, do we? You could go visit our various houses— the perfect summer getaway." Startled at how easy this had been, she couldn't think what to say. "Talk to Sabine about beginning with the Wyoming paintings, and we'll see how you do."

"Should I just arrange this with her now? Won't it look odd, I mean at a party and all?" Hull stared down at her, uncomprehending. "Minutes ago you pretended not to see me. Maybe she'll do the same?"

"What are you talking about? You're much too sensitive, you know. Get going, you silly girl, get to it." He appraised her critically. "Afraid of her, are you?"

"No, not at all, but. . . ." She couldn't possibly tell him what she had witnessed at the hotel.

"I don't have time for this. Follow me."

Jenna trailed behind his formidable back, as he returned her to the room where the party rattled along noisily. They found Sabine Hull in conversation with Tasha, close to a massive window that looked out toward Central Park, and her boss guided her to them swiftly, now pulling Jenna by the hand. She looked around in torment, certain the guests were watching this scene in amazement, but all she could do was cling to Hull and focus on her mission. At first, Mrs. Hull did not look up, but when Vincent announced her, Tasha leaned forward and kissed Jenna on the cheek.

"I didn't mean to interrupt. . . ." she started clumsily.

"The new mistress of the letters," Tasha said, effusive and charming and only briefly noticing when Hull walked away.

Turning to the Frenchwoman, who stared down at the floor, Jenna leaned forward and spoke as quietly as she could amid the noisy drinkers and partiers. "I'm supposed to do an inventory of your artwork, Mrs. Hull, and I wanted to ask—that is, Mr. Hull asked me to ask you—if I could take photos of all the pictures in Wyoming, as well as in the other residences. Plus get all the original paperwork. I would need that too."

The chic, slight woman finally lifted her eyes, staring at her with a strange look on her face, as if she had just come out of anesthesia and suddenly felt every knife that had cut through her flesh. Jenna stepped back, certain that Mrs. Hull remembered the circumstances of their previous meeting. Nevertheless she looked Jenna in the eye and spoke calmly, as if reflecting, with only the trace of an accent. "We have all the bills of sale somewhere, but not too many photographs. You will have to start from the beginning with those, I fear." She stared off over Jenna's shoulder, toward Tasha.

"It's no trouble, my job really." Jenna tripped away as fast as she could, and the two women once again bent toward each other. She immediately headed toward Inti. "Oh great, oh wonderful," she prattled into her wine glass, in front of the astonished young man. "I achieved my mission."

"What mission is that?"

"To get out of here."

"Yes, let's blow this joint."

"No, I mean out of town."

"That too." Without a word to anyone, he escorted her through the hall and down the incredible staircase. Once outside, buffeted by a hot wind steaming up through the subway grates, the two of them shared a final, narcotizing cognac at a café on Madison Avenue. There she explained more fully her get-out-of-town mission, so much more exciting than sitting in an office. Inti felt somewhat unsettled about this roaming inventorying, but didn't want to suggest dark motives on Hull's part. After all, he wasn't sure. "You can come and see me in Rye. It's beautiful up there, basically a suburb of Manhattan but like another world."

"I'd love to do that, someday." She felt shy, though, because their intimacy certainly hadn't yet stretched that far.

Inti sipped his drink and looked intently at her. "Be careful. You'll become his slave. From what I hear, he's got a lot of those."

"Oh come on, he's cute, in an old sort of way."

"Like a vampire."

She grimaced. "Not to worry, I can hold my own." She realized the liquor had encouraged her inner temptress, for this man and another, perhaps not for the good.

FIVE

To her great disappointment, Jenna's journey to catalogue art in Wyoming was thwarted, since both Hulls had once again decamped to France. "Maybe I should remind him, not the wife? He seems more approachable."

Jorge regarded her sharply, looking skeptical. "Jenna, stop it. You're acting nuts, and stop complaining about the heat and the smell."

"Easy for you to be so snooty. You go to the Jersey shore every weekend." Jorge had regaled her many times with his adventures in Cape May, with a brother he had to force out of the house and a mother who needed help walking down the stairs.

"Okay, here's how you do it. You email him regarding the extreme importance to the project of having photos. He probably thinks of this as a make-work deal I dreamed up for you, but, you know, later, when he—um, um—" Here Jorge gagged and then drew his finger across his throat in a slashing manner—"or in case he ever, you know, dies, not that he ever will, of course. . . ."

"No, no, obviously not."

"I would take care not even to get near a subject like that."

"I never would. He's young."

Jorge began to laugh. "Tell that to his wife." But this was a remark Jenna chose not to pursue. "In any case, someday the heirs will need this information, and he knows that."

She prepared a very careful email that outlined her plans but heard nothing for a few days, until at last a blessed, wonderful reply. "I'm coming into town day after tomorrow, just briefly, but then will be flying out to Wyoming for the weekend to check on some architectural studies for an addition to the house. Why don't you come along?" At last she could indulge her long-held fantasy of sitting by a wooded stream fishing for trout or whatever else swam around there, and so she sat at her desk picturing water cascading over her waders as she cast her glowing little fly expertly. Of course, she knew nothing about fly fishing, only hoped it would be that way. She didn't honestly picture a male person at her side—her mind had not yet flown in that direction—and yet anyone, especially Jorge, could see she was susceptible.

He watched her when she told him of this so-called plan and felt it wise to warn her. "I'll believe it when I see it." Jorge was used to these time fucks, and he had given up trying to make an exact schedule in anticipation thereof. Time fucks went a certain way, as he explained now to Jenna. Hull called, set an arrival time, called back an hour later with an update, then failed to call at the putative arrival time. He preferred to show up when least expected. People waited, babies were born, news was made, and still they waited. Chunks of a glacier calved in the great North, and Jorge just sighed every time the cycle reasserted itself. He couldn't really understand why Hull attempted to control time, especially everyone else's, but he thought he should write a book about it in his old age, to which end these time fucks pushed him ever closer.

When Jenna showed up at work the next morning, anxious to see what news of the great one, she barely got a chance to shove her purse into her desk drawer.

"Lunch, lunch," Jorge yelled at her and motioned toward the kitchen.

"Yes, lunch, lunch what?"

"People are coming in for lunch!"

"No one at all has eaten lunch this summer, Jorge, since I got my so-called assignment to manage Martin. He just feeds *us*."

He kept shaking his head and handed her a printed out email from Hull. "Read me some names. I'm afraid to look."

She rattled off a few, and Jorge crossed his arms in front of him and then jabbed up at his forehead with his pen. "Jesus, Mary, and Joseph, fifteen people. And Howard Stern? Holy fuck. Some of these guys are important . . . wait, is this the Secretary of the Interior? Give me a break!"

"Calm down. What's the big deal? We just give Martin the list, and he'll take care of it."

Pointing an accusatory finger toward the kitchen, Jorge sputtered, "The son of a bitch quit. Supposedly Hull told him he could be the chef at his new restaurant. Did I tell you about this? Anyway, he's really the *sous* chef or the sub chef or some such thing. Jesus, what are we going to do? Howard Stern?"

"I've heard of him, though not sure. . . ."

"The so-called shock-jock, the radio guy, insults people. Why would Hull even invite him?"

"Don't panic. Let's just do takeout."

"Are you insane? These people have memorized every single takeout menu in the city. Anyway, Hull insists our food be the best in the land, totally original. People kill for these invites. Why go to Le Bernardin when you can eat something fantastic here?"

Jorge and Jenna finally determined that an attempt

should be made to get Martin to come back, at least to prepare one final lunch. First Jorge called him, but the conversation was short. "He hung up on me. You call. He likes you. You're the only person who cleans her plate."

"Are you saying I'm fat?"

"No, absolutely not. But you actually seem to enjoy food, instead of being on some weird diet. The last girl here ate only nuts and twigs."

Jenna sucked in her stomach while trying to figure out what to say as she dialed Martin's number. Chilly, nearly silent during her heartfelt pleading, he finally said, "I can't help you. I've had it—years of great food, and then he goes behind my back. He's not a well man."

"What are you talking about?"

"Nothing, forget it."

"Hull will probably fire me if you're not here."

"I'm trying to care about that, but I can't even get my head around it. Besides, he likes you, thinks you're just great."

"Right, sure he does."

"He does. And believe me, 'like' is a major term of endearment for that guy."

"Please, Martin, please, I'm begging."

"I am as stone." Their former chef hung up.

"Do you know how to cook, Jorge?"

"I could do my mother's enchiladas Suizas, that's it. We usually have it with guacamole and some stray pieces of cucumber. He'll know old Martin didn't come up with this."

"He'll know he's not here, Jorge. He almost always drops into the kitchen and talks with him before the lunches."

"That depends on what time he arrives, and we don't know that yet, do we? I told you, he may not even show up at all."

"Do you ever call him to see what time he's coming in?"

"Never."

"I've got an idea. I could make my grandmother's lamb stew and boxty."

"This is nuts. We'll have to order something from a restaurant, somewhere he's never been, though for fifteen people and in now, just two and a half hours . . . Jesus."

"'Boxty on the griddle, boxty on the pan; if you can't make boxty, you'll never get a man,' an old Irish rhyme." Jorge stared at her in horror. "No, the stew is really good, especially if you pour in a lot of stout. Makes it full and rich. And the boxties are like crispy potato pancakes, they're delicious. Let's make a list for the Food Emporium down the corner."

Jenna was fired up. From the short time she had worked at *NewsLink*, she had divined Hull's private code, both from the letters he wrote and the phone calls he made. He always praised the professionally skilled, seasoned practitioner of any art. Carpentry, plumbing, window washing, writing, it made no difference what the craft, or the person's rank in society and, in fact, he seemed to worship his daughter's meticulous and dedicated violin teacher. Poor performance, sloppiness, gross mistakes, he had no time for them professionally, and he had bragged to her about firing several members of the staff for such ineptitude. This mini-crisis made her want to show Vincent Hull that she could not only survive but actually triumph, if only through her grandmother's Christmas dinner. Not that he would know who really did it, but would he?

Three full boxes of groceries arrived within the half hour. Jorge took over all office chores, while shouting encouragement to Jenna as she cooked, chopping onions, brushing mushrooms, slicing the lamb. She needed left-over mashed potatoes for the dish but had instead gotten garlic instant mashed ones. Only occasionally did she take a swig of stout to keep up her spirits. The stew filled up two platters, and the boxties rose like crispy skyscrapers. The dessert came from the store, an ice cream cake covered with lemon frosting and dotted with yellow rosettes.

When he eyeballed the mountain of food, Jorge narrowed his eyes and said in a low voice, "I think we're saved." According to Angelo, who had just called, Hull was indeed coming in for the lunch. Maybe he wouldn't ask any questions, as accustomed as he was to the seamless web of his own importance. Jorge stood beside the steaming saucepans, tasting everything. He pronounced it "fantastic, better than Martin's. Maybe you can be the new chef."

"Don't get nuts." But Jenna felt accomplished for the first time since she had arrived in New York City.

Just as Jenna said this, they heard the heavy footsteps of Vincent Hull and the de rigueur chorus of greetings from staffers. It was nearly twelve thirty, and the big man barely looked at either one of them, striding toward his office. "Hello, guys," he muttered.

"Hello there," Jenna said brightly. Hull slammed the office door behind him, while she and Jorge made anguished faces at each other.

They had a half hour until the lunch, and now Jorge compulsively hovered over the warming of the food. "I don't know. The meal's always cold when we serve at Thanksgiving, I mean, it's impossible to keep everything hot together. Martin's some kind of genius. I take back everything I said about him."

"I do too," Jenna said, sipping what had to be her fourth cup of coffee in less than an hour, attempting to counteract the heavy brown Guinness. Her head jangled like a tin pot, and she felt as if she would jump up and scream.

A tall man with a thick head of black hair arrived, "the dreaded Howard Stern," Jorge whispered. The man barely looked at them, as Jorge indicated which door he should walk through. Several frightened junior writers appeared, right behind the Secretary of the Interior, an intense, gray little man. While Jenna stood at the door with the plate of lamb stew, Hull entered the dining room and seated himself at the head of the table, shaking his head at her as if mystified, and when Jorge appeared with plates of piled high boxties, the big man frowned. He said nothing, however, after a cough and a signal for some wine.

Jorge and Jenna lost track of time, and they even had fun in a madcap, end-of-the-world sort of way. Later Hull appeared at the kitchen door, leaning into the door jamb on his elbow. He grinned at them, looking strangely gleeful. "Well, well, hidden talents from you two."

"Thank you," Jorge said, at a loss really. "Jenna did it. I just helped."

"They were my grandmother's recipes. We had that meal every year at Christmas, but this is the first time I actually made it myself."

Vince laughed. "I'm guessing Martin didn't show."

"That would be a yes," Jenna said. "Actually, he quit."

"Don't do any more cleanup. I've called the Regency, and they're sending over a crew. You guys relax."

For the rest of the day, Hull worked in his office, asking Jenna to take no calls. She worried over this, quivered almost as she kept checking the panel of ever-blinking lights. He was even placing calls himself, unheard of since she had worked for him. Where oh where was the Wyoming plan in all this? Had it evaporated?

Around six, Jorge came over to her desk and swiveled

her chair so she faced him. "We took one for the team today, McCann. You're a pro, I've got to say that."

"Thank you, Jorge. It's good to know I can do something." She stood up and kissed him on the cheek, while he laughed nervously.

They didn't notice Hull watching them until he cleared his throat. "If Martin were here, which obviously he is not, I'd shoot the son of a bitch."

Buoyed by her triumph, Jenna giggled. "Oh, you can't do that. Think of the lawsuits." She had visions, yes she did right at this moment, of all the great things she could do—scale a mountain, wave to a crowd of people wishing her well, the world saluting her goodness and expertise. She could rescue everybody, and each person would be grateful.

Jorge put on his coat. "I need to go home and walk the dog."

Now Jenna found herself alone with Vincent Hull, who showed no signs of leaving. "It's been a long day for all of us."

"Yes," she answered, conscious that she looked sweaty, a bit like somebody's maid, as she was, pretty much.

"I loved those potato pancake things."

"Boxties. With those you could take over the world."

"I certainly hope so."

"I guess they won't have any of those in Wyoming."

He looked down at her now, in kingly fashion, "Not at my restaurant there." Just for a moment Jenna thought he stared at her breasts.

"You have another restaurant?"

"More of a diner. I'm going out to Water Mill this weekend, but maybe next Thursday or Friday, I'll show you the wonders of Jackson Hole."

SIX

Another four days went by with no Vincent Hull and no weekend trip to Wyoming. The pavements of New York stank, the corners filled up with trash, and the subway blasted hot air through the even hotter air above. It seemed like a concrete oven. On this particular Thursday, two bags of letters sat directly in front of Jenna's desk. "Nothing really changes in the summer here, does it?" Now of course, she was freezing, as the air conditioning blasted away.

Jorge sighed and looked down into his coffee cup. "Not really."

On the fifth day of the painful wait for her boss, all in vain, the fashionable Tasha appeared in a long red skirt with a black tank top, showing off her shapely arms and remarkable breasts. Jenna had never known anyone who looked as dashing as this woman. "I'm taking her for an iced tea, Jorge. I mean, how much more of this can she take?"

Jorge seemed surprised, but then went quickly back to his work. "Don't talk about me, that's all I ask."

"Never." Tasha waved Jenna up out of her chair and walked arm in arm with her down the hall, toward the coffee cart, where she did a sudden about face, "Let's go to the deli outside. I've got to get out of here."

At a table under the atrium in the noisy center of the little café, where a fountain spewed water to cool them, the two sipped big glasses of iced green tea, trying to talk above the din. Jenna couldn't stop looking at Tasha's velvety chocolate-colored skin and her long, ruby red fingernails. The elegant woman didn't talk much, seemingly absorbed in some inner drama, but finally she laughed abruptly at nothing at all, then stood up and sat down again, a very strange move in this location, magically in possession of an uninhibited self that Jenna had not seen before. New Yorkers just commanded space because they had to, with so many others vying for it. "Hull's one of a kind. You'll be surprised." Jenna let this pass. "So how have things gone with him?"

"Great. As of now, I'm promoted, sort of. I'm running the executive dining room."

Tasha smiled and chewed on a madeleine, offering one to Jenna as well. "He and Martin fight a lot. We'll see if Martin comes crawling back."

"Mr. Hull is attractive in some way I can't quite figure out. From one side he has this fantastic profile—I mean, for an older guy. Full frontal he's almost ugly. . . ." Jenna paused when she saw the shocked look on Tasha's face. She added quickly, "Not that that has anything to do with my job."

"He's not smart enough to avoid the big tragedies, and he savors the small ones."

"The small tragedies? I wonder if I know what those are?" But talk of their mutual boss, at this level, seemed like a seriously bad idea, so she turned back to her own humble piece of the world. "Have you eaten in the executive dining room much?"

"Three or four times, maybe, always with a group."

Of course Tasha would have attended many events that others might not. She was a person of fashion, of grace, and Jenna felt instant admiration for her, and by way of contrast, dissatisfaction with herself. Like many unformed, embryonic young women in their twenties, Jenna knew that she must "do" something, "be" something, but nothing came quickly to mind. She was only ever escaping something, that being her dreary, painful youth in the hinterland.

After her father's early death from some infection her mother could never quite name, Eileen McCann had remarried not once, but twice, the second time to an angry, jealous man, a lawyer in Youngstown, Ohio. Perpetually in a rage, annoyed at Jenna for being "sassy" and a "smarty-pants," he regularly got drunk on weekends and beat her mother up. After one drunken rampage in which he tried to throw her out the window, Jenna actually called the police on him. This triggered a series of moves by neighbors and officials, until her grandmother stepped in and took her out of that house forever. She got legal custody and moved the two of them to Burton, a peaceful, unnaturally quiet landscape in the northeast Ohio hills, farm country, but Jenna's dream had always involved the big city, nothing even remotely close to Burton, where winter lasted nine months at least. A gray, lowering sky, that was what passed for "fine," as the weatherman on television would put it, because at least it wasn't life threatening. Her college years in Athens, Ohio, remained the happiest memory of her young life.

Tasha seemed content with the silence, until, as they sipped their tea, she asked her about boyfriends. "Any of those floating around?"

"I did just meet someone, a journalist. He's very cute. Not important or anything. He's been writing about zoning somewhere upstate, Rye I think."

"That's a posh suburb . . . really."

"It is?"

"Just be sure not to tell him anything."

"I don't know anything." Jenna giggled but stopped short. She didn't want to appear a complete rube. "What about you and boyfriends?"

"No one at the moment. I don't have time, and I don't want ties of a certain kind. It's too much trouble."

And wouldn't she just feel that way, Jenna thought. A woman as beautiful as this wouldn't really need male attention, the way she knew she did. Jenna felt nearly desperate, inside herself, that is. She tried too hard in social situations. She laughed and smiled too much. She wanted to please, whereas this gleaming personage before her wanted to be on the "pleased" end of the spectrum.

"Mr. Hull promised to take me to Jackson Hole, Wyoming, one of these weekends. I'm supposed to inventory his paintings there, but I'm not sure when. I can't wait to get out of town."

Tasha stood up now, abruptly. "Gotta go."

Jenna feared she might be angry, but to her surprise, they walked down the street once again arm in arm. Such a companionable thing, an Ohio thing almost, and she felt grateful for her stunning, sophisticated friend, way cooler than her dreary roommates, who were the opposite of companionable. Right then and there she pondered friendships in New York and resolved to have more of them, more of any and all that came her way. "How long have you been at *NewsLink*, and why? It seems like all white people to me."

Tasha didn't appear offended, but instead rather proud. "I've been in publicity forever, since I first got there and started out as an intern. They've been great to me; I don't know . . . affirmative action at work, but why should I care?" She fingered a green-and-red coral necklace that hung down low over her neckline. "There are perks and stuff," she added, smiling mysteriously. "And

I'm good at my job." She seemed a happy woman, but then Tasha turned thoughtful. "You don't want to cut yourself off from other men. That could be a problem with a job like yours. You'll meet famous people, important people, and that may come to color your view. You know, no one ordinary will be good enough."

"You mean I'll go 'New York'? I don't think so." Jenna truly couldn't picture one of the captains of industry copping a feel off her under any circumstances, constrained by lawsuits or just deterred by her hopeless appearance.

"Seriously, opportunities come up, if you know what I mean, and you should be careful. There are big dogs barking everywhere."

"Not at me, but they must bark at you all the time."

Tasha hiked her purse up around her shoulders. "I'm saving myself."

"For what?" Jenna wanted to ask, but she was cut short by the harsh squeal of a cab slamming on its brakes in front of them.

Back at her desk, digging once more into her letter pile, she pondered how Tasha made her way in this very expensive world. While publicity must pay a lot more than her own pitiful salary, Jenna knew from Jorge's remarks that nobody except the major editors made much money at the magazine. Either she had resources of her own or came from a prosperous family, or maybe there was a sugar daddy, because at her salary level, she would have to be the best shopper on earth to get those clothes.

SEVEN

After another week of not seeing or hearing anything from Vincent Hull, and after going home early on Friday because there was nothing at all to do at work, Jenna got a frantic call from Jorge. "Pack your duds, Missy, you're on your way out to Teterboro. Hull came in from Water Mill and asked me to give you a call. Angelo will pick you up in twenty minutes."

"Yay!" Jenna sang out happily to the four walls of the apartment as she flung various outfits into her suitcase while her roommates looked on in bemusement. They considered her a naïve girl who probably had no idea what to expect, what to wear, even what to say to whomever she might encounter on this little junket.

"Be sure to take pictures of everything. I'll bet the house is fabulous." Vera picked lazily through the clothes Jenna was putting in her suitcase. "What about the wifey? Will she be there with the kids?"

"No idea, no idea about any of this. But I'm on my way to Big Sky country."

"That's Montana, actually." Allyson peered through the doorway while she stubbed out another cigarette in her Coors Lite. "Are we going anywhere this weekend, Vera?"

"Fire Island is a very real possibility. I know a whole bunch of people who have rented a house."

"Wherever I'm headed, it's going to be great," Jenna crowed in delight, knowing her roommates would have sliced her up with a knife and fork to get such an opportunity. Her own father had dreamt of such adventures but had never had the money, nor, it turned out, the time. He died at age thirty-eight. Now she was living the best part of his life for him.

Angelo arrived promptly, and as she sank down into the limo's fragrant black leather backseat, she struggled to contain herself. Finally she leaned forward, "This is so exciting. I've hardly been anywhere."

"It's beautiful, I can tell you that. I've been there a few times, took the wife and kids."

"Oh, my gosh, how was the house?"

"Fantastic, but we stayed in one of the guest cottages along the river. It was incredible. The kids wanted Mr. Hull to adopt them."

Jenna shivered with anticipation. She was journeying to a place she had dreamt of, this time in a private jet, ooh, but would it be small? Vera had said that when she rode on one, she couldn't even stand up in it. Jenna was an infrequent flyer, both by choice and by pocketbook, and also because she could all too easily picture herself smashed head first into the ground. As she wondered and worried about the plane's size, the limo wheeled up behind a two-engine plane, a jet anyway, though not as big as a commercial plane. It had the characteristic Hull logo on the tail, a red block letter H with a black arrow slashed through it.

While Angelo helped her with her bag, she managed to inspect several sides of the plane for dents or something unattached. Always helpful, that's how she thought of herself. She climbed up the steps and didn't even have to bend her head to enter, but when she did, she encountered a world of soft beige, cream leather seats surrounding the wooden tables, and even the curved walls were of leather. It was wonderful, a dreamy man cave, like something she'd seen once at a cigar bar near the Plaza Hotel. Unaccountably, two unknown males were sitting in the two seats at the back of the plane, talking intently and pulling papers out of briefcases. They barely looked up when she entered, one only waving his hand in her general direction.

Which seat to take? She looked to her right and then lurched herself into the nearest one, located as it was before a small table. She had spotted a single, lower jump seat near the back, along with a bar or some kind of galley. A comely woman in a navy blue uniform came over to introduce herself, "Carole," and to offer Jenna a drink. "No thank you, or well, maybe a Diet Coke." She was on the job after all, not really going off on a fun weekend, though that's what she hoped for. But where was Vincent Hull? He planned to join them, did he not? She certainly didn't want to ride alone in this, face it, small jet with a flight attendant and two businessmen-type guys. They might object to her wails during turbulence.

The engines throbbed into life, and shortly thereafter the impressive figure of Vincent Hull appeared at the entry door. He wore a dark gray suede jacket and blue jeans, restrained cowboy getup, no boots, thank goodness. Granny Mac always advised that men in cowboy boots could not be trusted. Trailing him on a leash was a big golden retriever that he led into the cabin and motioned to lie down. Smiling at her briefly, he went to the back, and through various mutterings and mumblings, she could divine that the men he talked to were not, in fact, going with them, only there to go over some papers before departure. She leaned down to pat the doggie, who eyed her sleepily and then licked her hand. A moment after she buckled herself in, Hull came up and sat in the seat directly across from her on the opposite side of the plane. She smiled self-consciously, noting the hurried departure of the two men, holding jackets and briefcases as they rushed toward the door.

"This is Duncan," Hull said and picked up his paw to shake it. "He always goes with me out there, likes the weather, the birds, and all the places to sleep. He's very old, almost thirteen, about eighty, I think, in people years."

"He's a cutie," she managed above the din of the engines. Now she appeared to scream, "I really like dogs!" He smiled and nodded her way, then threw his head back and fell asleep as they took off.

Jenna was too excited to sleep, and she watched out the window as the plane climbed up over the Hudson River. The evening sky glowed pink and velvety blue. Heading west, they flew toward the setting sun as it moved almost imperceptibly down the horizon. In a few minutes, the flight attendant came by and asked what she would like for dinner, mentioning a choice of steak with fries, curried chicken and basmati rice, filet of sole with pilaf, or "any combination of these if you would like, or something else altogether."

She chose the chicken and, when it came, ate in silence, occasionally sneaking glances over at Vincent Hull. She wasn't here to socialize, after all. Hull ate a sandwich and drank Scotch as he worked on through the hours writing notes on a yellow legal pad, never looking up from his papers at the magnificent, muted, gold twilight sky. At last even Jenna shut her eyes, lulled by the engines, rousing herself now and then to lean over and pat the dog, and at last she fell asleep. She didn't know how long she slept but awoke suddenly when the plane pitched sideways, then jolted heavily downward. Jenna tried to spot the ground in the darkness, but she could only just make out jagged mountaintops and deep canyons. Several more heavy bounces and a leftward roll had her gripping her seat. A bright light over his head, Vincent Hull kept on working the whole time and didn't even glance her way. Finally Carole came by to check her seatbelt but other than that said nothing, so Jenna figured they weren't going to crash, at least not right at that moment.

The plane bucked forward and then surged downward until one of the pilots emerged from the cockpit. With some difficulty, he bent down to whisper into Hull's ear, and Jenna leaned in to hear, but she couldn't. Finally Hull turned to her. "We're going to try for a landing at Jackson, but a storm has kicked in, so we're not sure."

"Not sure of what? Are we going to crash?" she wanted to shout but couldn't get any words out.

Her face must have registered extreme fright because in the next moment he tried to reassure her. "Relax, there's nothing we can do about it."

What was "it," Death? Jenna desperately needed a drink, and, as if reading her mind, he yelled, "Carole, a Scotch for Miss McCann here and another for me."

Wobbling from side to side like a drunk heading for the bathroom, the flight attendant made her way down the aisle and returned shortly with the Scotch, while the dog never even awoke from its slumber. Jenna took a gulp of the stinging liquid, choking on it, and then drank some more, a fire in the pit of her stomach. Subdued banging had started somewhere beneath the belly of the plane, and at this point even Duncan lifted his head. As the jet strained ever downward through the storm, it rose up seemingly just as high a moment later, and Jenna gasped, suddenly aware that she was holding her breath. Vincent

Hull looked over and put his big warm hand on top of her clenched fingers. "Don's a good pilot." She pulled his hand closer and held onto it while they attempted to land, but it was not to be as she felt the plane climb at a steep angle, swirling its way back upwards, banging still.

"Oh, my god!" she cried, flinging his hand away.

Moments later the pilot stuck his head out of the cockpit, "Want to give it another try?"

"Definitely." Hull turned to the terrified Jenna. "He did a go-around, good move. Now he'll try landing again." He noted the look on Jenna's face. "Don't be afraid. I'm not afraid. This happens all the time in Jackson Hole. What the hell, I've lived a terrific life." He waved his half-empty glass of Scotch at her.

"What about my life?" she wanted to yell, angry, in the middle of a nightmare, the kind in which you try to scream but you can't, you're just an agonized open mouth. She looked over at him with tears in her eyes. He again reached for her and clutched her hand even harder. She held onto him now with both of hers.

The plane rocked sideways, until at last she heard landing wheels lock into place. She let go of her boss and strained to see something out of the window. There, blessedly, beneath them was the runway, and they touched down moments later, still shimmying from side to side in the wind. Jenna knew nothing of Wyoming storms and even less about Jackson Hole, its notorious history of bad landings and even scarier takeoffs, but she wanted to cry out to the heavens in gratitude.

When they at last deplaned, she feared to look at the man, linked as they had been in some momentary intimacy. She was about to pick up her small bag, when Vincent picked it up himself and led her to a waiting black SUV. Inside the car, she still refused to look at him or at anything much of the surroundings, except occasionally at the ground in gratitude. At last, though, she roused herself to peer at an elk preserve just outside the airport. The big animals huddled together in the cool air. A huddle, that's what she needed, but no one very cuddly occupied any space near her, except the dog, who rested at Vincent's feet. She rubbed his head, and Duncan crawled over and stretched the length of his body across her ankles like a nice, warm doggie blanket. Hull barely looked at her; instead, he too stared out the window.

The Hull house had the air and trappings of a log cabin, but an incredibly large one. It rose up majestically on a hill perched above an expanse of flat land, beyond which mountains loomed. As she got out of the car, she could hear the rushing water of a stream nearby but couldn't see it. Her boss went on before her without looking back, because, no doubt like Jenna, he found himself in that odd state that exists between people who don't know each other but have been forced unnaturally close by circumstance.

Once inside the imposing residence, Hull disappeared without a word. Jenna turned uncertainly, cowed by the floor-to-ceiling windows and the extraordinary view they afforded, not to mention the large numbers of antlers and trophy animal heads that perched above her on the crossed timbers. Everywhere, the house was vibrant with brown and green, the velvet couches, the mottled golden wood above, below, and on the walls. She thought, "I could rule the world from here." Within moments a diminutive Hispanic lady in a white uniform led Jenna upstairs to a cozy bedroom with a fireplace and a bed covered in a red, white, and blue quilt. Modern cowboy seemed the theme, but understated. On the mantle above the fireplace perched a large oil painting of grazing cows, unlike anything she had seen in the New York collection so far, and she didn't recognize the name of the artist squiggled on the right-hand corner. This was her first and last stab at any kind of work that night, and she crawled under the covers into a warm, blessed sleep.

In the morning, she awoke to blazing sun outside her window, and now she could see more of the landscape that surrounded her. Off in the distance, the river glittered as it rushed over rocks, while even farther away the Grand Tetons rose shimmering in the morning light. She could smell coffee and, though not too sure of what to wear here, put on her jeans, a crisp blue shirt, and a cropped blazer. She wanted to strike a look somewhere between dude ranch and cowgirl, though this was all pretty tricky. She feared she might have lurched too far toward novice park ranger, but she wasn't sure.

Breakfast was arrayed on top of an enormous half-moon-shaped granite countertop surrounded by black leather barstools. No one seemed to be about, so Jenna gingerly took off the tops of the chafing dishes, marveling at the omelets, the bacon and potatoes and grilled tomatoes, just like at a restaurant. She piled food onto her plate, poured herself a cup of coffee, and stared out the window toward a corral and horses. She shivered with pleasure, enough almost to get over her night tremors after their horrendous landing, but not quite. When it was time to leave, maybe she should rent a car and drive back to New York.

Duncan wandered in, wagging his tail, and placed himself near to her stool, only once looking up in hopes of bacon, which she handed him. Finally another human being appeared, a different lady from the preceding night, who smiled and said hello in a Spanish accent and started immediately to clean up. "Has Mr. Hull had breakfast yet?" Jenna said.

The woman nodded. "Oh yes, an hour ago." It was only seven now, nine by New York time. "He said he would catch up with you sometime during the day. But also, he left a camera for you in the study."

"Thank you." Jenna jumped up out of her torpor, but then turned uncertainly. The woman pointed to a door off in the distance.

The library struck a solemn note much like the Hull office in New York, but with Western-style paintings, a bronze sculpture of a bucking horse on the desk, and yet again, scattered about, more antlers, though smaller ones. Already she had seen a multitude of paintings, most of them not at all in the eclectic mode of his townhouse. They were realistic pictures of mountains and streams and horses, mostly the product of the nineteenth century, not at all bad or folksy, instead mirroring the landscape. So many books—two ladders were placed to reach them. On the enormous desk, Jenna saw what had to be the camera, and she pulled it gently out of its heavy leather case. It looked old fashioned, complex, and had "Leica M6" written on the top. She'd only ever had little point-and-shoot numbers and had no idea how this object might work, but she slung it over her shoulder without checking for film or any instructions, just for the look of the thing. She wanted to fit in, whatever "in" that prevailed, and headed outside toward the sound of horses.

In the corral, the big animals pranced and nipped at each other, but several just munched on hay from the trough. A bay and a chestnut nuzzled together, while a black horse with a white star kept biting the tail of a pregnant-looking mare. Suddenly she heard Duncan rush up behind her, barking. He scooted under the fence and began chasing the black horse away from the mare. "He always does that," she heard Hull say as he came up beside her. "He wants to be top dog." Jenna smiled into the distance, afraid to look him in the eye, and then began to fiddle with her new camera. "Watch out with that, only five hundred of these were produced, hand-made out of titanium."

"It smells like a new car."

"It's a classic. I'll show you how to use it later. Don't drop it down a well or throw it into horse turds." Jenna gave him a look. "You survived last night, I see." Now he put his hand on her arm, lightly, then took it away again.

"I did." She sighed but didn't want a defeatist attitude to mess up her life, more importantly her job, and so she brightened. "But I love it here. The heat in the city never did anything for me but wreck my hair."

"Obviously a major reason to get out of town. Wait." Hull disappeared behind a door into the barn. He came back with two gun cases, and this time she easily recognized the firearms. With a chamois, Vincent rubbed the barrel of a .357 magnum revolver, placing it on top of the case, after which he pulled a smaller gun out of the other box, a Ruger .22. "Choose your weapon." She looked up at him, confused for a moment, but he took hold of both of her hands and placed one gun in each, next a pair of earmuffs.

She had to laugh. "I'm a two-fisted gunslinger, all right. I'll keep the .357 magnum."

"You really do need to know how to shoot out here, just in case a bear comes at you from nowhere. A little like New York. If you see any wild animals, remember to make yourself big." He smiled warmly at her, and for the first time she could see why women might adore him. What followed was an hour's worth of shooting at paper targets set up on a hill not far from the corral. After a few bull's-eyes with the magnum, Hull took it from Jenna's hand, said, "Not bad," and gave her the pistol. "This is what the Mossad uses to kill people," he said.

As his custom-made New York rifle had well indicated, the man was an accomplished marksman and expertly lined up his sights again and again. Such activities gave her a chance to observe his muscular arms and physical stance, a glimpse of his body she had never seen before, a bit of a shock too, as she considered his age. But before very long the horses grew agitated, and she began to slow down, then stopped shooting altogether. For a time Hull ignored her, but finally turned. "What's wrong?"

"We're scaring the horses."

"They need to deal with being scared. All of us do."

"They don't have earmuffs."

He gave her a look of disdain. Still, he packed up the guns, and she followed behind him as he tramped back to the barn. He waved her away, though, and she realized that it wouldn't do to depend on some sympathetic contact in an airplane that had nothing to do with her job. "You can start your work now with that fancy camera you left sitting on a rock. I think it would be a good idea. My daughters will be here day after tomorrow, and then I'll get the plane to take you back to New York."

"How about a bus ticket?" He didn't even look back at her.

EIGHT

Vincent Hull's obsession with controlling time extended also to his marriage. Over the years Sabine Hull had resigned herself to his temporal fencing, the constant changing of the time they should meet, when they should dine, when he would come home, the reason for which was never given. Periodically she would flare up about this exotic form of abuse and protest, but it did her little good. Often as not, the control-time thing played out, somewhat comically, in her husband's endless phone calls. He stationed her at a distance but kept phoning because, down the line, he did not want his empire diminished by half. Now he realized that even in this area, he had been neglecting his duty to stay in touch, and so, sequestered in a small aerie on the second floor of the Wyoming house, an octagonal room with a telescope, he poured more eighteen-year-old Macallan into his glass and stared at the phone. Glumly he registered the books that spilled out onto the mahogany table in front of him. How many had he actually read? Perhaps a third, not too bad.

He picked up the telephone and dialed the Water Mill house. Amelia, his younger daughter, answered: "Hi Dad, I'm on the phone with my friend from school. Can you call back?"

"No, I cannot. Is your mother home?"

"She is, I think, somewhere, but I don't want to hang up on—"

"Amelia girl, you can call her on your cell."

"I don't have a cell. You told me I was too young.

"I think you do have one. It should be on the front hall table with the mail, in a FedEx box."

"You got me one? Oh, you're the best. I love you, I love you."

"Put your mother on now, sweetie." Vincent waited. He knew that his recent behavior had caused his wife anxiety, and for the first time, real fear. Perhaps he had erred in the display of a large drawing he had sketched out one day while contemplating his own future, a doodle really, aptly titled "Vince's Empire." Why he had done so was perfectly clear to him, but he knew that his wife's French mind would immediately get to work on the fact that he was counting up his possessions; nevertheless, he had tacked it up on the wall of the Water Mill study. There he stood, a small stick figure in the middle. Like spokes from a wheel with him at the center, out of each limb dangled a bubble of wealth: his mines, his agribusinesses, his hobbies—that would be newspapers and the magazine—then finally yet other hobbies, a bar in Clyde Park, Montana, a diner right here in Jackson Hole, several pieces of property in Sedona, Arizona, and lastly the new restaurant in Manhattan.

"Allô," Sabine said, in the French mode she always adopted when answering the phone.

"Hello, darling, it's Vince."

"I see by the phone number that it's you."

"We had a nightmare of a flight, had to go around after a failed first try."

"Nothing can kill you, Vince." She said this as if she might like to try.

"It's good of you to think so, a vote of confidence."

There was another pause, weighted, for him unpleasant, and then she said, "We?"

"That new little girl from the office." He made Jenna sound almost like an infant. "You met her at the fundraiser." "Oh, I do remember, but I meet so many people. She was cute, *quelle gamine*." She certainly did not mention the scene the "new little girl" had observed at their hotel suite. "The usual kid in her twenties, doesn't know much, seems at a loss." He hurried on, somewhat irrationally warding off further comments from his wife. "Neurotic too, if I'm not mistaken. She's the one doing the art inventory. I hope she can do it, probably won't even be able to work the camera. Given what I've seen so far, she's not so brilliant, a bit of a *boudin*." He wished he could tell her she was a three-legged dwarf with a hairy chin, but of course his wife had actually met the girl in question. He had given some thought as to whether he wanted to make his wife jealous of this young person but had decided against it. He sometimes did and sometimes did not wish to inflame his wife's passions.

This same little girl, needing help with the camera, was poised at the door to knock, but when she heard him speaking on the phone, she had waited, listening. Now she jumped back from the door as if she'd been punched. Up the endless hall she ran, until completely out of breath, she finally found her room, where she flung herself down on the bed, hiding her head under the pillow and squishing it against her ears. Then she sat up and stared at the ceiling. "Not so brilliant." And what did *boudin* mean? Jenna wanted to quit her job and leave this phony log cabin immediately, but she couldn't think how to get out of there. Whatever a *boudin* was, it sounded fat and unfortunate, and certainly nobody had ever called her that before, probably because they'd never even heard the word. She wanted to hide, but where? She was his little slave, one of a pile of them, clearly expendable.

How to get revenge, how to show him she was smart, yes, very smart. First off, all by herself she would master the hugely expensive camera. She could do it; she would have to do it. When she had seen the amazing thing earlier, it all seemed hopeless, and she had planned to ask him to show her how to work it, as she knew this was one of his fetishes. He collected old, medium-old, and new Leicas and had many of them displayed in his New York office, but there were five or six here too, perched on the shelves in the library. Her own little number, the M6, she had fussed and fumbled with several times, but knowing her highly developed ability to destroy machines of all types, she had been afraid to go too far. Yes, she did have a manual, but why waste time reading that? This one time she must. For the next hour, she sat on her bed and devoured every diagram in the book. At the finish, she felt at ease enough to photograph the quilt in her room, the view from her window, even her own pedicured foot, because she had always been quite vain about her feet. But how to get much work done without encountering the man? She would start with the cow picture in her room and work her way around the upstairs, while for all she knew he would be out killing more paper targets or even some poor elk.

So flew by the rest of the day as she matched each artwork with a receipt from her pile of papers. Moving upwards in the house, she was just getting to a sort of mezzanine area, what Vincent had called "his aerie," with telescopes and several rare books on a table, when she heard a familiar male voice calling her name. She moved to the top of the steps, where she looked down upon the cavernous room below. Vincent Hull gazed up at her.

"Come on with me. I'm going into town, meeting some buddies at the diner I own."

"I don't know, I'm working—using the M-6, easy really." That would fix him.

"Don't be silly. It's close to dinnertime. I'll need relief from all the testosterone that will be sitting at that table, and there are a few paintings there that you can put on your list."

"No, no, I don't think I should go."

"You're going."

"Okay, just let me change my clothes."

"No, no, I'm sure you're fine."

Nevertheless Jenna ran into her room, wiping at her face and pulling on a tight black jersey top and her short black jacket. She looked at herself in the mirror. Normally she was mostly pleased with her appearance, but this time she gazed with a critical eye. Could she somehow fix herself in five minutes, to change whatever offended, especially when she didn't even know what was wrong? Running a comb through her hair, she tried to laugh and said, "Fuck it." She stuck the camera into its leather pouch.

Outside the house, Hull was waiting for her in the SUV. She climbed in without even looking at him, without saying a word. He looked over, also silent, shoving the big vehicle into gear. This particular drive into town involved a torturous, twisting road, and she could feel herself growing queasy, but still she refused to speak. At last, he glanced over, saying, "You look just like a native. That's almost a uniform here."

"Did you say you were meeting friends?"

"They're what pass for friends here. Roger Bartel is an executive at Coca-Cola, the other's the town butcher. You've got to be nice to that guy or you get nothing decent to eat, unless you shoot it yourself, which I sometimes do."

"Oh." She looked out at the mountains in the distance. "The Grand Tetons, *Les Grands Tetons*, big breasts in French."

"I know what they're called." Jenna would have preferred to take one good shot at the man sitting next to her.

"How's the work going?"

"Fine, they're nice paintings."

"'Nice' is what I'm afraid of. We don't want 'nice.' We don't like 'nice'." She understood what he meant but didn't feel like agreeing, and her mind worked only on getting out of there. She seemed now to inhabit an actual nowhere, a place where neither car nor truck moved either with them or against them, and no planes of any type thundered down into the airport. Only the wind swept over the green land, fields that were dotted here and there with sheep and goats, but no more elk that Jenna could see. And before them the road ran unencumbered with signage of any kind. It was all landscape.

"It's very shiny around here," she said.

Hull looked over again at her. "Shiny how?"

"Shiny as two dogs' balls under a bed."

Hull erupted in laughter. "What the hell does that mean?"

"My late grandmother used to say this all the time. I think it means the balls dogs play with. If they're under the bed, they'd be clean. But maybe it means that their own little balls are shiny?" She giggled at herself for saying the word "balls." She was mad and nervous and nuts all at the same time.

"Tell me about your grandmother."

"Why would you want to know about Margaret Grace McCann from Burton, Ohio?"

"Because she knew about dogs' balls."

"I'll tell you when I know you better." Granny's sayings were secret information, of great worth, spoken silently only to herself. Hull stared at her. Whatever the request, no matter how outrageous lewd or expensive, people almost always gave him what he wanted, but now she had refused him.

"At least you could call me Vince."

"Maybe someday."

Their destination, what he had called his "diner," proved to be a largish tavern with pool tables, pinball machines, and seats at the counter in the shapes of saddles. The cowboy theme prevailed, and most of the people in the place acted like the real thing, cowboys indeed, cowgirls too. At least twenty men were playing pool, and the place was full, but Hull entered like the proprietor he was and sat down at one of the big center tables. Jenna wavered a moment, thinking to move around to the other side across from him, but he pulled her into the seat next to him. Up from behind came a tall, heavyset man wearing a worn-looking cowboy hat. He sat down next to her on the other side and pumped her hand vigorously. "Roger Bartel," he announced himself. "Once again, Vincent, I find you in the presence of a beautiful woman."

Jenna winced and gulped at a glass of water near her seat. No, she was just a big fat something or other. In due course another fellow plonked himself down opposite her, a fiftyish man with a red face and gray hair in a ponytail, the town butcher, he must be. He, too, seemed pleased to see her, unsurprised at a Hull functionary joining them for drinks and dinner. And what a dinner it was. Shrimp and avocados to start, surrounded with slices of lemon and small glass bowls of hot sauce, followed by seared steaks, piles of fresh sweet corn, salad with a dressing made of lime juice, garlic, and salt, slightly warm, served atop a magnificent heap of greens. Hull presided over the feast like a great king dispensing favors, consulting with the waiter, waving at guests, jumping up periodically throughout to shoot a little pool. The butcher pronounced the meat "perfect," as he himself had provided it, and the Coca-Cola man alternated between proclaiming the beauties of the wine and sipping from a Coke can. "I don't know how you do it, Vince. Hell, it's just a diner, but we could be at Le Cirque."

"No meat like this in New York," the butcher bragged, and even Jenna had to admit the food was the best she'd ever tasted. "Maybe even no wine," he added. It turned out that Hull stocked the tavern with bottles he had collected, so the locals drank better than many a prince.

"What brings you to our overpriced, overpopulated little hole in the wall?" the apparently jolly head of Coca-Cola wanted to know, addressing Jenna.

"I'm doing an inventory of Mr. Hull's paintings, and there are quite a few at his house here."

"Checking out his hobbies, eh?" The butcher laughed, while the Coke man punched him on the arm.

"Don't embarrass the girl." Hull took a long drink of his wine.

"I really just wanted to get out of New York. It's so hot there in the summer."

"And here I thought you cared about my artwork," Hull said, with a laugh. Both men joined in the joke, conspiring in something she only dimly understood, the secret male commentary on the sexual availability of the women around them.

Jenna wanted to get out of there, out of their presence, out of the overheated masculine need to be the center, the beginning, and the end, and the mental feasting on a woman's body. She wanted to look at them naked and tell them those fat bellies didn't get up the hormones in any girl she knew, but of course she just sat there. And Hull didn't have a fat belly at all, that she could see at least.

The party went on and on, and Jenna had never consumed so much wine in her life. Fortunately she interlaced the alcohol with a great deal of food, figuring if she just kept eating, she might not fall over in a heap. At some point the talk turned to guns and shooting, the men raising up their arms, pointing all over the room with imaginary sights, and clicking with their fingers, and this prompted her to leave the table. After all, she had a job of sorts, and she tried as hard as she could to canvass the room for artwork, slipping herself between intent pool players, wandering drinkers, and the dancers who side-stepped and reeled to country western music blaring from two speakers in the back corner of the restaurant. She found one very large rodeo scene, another possibly valuable Frederick Remington buffalo roundup picture, a beautiful photograph of an Apache Sun Dance by Edward S. Curtis, and at last, in a corner, a marvelous painting by George Catlin of moose at a water hole. These treasures, so vulnerable here to an outstretched elbow or a slop of wine, she neatly captured with the Leica.

Several of the pool players eyed her while she did her work, and for this she was grateful, as Hull's earlier comments replayed themselves endlessly in her head. Shortly thereafter a handsome young woman in a cropped T-shirt and low slung jeans that revealed a strip of her flat stomach, with short black hair tipped in purple, suddenly came up to Jenna and asked her to dance, putting her arm around her shoulder while she spoke.

Startled, Jenna said loudly above the din, "I don't know what to do to this music." So far only country western music had been playing, "jiggle music" she called it.

"Don't worry. I'll show you." The agile, leggy girl whirled her around in a circle, as everyone in the place watched. Out of two enormous speakers altogether different music began to sound, weighted with the rough magic of sex and sweat. The young woman, revealing herself as Helena, drew her forcefully forward, and Jenna found herself falling into a dreamy fog. At last she closed her eyes, conscious all the while that she moved her hips as if in love and in bed.

The music stopped. There was a silence, and the many who had watched erupted in applause. As they did so, Helena leaned toward Jenna and whispered into her ear, "You haven't lived until you've been fucked by Vincent Hull."

Jenna jumped back, blushing, in shock, afraid that over the din someone would have heard. She turned her head toward Hull, who stared back at her with a grave look on his face. "Thank you for the dance, but I just work for him."

"Yes, you do." Helena gave her a slight smile.

Jenna backed away, moving toward her table. Would these half-in-the-bag men have seen any of this in her face? "Watch out for that one," the butcher said as she sat down. "She's dangerous."

A slice of chocolate pecan pie awaited her, and she tucked into it, so as not to have to talk. With the last forkful, she announced that she felt "stuffed."

"Like a sausage," Mr. Coke said.

"Yes, like a *boudin*." Hull laughed heartily, but, for a moment not really believing what she heard, Jenna stopped breathing. *Boudin* was a sausage, and she looked like one. Heat spread from her face to her neck, and she pulled open her sweater, then touched her blouse at her breasts and fanned herself.

"What is a *boudin* exactly?" she burst out.

"It's French blood sausage."

"Made out of blood?"

"And a little head meat for textural contrast." Hull laughed again.

"Stop torturing the girl," the butcher said. Jenna stared down into her wine glass. She was as fat as a blood sausage.

And so the party broke up. No longer quite drunk herself, Jenna observed Hull to be completely sober, but how could he be after this? He was tall and broadly built, with room for booze without muddling his head. "I've had Manuel drive down from the house. He'll take us home and have someone else pick up our car," he told her. No matter how hateful he seemed, he provided the blissful protection of money, and that, at the very least, supplied peace of mind.

Outside, the wind had turned the air chilly, and Jenna and Hull very nearly huddled together, both silent. She bit her lip in dismay, the sausage image glued to her like something ugly and tainted. And then there was the sexy dancer's words, ". . . fucked by Vincent Hull," that rolled through her head like a challenge or a command, explosive. When he put his jacket around her shoulders, she did not protest. Up to the house, the ride seemed like a slog into her own peculiar hell, and so the minute she got there, she rushed up to her room without a word or a thank you.

In the morning, after a terrible sleep in which she dreamt of crying, skinny babies, Jenna awoke to find Vincent Hull gone. He had left a note for her saying that his daughters had decided not to come out after all and that the plane would be back for her in two days, by which time she should have completed her work. This information came as a tremendous relief, and she immediately got into her jeans and went outside, down the jagged hill that led to the river. There she sat, dropping her toes into the freezing water, wiggling them, and then dipping her hands in to feel the river's force. Up before her rose those Grand Tetons, so French and yes, sexual. The whole landscape, majestic with meaning, little tufts of green peeping out between the rocks, made this world infinitely desirable to her, and she closed her eyes to fix their picture in her mind. Once in New York again, she knew she would dream she was back here, water glistening on her feet, rushing over her with a sound she never wanted to forget.

In the remaining two days, Jenna roamed the big faux cabin, empty now save for herself, the housekeeper, and a small cadre of staff inside and out, cleaning constantly. Clipboard in hand, taking notes on every single piece of art on the main floor, she photographed each with the extraordinary Leica. Most works dated from the mid- to late-nineteenth century, by artists like Waugh and Church, not unknowns, but still not vastly expensive, at least according to the receipts she had. Several good-sized mountain landscapes bore the name Edgar Payne, a California *plein air* painter from the 1920s. He had captured the soft, burning twilight she herself had seen every evening. It was restful sort of work, the careful positioning of the camera, broken only by the sound of one of the maids vacuuming, and she liked the feel of something precious and vintage in her hands. The phone almost never rang, and she herself didn't answer it anyway.

In the wake of her personal isolation, she could think only of the words of that Helena person. Was it true, what she said about Vincent Hull's sexual prowess?

PART TWO

Late Summer, 1999

Ten percent of the nation's top executives are stockpiling canned goods, buying generators, and even purchasing handguns.

—MATT RICHTEL, "Mounting a Defense Against Millennium Bug," *The New York Times*, August 20, 1999

When you're dead, you're dead, as dead as Kelsey's nuts.

—MARGARET GRACE MCCANN

ONE

By the time Jenna got ready for the trip home, it no longer stupefied her that she would ride in a private plane. Amazing how one could get used to such luxuries. The previous trip was engraved on her mind, perhaps, more accurately, on her stomach and deeper down innards, but this time, when the pilot came out and greeted her, he apologized for the "landing mishap," and she acted brave and assured in this conversation, bolder than she really felt. "It was nothing. You did a good job."

All these thoughts swept away when she heard the engines roar on takeoff, but she didn't want to appear so frightened that the by-now-familiar flight attendant, Carole, perhaps a company spy, would report her back to higher-ups as a coward. Instead, she lay back and feigned sleep, until over the Gros Ventre mountains, that efficient woman returned and handed Jenna a Champagne flute, which she downed in a nanosecond. Jenna gave way to a feeling of "What the hell?" She got seriously drunk on the plane and didn't care who knew it.

Clearly she needed to go straight home when the plane finally touched down—it was now about seven in the evening New York time—but it turned out that Jorge had radioed the pilot and informed him that she, Jenna, should reappear at the office. This command she registered with a sense of panic, but almost nothing could contain her joy at landing without incident. Once inside the Town Car, she surveyed herself in Angelo's rear view mirror and fluffed some blush onto her cheeks, refreshed her lipstick, and crossed herself, though she had given up on the church when she was thirteen. "God bless," Angelo muttered, and she laughed, making a face at him.

Outside the car, she stood for a moment to steady herself, staring upwards at her place of work. The Hull companies occupied an entire building that rose with almost outrageous grace above Fifth Avenue, and since a noted French architect had designed the structure in the late 1930s, it sported zigzags and starbursts and stylized animals at play among other fanciful elements that marked it as the product of a highly developed but off-beat taste. Beneath the topmost spire rested an immense golden clock that ticked off the minutes with a sharp click. Even liquored up, Jenna thought the building didn't look quite right for a business organization, even less so for *NewsLink,* but now that she knew about the art scattered across the country in the Hull homes, she understood the look and its intent. "I'm not like you, not in any way gray or stolid or boring," that's what it said to envious men and women in suits staring up at it from the street below.

She arrived to find a party going full speed in Vincent Hull's office. A buffet had been laid out, exotic cheeses, chafing dishes of beef stew and veal *blanquette,* plates of warm French bread, and yes, still more wine, the red very dry, the white pleasantly bright and not too cold. Standing in the doorway, she looked about for Jorge, and spied in the distance her new friend Tasha, looking particularly delicious in a black sheath and a heavy gold necklace. That intriguing woman laughed and talked with Hull and some man Jenna didn't know. At least her boss seemed happy; he had to be, for it seemed that in every time zone, it was cocktail hour.

"What are we celebrating?" Jenna whispered to Jorge, whom she had finally found munching on a baguette slathered in butter.

"The opening of his new restaurant."

"I just ate at the diner in Wyoming."

"Hmm, this will be in a different style. He had a French architect work on the thing. You know, he loves all things French . . . mostly all things." To her eyes, Jorge appeared slightly tipsy himself and repeated, "Everything has to be French."

"So true," and as she spoke Tasha advanced their way, looming over them in a pair of black stilettos.

She reached out and hugged Jenna. "You had a good time, right?" She seemed at once knowing and curious.

"Just work."

"Oh no, I pictured you out there with cowboys and cows and elk and the buffalo roaming." Tasha, too, appeared definitely worked up with partying.

"I did hang out with a few of those."

"It couldn't have been that hard."

"Actually, it was fabulous, in a drunken, life-threatening sort of way."

"Here," Tasha smiled. "Let me give you some wine," she said as she swiped a glass off the tray of a circulating young woman in a black uniform. "Nothing but the best."

Jenna took the glass, also a small sip, amazed that yes, once again, what she tasted rose above anything else she had ever had, but sobriety was critical in this instance, and she merely pretended to imbibe. Tasha went away as fast as she had appeared, and Jenna watched as her newfound friend immediately reentered the charmed circle surrounding Vincent Hull. He had yet to look at Jenna.

Whatever her professional obligations, she vowed to leave that fiesta as soon as possible. It was simply too much to stand there and think of herself as a *boudin* while Tasha swanned about dazzling the world. But Jorge wouldn't leave her side, getting more and more effusive, finally confiding to her, beneath the noise, "I think he opens up all these restaurants so he'll have someone to eat with. Normal people don't want to talk to him." Jenna had no reply to this, but looked around to see if she could spot Mrs. Hull. Finally she had to ask Jorge. "Oh, she rarely comes to work things. They bore her, she gets bored easily, that's my impression. Plus her husband never seems to take much notice of her. There are distractions, if you know what I mean." She could guess of what kind.

How to get away, that was really all Jenna could think. "I think I'll go. I'm exhausted," but before she could make her escape, the elusive Mrs. Hull entered the room. With her chic, short dark hair and her graceful purple dress, she really put everyone else to shame, looking so self-contained, so confident, and several staffers joined her immediately.

Hull chose this moment to move toward Jenna, and when he did, the sea of people surrounding him parted almost biblically. "You made it." He observed her with care.

"Yes, another successful flight. I walked away from it."

"You sure did, and you're looking terrific."

"Really?" She had a bit more archness in her speech than might, strictly speaking, be appropriate for a young lady employee.

Before he could respond to this, Sabine Hull joined them. "Here you both are," she exclaimed. She touched Jenna on the arm and greeted her husband with a mock military salute. Hull seemed startled but leaned in and kissed his wife quickly on the cheek.

"Did you get what you needed in Jackson Hole?" she inquired of Jenna.

"Yes, I think so. Lovely paintings."

Sabine Hull made a face. "Appropriate to the place, I think." She looked down and wiggled one of her shoes on a small, elegant foot, then brightened. "I have some exciting news, a documentary, by a filmmaker I know in France. He's asked me to be in it. It's about young women who marry much older men, like you, Vincent. My mother always said you were too old for me."

Hull surveyed his wife up and down. "You're not young enough for that movie." He walked away. Sabine Hull gave Jenna and Jorge a sardonic little smile.

Despite the late hour and her fatigue, Jenna avoided Angelo and took a cab all the way back to Gramercy Park because she wanted to think about what she had just witnessed. "He should be shot with shit 'til he's dead and dirty," she said under her breath. That's just about what Vincent Hull deserved.

The following few days found Jenna back at the strange intersection between importance and irrelevance she occupied behind her desk in Hull's suite of offices, until a surprise came her way. Tasha called and asked her to accompany her to dinner at a fashionable eatery on the Upper West Side. Though she couldn't think why this entrenched inhabitant of Vincent Hull's world continued to single her out, she couldn't pass up a free dinner. She met her new friend at a sparse, white-walled sort of restaurant loaded with skinny young women in black, teetering in stilettos, all jammed up against the bar talking on cell phones and scrambling for drinks, young men hovering nearby. She wondered who they were, what they did, and how could they afford to live in Manhattan? But they seemed happy. Or maybe just nerved up? She looked down in horror at the piece of scotch tape attached to the buckle on her old green sandals, herself always in a state of disrepair. Why had she come? Mainly because Tasha was one of the few people who seemed to like her at all, and she worked in a place where almost no one except Jorge had had the nerve to befriend her, what with the Hull overhang of massive, total importance given to anyone attached to him. Inti had been the only male to brave that particular moat, and he had left town. At the very least, Tasha appeared to have good sense and clear advice, which she seemed prepared to dispense in this overheated atmosphere. "Don't cut yourself off. You should get out more."

"Right. After flying to Wyoming, almost getting killed."

"I know."

Jenna paused, "Wait, how did you know about that?"

Tasha took a sip of her gin and tonic, picking out a slice of lime and chewing on the rind reflectively. "I hear things. Hull told us."

"Us?"

"Everybody in publicity."

"From what I've seen, I can't imagine that he likes publicity."

"Our job is to make sure that nothing personal about him gets reported. He wants a carefully manufactured image for *NewsLink*, but nothing that will reflect on his own private doings. Even the seventy-five-million-dollar Mark Rothko painting he bought last month he tried to hide, but of course the auction house leaked it. It's an anti-publicity department, dedicated to personal paranoia and the putting-out of fires. We could craft a fabulous image for him because he is indeed revered for his philanthropy, not only in education, but also his commitment to very important medical research; and yet he won't let us talk about any of it. He just doesn't get how a carefully crafted image can overwhelm the modern world and make everyone forget the bad stuff. I should look for another job."

"Why don't you?" Jenna almost had to shout over the drinkers and diners.

"There are perks. And I'm very good at what I do." This lovely woman with the silken brown skin and high cheekbones stared down into the vastness of her drink. Just then two tipsy, well-dressed young men rattled by, stopping suddenly near them, as if hitting a wall.

"Whoa, where have you been since I last came here?" the taller of the two said to Tasha.

"Sitting right here, waiting for you." She gave Jenna a look.

"What about you, cutie?" The other man was a cheeky fellow sporting a pocket-handkerchief and a polka-dotted tie.

Jenna looked up into some very white teeth and a dazzling smile. "What about me?"

"Are you from around here?" The two men laughed.

"Not really. I'm a visitor from Ohio, just passing through."

"Thank you for stopping by," Tasha unexpectedly said and handed the first young man her card. "We'll see you later," she added, and he turned away.

"Why did you do that?"

"Just to get rid of him. There was no other way, really. Besides, as I said, you shouldn't cut yourself off. Working where we do, you can get a weird sense of things. Stuff seems normal that is actually bizarre. You need to be careful. It's all very seductive."

Jenna couldn't tell exactly what she was trying to say, except possibly, "Don't be swayed by all the luxury."

"Men know things and do things," Tasha announced cryptically.

"Really. I thought they just existed to cause pain."

"Now, now. Spoken like a woman with a past, and you're too young for that, aren't you?"

"Even a five-year-old has a past." At this Tasha looked away, embarrassed at what she pretended not to understand.

Along about her second martini, Jenna focused again on the bar, scanning it more thoroughly than before. To her shock, at the far end right near where all the olives and onions and lemons sat swimming in juice, she spotted none other than Inti Weill, looking extraordinarily handsome and happy. His black hair had grown longer and curled over his ears, and his face seemed fuller. Those lush eyebrows and deep dark eyes made him look exotic, out of another time, like an Edwardian actor, and his longish blue silk shirt hanging over black cords intensified the effect. After a moment he caught sight of Jenna, too, and immediately made his way to their table. "Hello, beautiful."

"I could have said the same to you. You look great. This is Tasha—"

"I know. We've sparred together over what can and cannot be said about the great Vincent Hull." He saluted her and pulled over a stray chair. Tasha seemed more than pleased to see him, enchanted almost, and asked him right away about his recent move. "Yes, I've decamped to the hinterlands, not an entirely unattractive place, though I do come back here for contact with the fashionable world, and with you two, of course. You never call or write, Jenna, what's up with that?"

"If you're ignoring this gorgeous man, I might have to step in." Tasha eyed the young man with such intensity that Jenna herself interrupted.

"I won't let you. He's mine, for this moment anyway."

Inti smiled at her and winked. "I thought you might go off with those two investment-banker type guys."

"Never. Now tell us about Rye." Tasha still gazed at him with her full attention.

What Jenna learned that night: Zoning was hell in Rye, history lived in the form of a pumpkin head hurled at Ichabod Crane, someone or something was killing small dogs and cats, and all the locals regarded their specific location in that town as the closest spot to heaven. After that weird evening at Hull's, she had never contacted him, but he hadn't called her either, and now she wondered how their uneasy threesome would split apart to get out of there. Fortunately, Tasha took the lead, kissing her on the cheek and patting Inti on the shoulder. "Just keep drinking, people. It's the only solution."

Inti stayed seated, looking at her in all his soft receptivity. He had barely glanced at the other woman when she left. "So, what about coming up to Rye?"

"It's a little far for an evening, isn't it?"

"Not really. Thirty-six to forty-four minutes on the Metro-North from Grand Central, but who's counting? Beautiful trip."

"What would we do up there?" Immediately horrified that somehow or other she was suggesting that only sex would make it worthwhile.

Inti just laughed. "I'm sure we can think of something."

TWO

Two days later at work, almost six in the evening, Jenna was finishing up the latest of her "dear concerned reader" letters. Jorge made several moves to leave, but then came around to her desk and sat on the edge, looking agitated. "Listen, it's getting pretty weird around here lately." He spoke in a low voice because Hull still occupied his office.

"Lately? It seems weird all the time."

"Shh. Wait." He pulled her into the hall immediately outside the office suite. "Mr. Hull comes and goes at all hours. Even though he mostly stays in New York now, he only comes into the office really late, like tonight"—he motioned toward the massive closed door—"and he's buying anything and everything he can lay his hands on. I've been watching the man for years. He starts buying stuff when he's upset."

"He's a billionaire, Jorge. Aren't they always upset? And buying stuff?" Jenna laughed at this and flicked him on the arm.

"How many billionaires have you known?"

She held up one finger, then waggled it at him. "What does he buy?"

"He bought a Porsche Boxster for his older daughter. She's fourteen now, but he says he's going to save it and use it as an incentive for good behavior."

"Oh boy."

"He bought three Patek Philippe watches, god knows for what."

"He wants to be on time? Or he wants to calculate everybody else's time and try to be late? That must be it. Listen, this is way beyond what I understand. I'm just trying to stay here and work. Job retention, the key to my personal happiness, that and getting out of town on the weekends."

At this moment Hull's doorway swung open, and the big man stood in its archway, his hands above his head, as if holding the building up. "You two still here?"

They nodded stupidly, but Jorge moved toward his desk, pulling his jacket off the chair, making ready to leave. Hull disappeared back into his office, and Jenna just sat, confused as to whether she should go home. "Maybe you should wait a minute," Jorge suggested.

"You're abandoning me."

"Mother and brother await."

She waved goodbye to him, opening up yet another demented letter from a reader. She was marveling at the fiery language and the small, cleverly drawn revolver squiggled just above the name Jared, when Hull buzzed her. She peered at the flashing blue light in alarm, straightening her blouse and pulling on her sweater, preparing herself—for what, she didn't know—and walked into his office. "Where are you on the art inventory?" He did not even look at her.

"Almost finished. I have all the papers and receipts from Lanai and—"

Hull interrupted her. "Not necessary to go there. Those pictures aren't worth much anyway, just fill in the blanks or whatever. Sabine picked them out."

"I still haven't done anything about Water Mill, because your family stays there almost all the time in the summer, but I definitely need to photograph those pictures, quite valuable I think." She let this suggestion hang for a moment, nervously, because it was crucial to any plan to leave town in this bright, brutal August. She had nowhere else to go.

"I thought you'd gone out there already?"

"No, how could I have?"

He gave her a stern look, but then his face softened, and for just a moment he seemed human, more than that, in need of something. But what, she couldn't tell. His deep eyes focused on the street far below. "We'll have to arrange that, possibly even this weekend might work out. You can call Sabine, and she'll fix it for you."

Jenna worried over this at her desk, but since she had to get the work done, she forced herself to call. The soft tones of the Frenchwoman scared her slightly, as if they were just a tiny hint of the screams and screeches yet to come should she upset her, or more likely someone else, like her husband. Fortunately, Mrs. Hull announced that she and her husband, along with the girls, would go out to close up the Wyoming house for the summer, so she should just come ahead next weekend. What? Could this really happen? A fantastic dream rose up before her that involved staying for two and a half days in a lovely small village in the Hamptons, alone in what must be a magnificent residence. Would servants be there, the golden retriever or maybe even more dogs? She was afraid to ask.

Packing for the next weekend with great care, Jenna could just see herself playing mistress of the place, or at least living out some sort of mistress fantasy. Hull had hired a livery car for her since Angelo was otherwise occupied, so she wouldn't have to take the jitney, which was a bus really, no matter how cute its name. The weather had gone exceptionally steamy in Manhattan, and her roommates had dropped down to mordant sniping about the life she led. They envied her, though they kept advising her that it wasn't "real." "Real enough for a weekend away from the city. I'll bet they have a pool." They surely had a pool and much, much more. Jenna did have a pang of guilt about Inti, though. He had called twice, and finally she had had to explain to him her mission in the Hamptons. In his voice she could hear skepticism of some kind, suggestive yes, but finally he told her that the following weekend belonged to the two of them in Rye, and she agreed, overjoyed at two such delectable prospects.

The Hull summer home occupied an acre of land on the edge of Mecox Bay in Water Mill, a hamlet in the town of Southampton, and as the Lincoln Town Car drove up to the front door via the long curving driveway, Jenna could hardly believe that this was what her boss sometimes referred to as the camp or the summer house. Two carved stone pillars framed the front door, and up around the vast structure, trees hid much of the actual shape of the house. Jenna pushed on the brass door-knocker, and a smiling black woman in a white uniform, presumably the housekeeper awaiting her arrival, took her overnight bag in hand and ushered her up an elegant, carpeted staircase into a bedroom with a window overlooking the lawn. Her room had a stone fireplace, exposed brick walls lined with dark wooden bookshelves, austere and grand, but, by way of contrast, there was a low, Chinese-style bed covered in painted yellow silk. Several grinning Chinese Buddhas sat on a chest at its foot. Jenna pulled up the bamboo shades and looked out at the bay across the lawn.

The evening air felt blissfully silky and full, at least inside, perhaps the result of whisper-soft air conditioning. She threw her bag into the closet, deciding to go to work, clipboard in hand, to check out the paintings. She crept down the immense staircase and determined that she would start in the living room. Almost eight by now, an evening summer glow filled the room, intensified by the blown-glass chandelier that swayed overhead, and she found herself surrounded by more exposed brick and great stretches of distressed wood, like a hideout of some sort, insistently masculine. Jenna didn't consciously set out to snoop, since there might be security cameras or possibly the housekeeper would be keeping tabs on her, but she wanted to see everything and learn all she could about this potentate's world. Descending three steps into the living room, she spotted a large square painting by the French doors leading outside. A presumably naked young woman stood submerged in a pool of water, her shoulders visible, her head turned away, a strong hand clasping a wet handful of hair, so wet that it looked real. Only a slight swell of breasts underwater indicated the rest of her body. She looked for the artist's signature and could make out M. Bélange in the left hand corner, someone she had never heard of.

Jenna found her quite beautiful, frozen as she was in her contemplative pose, but she quickly got distracted. When she looked out the floor-to-ceiling window before her, at once she knew she had to feel the soles of her feet sinking into that luxurious expanse of lawn. Outside, the wind brushed the trees like a hot sigh. Fortunately, she had worn a short cotton dress, and she could fan herself with the skirt. Jenna could glimpse parts of other nearby houses, one with a dock and a small boat, another incongruously rising up like a modern castle. She stepped onto the grass and heard something slap the water rhythmically. Walking farther down toward the water, she could see a lone kayaker flailing his way past her, and he waved. She waved back.

Overwhelmed with a sense of luxury and calm, she sank down onto the grass, watching as a runner passed by on the driveway of the house next door. She saw several children playing outside, barely visible but definitely audible, kicking a soccer ball, and here and now she applauded the life of the rich, even if only as an onlooker. Still, she had to work and started back toward the other side of the house.

But she stopped about halfway. Before her she could just barely make out a small infinity pool rippling in the distance, and upon closer examination, she saw that the bottom was black, so it resembled a spring flowing up out of the ground. It seemed almost menacing in the shadows, and yet she sat down on the side and dangled her feet in the cool water. "Don't worry," she said out loud. "A big hairy monster isn't going to come and get you." All around her the steamy air seemed to quiver, and sweat ran down her neck. She looked back toward the children—they must have gone inside, and she could no longer see anyone else out in the bay.

Without a thought, Jenna stripped off her dress, her panties and bra, throwing them over a lounge chair, and slid slowly into the blissful water. So good it felt, silky warm and smooth, but still she splashed around in what looked like a bottomless pond. Weren't there lights somewhere? In the darkness she could see a chunky steel box, and she swam over to it, spotting three square knobs. Would one sink her to the bottom? She laughed at herself. Only the Irish could think such things, so taking her life in her hands, she pushed the first knob, and behold, lights turned on all around her under the water. She swam now in a sea of shimmering light, and when she lay back, her white legs glistened, her recently painted red toes pointed up toward the sky, and she squealed in delight. Floating on her back for a time, she looked up at the stars.

Within her reverie, though, she heard a strange sound. Could it be, what, footsteps in the grass? No, not possible, but maybe the housekeeper had come looking for her? She straightened up and began to tread water, glancing feverishly about. Out of the darkness a tall figure strode down from the house toward her, a determined man, the one who owned this place, Vincent Macklin Hull. Panicked, she swam to the side toward her clothes, but then she would have to get out of the pool, naked as she came into this world, so improvising, she sank down to her chin, in a vain attempt to hide herself. Horrible man, always inserting himself into the lives of others. This was meant to be her own little weekend in the paradise of the Hamptons, but instantly she kicked her right leg against her left shin for being a fool and awaited with certainty the end of her time as a moocher off the privileged and the great.

Hull was dressed in khakis and an open shirt, holding a drink, and he looked more youthful in the dark, while Jenna's naked limbs glistened as if in klieg lights. She couldn't possibly hide them. As she held her breath, Hull, now directly above her at the side of the pool, began to laugh. In response, Jenna slid lower and lower, so deep she swallowed water, until at last the man spoke. "There you are. I've been looking for you."

Summoning up what little dignity she could muster, she kicked herself upward and sang out, "Your wife told me you would both be in Wyoming this weekend." At that she dropped back down into the water.

"Change of plans. How's the inventory going?"

"Great."

He really laughed now, as Jenna sank again, getting another big gulp of chlorine. When she popped up for air, he was stretched across one of the lounge chairs on the pool deck, taking another swig out of his glass. "I changed my mind at the last minute about going. Too much to do here. I don't know, I don't know anymore."

Given her own family's fondness for situations, Jenna knew right away that she faced one now, hers quite obvious, his not so clear. He raised his head, angrily almost. "Anything to say?"

"I'm just visiting, the house I mean." I feel out of place and prune-y, she wanted to add, but already she looked ridiculous and could not foresee any way to get out of that pool, like forever. "It's so damned hot outside."

Hull stood up and opened a nearby storage bench, pulling out a towel. "I'll turn around, I promise."

"I don't know if you're to be trusted."

"Nobody trusts me." It was her turn to laugh, but he did turn his back to her, so she grabbed onto the side of the pool and pulled herself up, throwing the towel around her breasts and tucking it in at the top, the way she used to do at camp. "Can I turn around now?"

"Yes." She grabbed her panties and bra and picked up her dress. Her shoes too she had to carry, as she didn't want to bend down. Together the two walked, without saying a word, back to the house.

"Have a drink," Hull said as they entered through the French doors.

"I have to change."

"Yes, after that."

Jenna flew upstairs, worrying that she was dripping as she ran, all over that lovely staircase. Fluffing her hair with the towel, drying herself off, she put on the only other dress she'd brought, a soft rose-colored shift. With a shock she realized it didn't even cover her knees. Oh well, it was a good dress to get fired in. She pulled out her little blue sweater and slung it around her shoulders. Her feet she stuck into cork sandals. Alas, her wardrobe was almost depleted now, and she'd been here maybe three hours. Staring into the mirror, she started to make faces at herself and laughed, because after all, she had managed to look not only dumb and lazy, but vaguely depraved. It's the heat, she said to herself, and prepared to meet whatever doom awaited.

As she descended that staircase fit for a king, she heard loud talking and followed it, only to find Hull in a book-lined library off the living room yelling into the phone. She hesitated in the doorway. "You're goddamned right it is, you son of a bitch. You'd better figure it out before I can your ass." He put his hand over the receiver and scowled at her.

"Oh . . . sorry," she tried to back out.

"Stop being sorry. What the fuck do you have to be sorry about?"

Pulling her sweater around her shoulders, she walked out to get away from that awful man. If this enchanted fairy tale place she inhabited was over for her, then it would end, and she could do nothing about it. She almost fell down the steps into the living room but stopped short when she spotted an immense painting that covered an entire wall. Black pillars of paint over white space and strange misshapen balls on a red background squashed against each, and she recognized it at once as a Robert Motherwell. She cocked her head to one side trying to fathom this immense expression of what—of harm of some kind? Of pain at being crushed by life? She didn't understand it. In the distance somewhere, she could hear her boss's loud voice. And then the voice stopped.

She waited in the silence, and then she heard footsteps. Hull strode into the room and, without speaking to her, went to the large wet bar in the corner, grabbed a glass and poured himself another big glass of Scotch. He looked down into it before he turned and acknowledged her presence. "There you are again." He glowered at her like a talking redwood.

"I could start to work now. It's a privilege to be in the same room with this Motherwell."

"Oh crap, lately I've decided it's a fake."

"What? No, it couldn't be." But of course it could.

"There are a lot of fakes out there, paintings and people." He poured another glass of Scotch and handed it to her. "It's a Friday night in Water Mill. No one should be working. Go ahead, it's a grown-up drink, you'll like it."

Jenna took a sip of the deep amber liquid, which tasted to her like medicine, and gave a small hiccup. She tried for a smile but wondered how long or how much he'd been drinking, and whom he had been yelling at? The big man stood now and reached out for her. "Come on. Let's go outside."

He took her by the arm. She twisted away as soon as she could and waited for him to sit, and he did, on the patio steps. She moved toward a rocking chair, but he motioned her to come next to him. He had brought the Macallan bottle with him and poured himself another half glass. As Jenna nursed her own drink slowly, warming to its smooth, sharp flavor, she began to feel more mellow in the soft night, to relax, and finally almost to sing inside. This place, this world, she had never experienced such before, and it caused her a sharp, unaccustomed pleasure. "Why do you have so many paintings?"

Hull observed her with a certain amount of charity. "That's complicated. It must be about beauty—that stays."

"Forever," she said, with something very near to a burp. Hull laughed, and as she scrutinized him he seemed softer, less imposing, much more handsome than she had perceived him at first acquaintance. It's the drink, she thought, as she tried not to take it in too fast. "My granny liked Irish whiskey."

"The 'shiny dogs' balls' woman?"

"The very same. One time I was dating this guy—well, I had been, but we broke up. Then I started to worry. Why hadn't I heard from him, was there something wrong? I told my grandmother the whole story, sort of whining I guess, and saying something about calling him or trying to get in touch. 'I've got an idea,' she said, 'send him a letter and say, Call me when you're dead!'" Jenna erupted into giggles.

"Did he call you?"

"No way, apparently he's not dead yet." Jenna put a hand on her stomach and paused to take a breath, since she felt an attack of hiccups in the offing. "This Scotch stuff is great. My roommates drink a lot, and they always want me to go out with them. They must really love me, ha, not!"

"You do seem like a girl waiting to be loved."

Had she heard this right? She didn't have time to react, instead he pulled her up beside him and led her down the steps, across the lawn toward Mecox Bay. His hand felt warm and strong, familiar to her now from their plane flight of doom, and she was embarrassed, couldn't even look at him, but she tightened her grip. Lights from the houses flickered across the water, and she heard the sweet whistle of a blue-winged warbler when it veered off in front of them. As they approached a wooden dock where a skiff bobbed in the night wind, Jenna muttered, "You're not a fisherman, are you? I could never kill a fish. . . ."

Before she could say more, Vince closed her in his arms and kissed her. She trembled but opened herself to him, and she felt herself warm and clinging, felt his arms and held on. When he finally let go, he pulled her again toward the pool. "Why don't you take those clothes off one more time?"

"Are you sure?"

But he didn't reply, instead he pulled two chaise lounge cushions out of the storage bench and laid them on the tile surrounding the pool's rim.

She watched him carefully, and then, with no hesitation, unbuttoned her dress and let it drop. Her bra and panties came off next. Vincent Hull drew her down onto the chaise and touched her slowly, cradling her breasts in his hands and then kissing them, moving over her body with a light touch, until he stroked her thighs and opened them. Jenna thought she would faint, not doing much herself except clinging to him. After teasing her with light flicks of his hands, he touched her soft places and played with her until she moaned loudly. "You're fast, girl," he said. "It must be because you're young."

Jenna didn't know what this meant and would have been embarrassed, except that she had lost everything except the wish that he would touch her again and again. Still in his own clothes, she could feel his hard, thick body against her, but at first she feared to excite him more. She didn't have to though, as now he moved his lips across her nipples, down her belly, to the curly red hair between her legs, and there he licked her until she gasped with an ecstatic cry. He stood up and slid out of his pants. Jenna was almost afraid to look, but when she did, saw a man in full with muscular thighs and a muscled torso. As he crouched down above her, she touched him, slowly too, gently, and he came into her body and moved with her until she cried out once more, at which he bent his head and groaned into her breasts. After a moment, he pulled her up and wrapped her in another towel, while he wrapped himself in one too, picking up her clothes and then his own. "Now you are so quiet, Miss Jenna."

She couldn't look at him. "I don't know how to talk to you. I don't have the right words."

"You'll find them, I'm guessing." He kissed her lightly on the forehead, leading her straight up back to the house.

"I don't know what to call you."

"'Vince,' but only when we're alone together." Right away this new man, this Vince said goodnight, though tenderly, at her bedroom door. She sank down into the pillows and fell asleep without showering or doing anything else to cleanse herself of his body. When she awoke the next morning she found a note on her bed. In black pen with a more florid hand than usual, he had written, "What a beautiful evening." That was all, and she learned later from the housekeeper that he'd gone back to the city. She didn't know what to make of their lovemaking but felt curiously complete and relaxed. She didn't worry for her job, nor for any gossip or problems or further romance. She had provided him some solace, for what she didn't know, but she had felt it in his mouth and his hands and his sex. She would just stay here and do the inventory, but still she didn't want to wash his smell off her. Why did everyone hate this man?

THREE

For most of that Sunday morning Jenna worked on the art project, energized and full of hope, for no good reason except a rested soul. The very discreet housekeeper, known to her now as Carmen, seemed to come and go, to vanish behind swinging doors, to tiptoe through halls like a kindly sprite, smiling all the while but acknowledging nothing that she might have seen or heard, not even the trace of a leer in her face. By now, Jenna had thoroughly mastered the Leica, which she had quietly taken possession of, and got so much work done that later in the day she called a taxi and went into town to shop. Her two little dresses had been through a lot, and she still had not washed herself or even taken a shower.

After a short taxi ride from Water Mill, she wandered dreamily along the quaint main street of Sag Harbor, randomly picking out items in the pricey boutiques that looked good but that she didn't even bother to try on. After two hours spending way more money than she should, Jenna took a second cab ride back to the palazzo she currently occupied and fell hot and exhausted onto her strange, Chinese-looking bed. She floated off into dreamless sleep, and when she finally awoke, the clock read six. She jumped up, pulled the two skirts and three T-shirts out of her shopping bag and decided to shower before traipsing down to what she knew would be a solitary dinner. She did not want any sadness or loneliness now, just the remembered pleasures that suffused her body and her mind. She stripped off her clothes and looked at herself from head-to-toe in the mirror. Everything the same but rosier, breasts slightly bigger. Really? The tummy flatter, the thighs taut. "Oh, you idiot," she said aloud as she contemplated the effects of love on her young and blooming flesh.

Inside the ridiculously big shower—the Hull bathroom was larger than her living room in Gramercy Park—she soaped herself all over with a sumptuous washcloth and luxuriated in the cleverly modulated streams of hot water cascading over her. Such bounty had never come to Jenna before, and while she knew it couldn't last long, she intended to enjoy every single minute of it. Out of a window large enough to show off the capacious lawn and the pool, she watched as once again the lone nighttime kayaker reappeared. She wondered who he was. Turning away to raise her face to the water, she didn't hear Vincent Hull come into the bathroom and sit on a stool near one of the sinks. When she turned, she saw him and gave a screech.

"Don't panic," he mouthed, and added louder, "I didn't see anything that I haven't already seen."

Jenna put her face up to the shower glass. "You again," she said boldly and then put her hands demurely over her lower body. Even through the foggy glass of the shower, she could read his intense expression, and as he fixed her eyes with his, he began to undress, pulling off his T-shirt, then letting his khakis drop, next his boxers. His thick, muscular body was not old looking, not wrinkled, but taut, as if he worked out, though she'd never heard of such activity. She dropped her eyes the minute she saw how vivid his excitement was. He opened the shower door and stepped in. As she turned toward the shower head, he caressed her from her shoulders, down to her back, to her buttocks, and then her thighs, curling his hands around front to excite her even more, while he moved into her from behind. After she could stand it no longer, she curved herself around and clasped him to her, while they shuddered together with pleasure.

Outside the shower, right away they started laughing at their bedraggled, possibly drowning state. Drying himself quickly, Vincent took the enormous towel in hand and with it covered every inch of Jenna's body, rubbing each soft secret place very carefully, until once again she moaned into his arms. Then he sat back with only the towel draped over his thighs and watched as she pulled her hair out of its scrunchie and combed it over her shoulders.

"You are really beautiful."

"Liar." She giggled. Actually she felt like singing, but then a strange silence fell.

"Who taught you to fuck like that?"

"What?" He had ambushed her, and for a moment she couldn't think what to say. Then, "It's an Irish thing."

Perplexed as well, apparently, he stared at her, until finally he lashed out. "There you stand in all your glory, while you betray a wife, a woman who right now sits probably waiting for a call from me, who met you and is secure in the knowledge that you are possibly too sweet and too kind to do what you did here today. Not that you did it to her, but you might as well have. And what of the children? You've seen them, or at least their pictures, innocent, loving, trusting. Do you think of them at all? Waiting at home for Daddy?"

As she listened, Jenna stopped breathing. He was right. She thought of no one but herself, nothing but her own pleasure. She was young, a kid, just turned twenty-four. She knew nothing, she thought nothing, she just longed and wanted and got and didn't care. Her eyes filled with tears, and she shouted, "Get out, get out of this bathroom. You bastard. They told me you were the devil. After all that we've done together, all we've—" here she stopped because she didn't know exactly what it was they had done. Earth-shattering to her, but perhaps to him, to anyone schooled in these arts, just ordinary. And yet, standing there half naked, full of sex and heat, she thought, no, it was important. She shrieked again, "My roommate Allyson always says, 'To me love is fucking.' I never knew what she meant, but now I do. I guess you don't." She whipped a towel around her and tried to run past him out the door, but he grabbed her.

"Stop, don't do that, I'm sorry. Oh Jenna, Jenna, you're the most loving person in my world now. I don't know why I said such ugly things."

"You don't know why you do anything. Why do you collect guns, houses, women, paintings? What are you doing with all this stuff? Maybe you're just a high-class hoarder." She ran out into the bedroom and flung herself face down onto the bed, leaving her damp imprint all over the yellow silk duvet cover, screaming her rage into the pillows. Vincent stood for a moment and then sat down next to her and began rubbing her back, but she rose up and shouted, "Stop doing that!" And yet she could see that he looked shocked, actually hurt. His eyes seemed to tear up, but she felt no pity and jumped away, pulling on whatever of her clothing lay about.

"Sit," he shouted and shoved her into a chair. She could not resist but refused to look at him, because in truth he was right about everything. She was a selfish, ignorant bitch who didn't care for families or children at all; she knew nothing about them, really. He sank down in front of her and tried to pull her toward him, but she pulled back. "Please forgive me, please. I say things, I shoot my mouth off. No one ever opposes me in anything. I've forgotten how to act like a civilized man."

Jenna stared into his eyes now, recovered somewhat. She pulled her T-shirt over her chest, though she was still naked from the waist down. Quietly, in a hushed voice, she murmured, "I was just part of your empire, the bed part of your empire. Who are you exactly? I mean, do you exist at all in the real world?"

Vincent dropped his head and wiped his hand over his forehead. "Forgive me."

"Just tell me one thing that's true about yourself. Can you do that? Do you know how to do that?"

Vincent Hull controlled thousands of people, owned treasure equal to that of kings, a world of possibility and freedom, and yet he felt so ashamed that he couldn't speak. Finally he clasped Jenna's shoulders in his strong hands, leaning in close to her mouth. "I am the faithless one. I am the confirmed, practiced betrayer, a traitor to those who love me."

Jenna stared at the man, and at last put out her own arms to him, and they held each other. "No, you must be good, you are, truly. Kiss me," she commanded.

He opened his mouth to her, but as soon as he did, she pushed him down on the bed. Pulling off her T-shirt, she tugged at the thick towel around his waist. When he was naked, excited already, she straddled him and pushed her weight against him. "Watch that, girl," he tried to joke. "My chiropractor won't like this."

Her breasts touching his chest, she began to slide very slowly from his mouth, to his Adam's apple, to his belly, and thence downwards, using them as soft arousing pillows that rubbed every part of the front of him. He moved as if to kiss her, but she shoved him down sharply.

"You do what I want now." With her lips and her hands, even her legs, she made love to him, flicking his penis with her tongue as he lay passive, not allowed to move because she lay on top of him, until at last he cried out so loudly that she had to put her hand over his mouth. Moments later, she slid down upon him so that he could enter her. As he rose inside her, she gripped with her strong pelvic muscles until he shouted in a frenzy. Only then did she allow herself her own pleasure. Exhausted, silent, at last he sat up, and Jenna let him go. He embraced her, murmuring, "Never in my life have I had a lover like you." She smiled, not saying a word, and curled herself into his arms, ready to sleep.

He stayed with her the whole night, but when the sun came up, Jenna arose before he did, soundlessly plucking up her purse and what she had been wearing yesterday off the floor. She gazed for a moment at his sleeping face, a great man, an awful man, both. She tiptoed out and dressed in the hallway, praying that the sweet housekeeper would not appear, but it was far too early for breakfast. She got out of that house as fast as she could, and when safely in the driveway, called a taxi, with her Vince-phone, as she had named it, telling them to wait for her on the road. Looking back for a moment at that glorious mansion, she felt a pang for the man still sleeping in the bed. Probably a lie, what he had said about her as a lover, something meant to keep her nearby, but the momentary flash of her as a betrayer of those around her had left a mark, like a newly formed bruise. Curiously, as she got into the cab, she thought of something Tasha had said. "He's not smart enough to avoid the big tragedies."

Whether she would return to her job, whether that was possible, remained a question. She couldn't afford to stay in New York if she lost it, but how dare she ever face the man again, his flesh still molded to her own? These matters she vowed to consider on the long drive home, and she told the cabbie to keep on driving all the way into the city.

FOUR

Late for work, she strode in with a new determination, glancing only briefly at Jorge, who was as usual working hard. He barely glanced up, but when he saw her, he looked twice. She was rosy, flushed, excited somehow, and she moved with an intensity that surprised him. Usually she just seemed panicked. "Good weekend?"

"Long, but I got the inventory done, at least insofar as the stuff that exists in the United States. I doubt they'll send me to Paris, and Hull said the pictures in Hawaii weren't worth much." She flopped her purse down, conscious that this new dress wasn't quite the thing she usually showed up in. After the initial shock of being back at the office, the same place, the same setting, yet now she had an entirely different location somehow, at least in her own head. Jenna began to worry about when Vincent Hull would reappear. Would he burst in on her, once again yelling orders into the phone, threatening everyone in his wake, as he had before? Would he show embarrassment about their weekend, worse yet fire her in front of Jorge, thereby letting him know what they had done together?

And then Sabine Hull called her at the office, on her very own designated phone line. She demanded to know why her husband had had six antique Audemars Piquet watches overnighted to the old family home she and the girls now shared in Villefranche-sur-Mer, on the French Riviera, having gone directly there from Wyoming. "I'm sorry, I have no idea about this."

Jorge watched her as she looked over at him in dismay, indicating, "Say what?" with a wave of her hand. Sabine's warm soft voice and restrained manner didn't seem threatening to Jenna at all, but she wondered about the timing of these purchases and what she could have had to do with them. Did the wife think she had picked them up at the store or something? "Truly, I don't know, but he did buy some other watches several days ago. I'll speak to Jorge. Do you need them returned?"

"No, no, of course not, but I haven't been able to get hold of him lately, and I thought you might know something."

"I did do some work at the Water Mill house this weekend, the art inventory, but no shopping or anything." She really wanted to burble out some long excuse about having not seen him since the last Ice Age, but even she knew that when hiding a lie, short works better than long.

The Frenchwoman sighed, and there was silence, until, "Oh well, thank you. We will see what this all means."

Jorge came around to her desk and shoved a piece of paper in front of her. "The great man is off to Paris today, not back for a whole week." Jenna looked at the elaborate itinerary and burst into tears. "What's wrong, sweetie?" The usually restrained man bent down and knelt before her.

"We should tell his wife this," she managed through her sobs.

"Never interfere in their scheduling or lack thereof. It's a no-no. Look on the bright side, we'll be free as birds around here. We can move some of his Buddhas around and see if he notices. After all, it's the small little triumphs that make the world go round." She kept on snuffling into a Kleenex. "I'm trying to make you laugh."

"I know, and thank you, Jorge. It's fine, I'm just. . . ."

"A weekend at that house in Water Mill would make anyone crazy. Envy, lust, greed, at least half of the seven deadly sins got me going when I was there. It's too much for anyone in this world to have, and yet that S.O.B. has it all, and I do mean all, plus the wife and kiddies."

But Hull had certainly not had the missus for much of the summer, and this was by her design. She wanted him to feel her absence, to let him worry and wonder across a transoceanic distance because she had been particularly miserable of late. Several times a week she journeyed up to the almost always empty Saint Thomas More Church on 89th Street, dropped herself down into a pew, and just sobbed, reflecting up at the magnificent stained glass windows for a moment and then sobbing again. All she could do was relive those wonderful days when she had first met Hull at the tennis club in Villefranche-sur-Mer, where she had been a young and obsessed player. "How do you improve your game once you hit a plateau?" This she had asked Hull on a hot, windy day in 1983, he looking carefully at her taut legs, she watching the golden hair that he brushed away from his face.

"It takes time, small steps. You must be specific with your coach, if you have one."

"I do."

He had taken her by the arm and drawn her away from the scrum of people at this exhibition match. "What bothers you most about your game?"

"Return of serve and my net play. I'm afraid to run up there."

"Tell the coach only these things, not anything vague like 'I'm at a plateau,' just the specifics. You will get better, I promise." He had smiled down at her in all his splendid self-confidence. She didn't seem intimidated by him, despite the dazzling aura and the gossip about his money, and once when the two had played a game to-gether, he had noted this fact. "Nothing really impresses you, does it?"

She had taken his hand in her own, turned it over and kissed his palm gently, "You impress me."

By the time their second daughter turned five though, silence and anger had closed in around them. During one particularly ghastly summer, for reasons Sabine could only dimly understand, Vince became obsessed with their gardener in Water Mill, with the fact that he wouldn't do what he wanted him to, specifically cut down the neigh-bors' salvia plants that marred the view on the south side of the house. Said gardener, a noble-looking man of thirty, himself with a wife and three children, humbly and re-peatedly refused. Sabine took the man's part. "You can't just cut down other people's plants, Vincent. It's illegal. Go talk to the neighbor and see what you can do."

But Vincent didn't want to be that "known" to his next-door neighbor, so he persisted in this now-doomed campaign to get both his wife and the gardener in ca-hoots with his plan, but they stood fast. He often spotted them talking together in the garden, heads bowed over the salvias, and in the dark hours of the night, riven with Scotch and suspicion, Vince decided that the two of them were having an affair. Once his wife realized what he thought, she found it incredibly funny. After all of Vin-cent's own secrets and lies, she supposed that it did make some sense to suspect such a thing, but really, it was too much even for Sabine, who had a highly developed sense of irony. She never formally disabused him of the notion, but at the last, when Vince ventured out at two in the morning with a large pair of hedge cutters to cut down the plants himself, she told him he needed therapy.

Sadly, Sabine saw the plant-cutting business as symbolic of a permanent break and that she must live and act alone, even while the powerful, relentless personage who occupied her house—rather houses—came and went at will. So her rare phone call to the office struck both Jorge and by now the very guilty Jenna as an anomaly that must mean something.

Jorge seemed genuinely concerned. "I've got to say he's been acting strangely for the last couple of months— manic, then depressed, then, I don't know, sick somehow, or sicker. Tormented, dare I say it? I've always wondered who or what could bring him down.

"He needs someone like you to look after him," Jenna said.

Finding this a startling remark, Jorge stood back a moment to survey her. "Hmm, yes, maybe. Listen, I've got an idea. There's a new wine-tasting class, high atop the World Trade Center downtown. Why don't we take the class together? We could actually learn something, and then we could gaze down in complete condescension as people run around below us like rats. I could sign us up, if you don't mind being seen with an old fart like me. It starts tomorrow night at Windows on the World, a fantastic restaurant with the best view in Manhattan."

"Let me think about it. It sounds great, but I need to hunker down for a while and just do nothing. I'm exhausted."

Interrupting their tête-à-tête, to Jenna's great surprise, the long-absent Martin reappeared with a tray of pastries. "Did I hear crying? That's my job, to cheer people up with food." He handed her a chocolate croissant and a cup of coffee.

"You're back, as in back back?"

"That's right. I decided to give the great man another chance to slap me around, and this time I got him to sign on to a raise and more vacation, so screw him and that gauche restaurant of his. Baby back ribs, my ass!"

Jorge plucked a pastry off the tray. "You'll get used to this revolving door routine. Hull can't bear to let anyone go. Everybody just keeps coming back, like Lassie."

Both Martin and Jorge recognized that something major was amiss with Jenna too, but they didn't discuss the possible source of her troubles. All the while she sat at her desk, plowing through the vile letters that arrived without fail every day, only this time she agreed with every word. "I'll rip your heart out, you should be deported to Rwanda, give all your filthy wealth to the poor, die you stinkin' fucked up bastard. . . ." It all made sense, and she actually started to laugh, but in her heart she waited for Vince. Waiting for what, she didn't know.

While she pined, someone else altogether waited for her, noticing that she might like to get out of town, and he could help. He had no ranch, but he had a mystery on his hands. "Come up to Rye, you promised," Inti spoke into his new Motorola StarTAC cell phone. Only four days since her Water Mill junket, it seemed months longer, and the suspended animation of Jenna's heart made her angry and lonely at the same time. She wasn't sure she even liked Inti. Still, he was an enticing guy with a real job, and he seemed to be interested in her.

"Is there anything going on up there? Isn't it just a suburb?"

"Oh, but what a 'burb.' And we have a mystery of sorts. You could help me figure it out, since I definitely need a scoop of some kind to ratchet myself upwards in the hierarchy. Much as I love having no real future at the *Rye Register*, it's beginning to eat away at me."

"We can't have that, now, and you haven't even been there that long." Jenna was tempted.

"Come on Saturday morning. You'll need to pack some jeans, a jacket, and good walking shoes, socks and all."

"We're not going camping, are we? I did way too much of that in Ohio."

"Camping crossed with sleuthing, more likely. I don't want to say more. Somebody could be listening."

"Who? Our phones aren't bugged."

"For all you know they are. Listen, please bring that camera of yours. I need pictures."

Jorge had tried to listen discreetly to Jenna's half of the conversation, hoping that Vincent Hull did not occupy the other end of the line and finally became convinced that he did not. No woman was safe around the man, and he knew this from long experience. He felt protective toward his fetching office buddy, and while none too sure, he had uneasy feelings about the increasing proximity of this woman to his boss. She wasn't the man's type, but still he worried. This one was special. If he could see it, so could Hull, but perhaps he could stop him from getting his hooks into her. When finally she hung up the phone, he offered, "Rye is fantastic, I mean beautiful." He didn't want to oversell the town, since he'd never actually visited it.

"I don't know much about it."

"New boyfriend?" There, he'd committed himself to snooping.

"Not really. A friend, a journalist. He's at the *Rye Register*."

"If you'd wanted a writer, you could have had your pick of these guys hanging around here. They'd have been thrilled."

"He did work here, Inti Weill."

"Not familiar with the guy." He had long since given up on the world of the scribe, the kind that he met at *NewsLink* anyway.

FIVE

No word from Vincent, and nothing from the man to Jorge either, so Jenna prepared herself for a suburban junket. While her roommates scurried off once again to Fire Island, she packed her duffel for some sort of outdoor encounter, her ultra-cool camera packed in its case very carefully. She could feel her sometime lover in its heavy leather strap. Did he know she'd absconded with it? No doubt yes, but so far he hadn't said a word, nothing at all to her after what they'd done together. Though manifestly a crazy idea, she felt nagging guilt about Vince. Was she being disloyal, venturing off with someone else? What a mad thought, one that should be emphatically rejected, so she made her way to the Metro-North railroad line leaving out of Grand Central Station. On this Saturday, everyone else in town had also had the clever idea to avoid a Friday train, and the mayhem was total. The crowds, the vendors, even the man playing the violin, soliciting coins looked especially haggard. When finally she sat back in the cool railroad car, though, she felt blessed, freed at last from every care of that strange building she inhabited and the world of its ruler. About Inti's world she hadn't a clue, but she didn't think it would lumber so mysteriously through her soul as Vincent Hull's did right this very minute.

Inti stood waiting for her at the Rye station, reading a book and sipping on a soda. As the locomotive crawled into the station, Jenna watched anxiously through the window, and with sudden anxiety wondered whether this little outing would possibly involve sex. She wasn't prepared for that and didn't even want to let it enter her mind. Other people thought of these things, but she had been living in her own little Hull fantasy world, much removed from the reality of something like a real date with an available male. Now as she watched the young man standing there, she realized how beautiful he was, soulful but also slightly goofy, unlike any "face man" she'd been tempted to go out with in college. He had the sort of grace she associated with men in magazines, in his usual uniform of a blue T-shirt and beige linen trousers, but he didn't seem vain or affected, or even really conscious of how good he looked. Instead he appeared preoccupied, a bit out of it.

Over fried chicken and biscuits at a diner, she learned more about him. The sheltered product of two professors at Evergreen State College in Olympia, Washington, he had grown up on eccentricity and granola, at least that's how it sounded to Jenna, and he played the cello. "My mother taught child psychology, my father anthropology, a people-of-many-lands thing. He was into the Skokomish and the Puyallup, all their artifacts, their way of life. One Christmas he put a teepee up in the back yard, and my sister and I had to spend the whole weekend there chanting weird songs with them about various gods. It was our version of a sweat lodge."

She could barely imagine such a world but envied the idea of cultivated parents with interests beyond beer and bowling. Her own ever-shifting set of adults, some of whom appeared to have just wandered off, had never focused on any interest whatsoever, with the dramatic exception of her grandmother, who had concentrated on her. "How eccentric," Jenna said, unsure what all this meant.

"Where we lived, we didn't make too much of it. The Pacific Northwest, you know, home of the brave and the strange."

"Really?" Jenna felt unbelievably ignorant about at least sixty percent of what he was saying. "So what's the big mystery in Rye?"

"Small dogs and cats are disappearing at an alarming rate. Is there a pet killer about? Someone or something is going after them, always at night, and they end up mutilated. That's why we have to camp out and watch and photograph at the epicenter of all this, if possible. Are you up for it?"

"Sure, I guess. Will there be any violence involved?"

"I certainly hope not, but just in case I have some Mace here, also some salt. Let's see, a Snickers bar, hmm, a little pot. Want some?"

"Not right now."

"We really lived on weed in Olympia. I think it was meant to combat the rain."

"Any lasting damage?" Jenna said as he threw his coat over her shoulders even though it was a balmy night in Westchester County.

"Hard to tell. I am as you see me." He lifted his arms out wide and gave a quick salute. "I consider myself blessed because you're here." This winningly nerdy speech made her laugh, and at once these last few weeks lost a touch of their fire. She vowed to enjoy herself and find more people her own age.

Armed with a bottle of wine and their duffle bags, the two set off into the woods of Rye. Inti had arranged for them to camp in the spacious backyard of one of the city fathers, not in his own guesthouse rental. That would have been too much sharing for him right now, but also there had been no disappearances in his area. Behind the white colonial house, they spent the next hour setting up their tent under a voluminous red maple tree, building their small, regulation fire, and setting out sleeping bags. Inside the tent, it was cozy, so much so that if she had not had on clothes meant to deter ticks and other critters, Jenna might have been tempted to take them off. Almost immediately Inti stripped down from his fashionable getup into a sweatshirt, and at that moment she saw the torso of someone seriously in shape, but she tried to look away. Sex occupied her too much of late. Vince had started her up again, and the engine thrilled at being able to turn over at all, like a car too long parked in the garage.

Once they settled in, Inti handed her a flashlight and a plastic cup of wine. "Two essentials for the night."

"Don't tell me about the little pets who died. I couldn't stand it."

"I know, Fluffy and Pooki and all that."

"They deserve to live, too."

"I'm a friend to the animals; why else would I be doing this? It would be a major scoop, at least around here, but also I'm guessing in the city as well. There have been several attacks there too."

They waited for about an hour, during which time Inti told her his history as an aspiring cellist. All the while he talked, Jenna focused on his long dark eyelashes and his very nearly black eyes. He had a lovely passivity about him, not always moving forward, but sideways into the wind as it were, and he laughed a lot, in this instance very quietly, so unlike Vincent in every conceivable way. "My mother asked my famous Russian cello teacher whether I could be a professional someday. He said, 'For a cellist, he would make a good insurance salesman.' That did it for me. I switched to English literature."

Silent now, they waited together a long, long time, watching at a tiny opening in the tent, listening to every waving branch, every twitch in the grass, anything that moved. After about twenty minutes, they heard one high pitched whine, then another fearsomely loud, inhuman scream. Inside, they huddled, hardly breathing. Inti opened the tent a crack and peered out. He saw a white tabby scampering away. "Just a cat making those terrible cat sounds," he whispered.

"I've got to admit it, I don't totally love cats. I'm more of a dog person."

"Me too."

They settled back to listen, and Jenna lay on her sleeping bag, exhausted by just about everything in her life, dozing. Inti stayed wide awake though, and after about an hour, they heard at once a rush, a pounding over leaves, and then something like animal keening, but after several moments, the eerie cries vanished into the night. In another instant they heard scratching sounds behind the tent. Jenna grabbed her camera and whispered, "Too bad we don't have a gun."

"Shh." Inti put his hand over her mouth. The crunching of leaves grew louder, but then again more silence. He pointed toward the sound as he gently opened the tent wide, while she raised the Leica. Then a soft movement around them grew louder, and finally they heard the whiny meow of a cat slinking right across their field of vision. Out of the darkness a mangy dog-like creature sprang out toward the cat, who howled in terror, and at the same moment Inti leapt toward them and began shouting and waving his arms. The cat appeared ready for the fight and held its ground, slashing about with its paws. The wolfish thing lunged to bite but then unaccountably staggered backwards and fell down, dead it seemed. Jenna had jumped out of the tent, camera in hand and shot a number of pictures before the cat scooted away. "Damn, it was a coyote." Inti stared down at the limp carcass.

"I got some good shots, I think. I might have caught a glimpse of the pack."

They explained the whole scene to an animal control officer, who was accompanied by a policeman, and it seemed they had suspected coyotes for some time but hadn't caught any. Now this female who got so close to a house and to people was probably sick. The animal was bagged for testing, even though to Jenna's sympathetic eyes the poor creature just looked sad and starved to death.

"Poor creature, my ass," Inti chided her. "She could kill a dog or even a small child."

"Not any more, but still, I feel sorry for her."

"And where did you get that incredible camera?"

"A perk, of sorts, for the work I do for Vincent."

"Vincent, eh?" Inti didn't have time to explore this thought, but instead put his arm around her while the officers tried to convince them not to stay in the tent that night. He refused to budge, didn't want to miss a scoop, even if it was only for the *Rye Register*. "Be on the lookout for more of them. They normally travel in packs, and you'll need shots if one of them bites you. Just make a lot of noise and expand your physical presence," one of the animal control guys advised, throwing out his arms and flapping like a bird.

Jenna watched the officers retreat with their frightful prey wrapped in a towel, its tail sticking out. She, at least, was shaken, but Inti appeared energized. "It's a terrific story. I was there first. And you've got pictures with that fancy camera of yours."

What with the fear and the animal screechings and the officers, it all made for an emotionally-charged situation, and Jenna could feel this as the two settled into their respective sleeping bags. It was too much for her, and she wanted to defuse it, so as she snuggled a bit closer to him, she pulled her hoodie up over her head. "Want to tell ghost stories?" He ruffled her hair and pulled her toward him for a kiss. She responded, warmly, but the two were exhausted and covered in clothing. They fell asleep almost at the same moment.

The next morning the birds woke them before the sun, and as Jenna turned she saw that Inti was looking at her. She started up, uncomfortable from a night on the ground, but he gently pushed her back down. "Stay and rest. I'm going to look around the property for the cat and see what else might have happened." She listened as his footsteps receded and, after what seemed like a long time, she fell back to sleep.

Inti was a man for whom women had done a lot. His mother had made him a fresh and often exotic sandwich every day for school. His sister, who bossed him around at every stage of their relationship, thought him her truest and best friend, though she had conditioned him on how to behave. She conceived a game called "Strongling and Weakling." Whoever called out "Strongling" first meant that the other person had to fall down right away, crying "Weakling." Inti was always the weakling because he never shouted the words first. She lurked and waited, the essence of the game, while he never gave it a thought until she screeched at him. He was greatly loved, though the cerebral atmosphere at home contained within it not a little pure coldness. His father lost himself in books and artifacts, and on the walls of their home grinning, ghoulish masks glared down upon them all. Things cheered up around cocktail time, and Inti had certainly noticed his father's big cigar box of marijuana, the rolling papers, and the expert handling thereof. Until Inti became one himself, his parents regarded journalists as children of the damned, but their son persisted, longing to exit that damp, boring sinkhole, as he called it to his friends, and move right along to a regular city, the bigger the better. No more government bureaucrats, no more chainsaw sculpture or people weaving lanyards out of painted leather. No, the homespun and the relentlessly artsy had lost their charms for him. He wanted new and clean and dry, though he remained a semi-committed expert on pot and its peculiar delights. Rye was the best he could do for now, since he distrusted Vincent Hull in whatever small dealings he'd had with him, worse yet had grown to detest the job at *NewsLink* and had gotten only a modestly positive reference from them for "good work in the field."

Inti recognized Jenna as another lost soul, even more forlorn than himself, and it fascinated him to think of her swimming along in the dangerous fish tank that the *NewsLink* organization surely was. Also, he knew much more about Vincent Hull than he let on. The man had once been a hero to him, not just a rich dabbler in the magazine world, more like a force of nature willing to push and pull and grab and wrestle to the ground the beast that was a certain kind of journalism, that of the opinion piece. Of late, though, *NewsLink* had become more and more a tabloid, available to whoever shouted the loudest, and its headlines habitually regurgitated blood, guts, murder, revenge, big money, and any horrible person currently making noise. No matter how much serious reportage was done, print got overwhelmed by dead men and hookers. He didn't necessarily want another job with the man, but he didn't not want one either, and should the opportunity arise, he might even return to *NewsLink* once he had more credits. Coyotes were rumored in Central Park, so this subject had legs in more ways than one.

Inti didn't share these views with Jenna, but on their way back into the city he rubbed her neck affectionately and kissed her now expertly and often. As the train pulled into Grand Central Station, he felt mad at himself for not having made a serious pass at her. "I'll send you the pictures right away," she promised. "Though don't have high expectations, please."

"I only have high expectations of you," he said, but she was already walking away from him.

SIX

Another week went by, and Jenna had to climb down from every wild thing she had done during this perplexing time. Her nerve endings seemed on fire, and while she had much to do, little will to do it. Inti's photos for one. She felt she should rush this job with the studio she had used for Hull's art inventory, but she had had to wait for the negatives to be processed. The camera might be "perfect," as Hull had said, but it was not easy or particularly fast when it came to the final images used for the prints. While she had no word from Hull, she assumed that Jorge knew something, but he only occasionally remarked on how blessed they were with his absence. Did Vincent pine for her, lust for her, gnash his teeth in demented longing, just as she felt like doing?

After more days of agonized waiting, Jenna wearily plodded through the *NewsLink* lobby, where she spotted Tasha with Mrs. Hull. Deep in conversation even as the crowd of employees elbowed past them, the two women waved her over. Jenna didn't want to move their way but did finally because the diminutive wife of her boss looked at her so intently. "We're going out for a drink. Want to come with us?" Tasha said.

Mrs. Hull smiled softly. "Yes, please do."

"I'm Jenna McCann, your new husband's assistant," she stumbled and corrected herself, "I meant your husband's new assistant."

"I know you. And I knew this already."

Jenna stopped breathing, but managed to get out, "That's right."

"You came to the foundation party."

"Yes."

"And once at the hotel." Jenna barely nodded. Why on earth did she keep telling this woman who she was, as if she'd been somehow invisible every unfortunate time she'd met her.

Angelo and the Lincoln Town Car awaited them, but Jenna decided to run back up to her desk to get her inventory, just in case Hull himself showed up. She had to have some reason for being in their company, and after all, it could be weeks before she saw him again. "Five minutes," she said loudly and left them standing agape. Did she really care if they left? No, but she held her breath while the elevator ascended.

At last, thick leather binder in hand, Jenna curled herself as far as she could away from the other women in the back seat of the Town Car. Tasha leaned over across Mrs. Hull, who sat in the uncomfortable middle, and said, "When we go out for drinks, we're all in this together. Don't forget that."

What could this possibly mean? Would she have to pay her part of the tab? She'd better watch herself and not drink too much. "Do you enjoy the job, Jenna?" Sabine Hull looked closely at her.

"Very much. It's a great change from Ohio, pretty glamorous and all, and taking the photographs of your art has been wonderful."

"Too much, all too much."

"Excuse me?" Jenna pressed herself back against the seat.

"We have too much. I tell Vincent all the time, but does he listen? You know where he is now? France, looking for a chateau to buy, if you can believe that, in the Champagne region. It's his favorite place but so cold there, cold and damp. Still he is determined." The woman smelled of a light, sweet fragrance, and wore a lilac-blue dress, maroon pumps on her slender feet, and carried a small purple clutch. Put together, contained, but Jenna still tried to shrink herself away to the side, as if the woman could smell what she had been up to. "We always go to the Plaza," Sabine Hull said brightly. "The Oak Room."

"Oh no, I should get home. . . ." But Sabine interrupted her. "You must come. Tasha and I do this every Friday, and we need some new blood. We're getting bored with each other."

"Do, Jenna. Everyone's afraid of Sabine because of who she's married to, and they just can't stand me. I've been around the place too long, and I think I've dated every writer there." She laughed and patted Jenna on the knee, and up front Angelo laughed too. "Stop that, Angelo. You're supposed to pretend you don't know as much as you actually do."

"I'm saving it for my book," he called to them over his shoulder.

"Very funny, mister," Tasha called back.

Jenna had to agree and figured, no matter how much it cost, maybe she could just get drunk and blend into the wallpaper. And she'd never eaten at the Plaza but felt pretty sure that some major dinner loomed in her future. Angelo's car phone rang, and he picked up. Pausing a moment, he said, "Yes, sir, of course. We're headed to the Plaza now, so I'll tell them, Mrs. Hull, Tasha, and your new assistant."

Jenna felt her head go fuzzy, but Sabine looked even more upset. "What's this, Angelo?"

"Mr. Hull just landed at JFK and said he'd meet you in about an hour."

The three women sat silently until at last Sabine remarked loudly, "Oh crap, *merde*, merde, merde."

Jenna just looked over at Tasha, unsure about all this but praying for divine intervention, as in a quick bout of the flu or some other excuse to get out of this dinner. Tasha stared her down expressively, as if to convey, "Say nothing, just go with this."

The three traipsed through the sumptuous gold-leaf-covered lobby into the wood-bound luxury of the Oak Room, and Jenna stopped at the threshold, staring up at the carved ceiling. This place looked and smelled like a heaven of food and drink, a kingdom all its own, and she vowed right there to enjoy every single part of it, up until the moment she had to slip Hull the inventory and flee. Whatever else happened, she would stay sober long enough to savor roast beef and all the trimmings, which she had already seen flash by her on an elaborate cart covered in huge silver serving dishes.

The vodka martini Sabine—yes—she was directed to call her by her first name—Sabine had ordered for her went down like cold syrup of the gods. By the time she finished it, she had gawked at every diner in the place, had listened to a long discussion of a sale at Henri Bendel's and the virtues of a purple over a green purse, and had spotted a television personality in the corner of the room. The one problem: Sabine had decided they should wait to eat their main course until her husband showed up. "I warn you now," the lady said sharply, "he's always late. It's his way of telling you how important he is," and she laughed. "His Goldenness, that's what we call him." Tasha smiled, while Jenna looked away. It wouldn't do for her to join in any criticism of him.

They ordered a second round of martinis, also three shrimp cocktails and a Caesar salad to share, but by now Jenna wasn't sure she could eat anything or even that she wanted to. "These martinis are terrific. Where have these been all my life?" She giggled, and the two stunning women, each in her own way, seemed to laugh right along with her. The medieval-looking chandeliers twinkled down upon her, and she nibbled on a shrimp, dipping it into the very hot sauce, and then kept swiveling her head, at least that's how she experienced it, while taking in all the glory of the room. A king might preside here, and alas they awaited one. The minute she thought this, she vowed to eat even more to dilute the vodka, but soon enough the hors d'oeuvres disappeared, and Mrs. Hull's phone pinged insistently. *"Oui, Vincent, c'est dommage, l'heure, l'heure. Pourqoi tout le temps?"*

"The always-being-late problem," Tasha whispered above the other woman's conversation.

"Time fuck!" Jenna spluttered, quite pleased with herself, but thank god the other two didn't hear her. She looked down at her watch. It was nine thirty. If you didn't eat by six thirty in Ohio, something was wrong with you because then you'd have to sleep on a full stomach. You would undoubtedly have nightmares, a piece of information she managed to get out in full sentences to the two sophisticated women she was supposedly dining with. Fortunately they didn't look any too sober either; in fact, they were all pretty much in the bag because by now they had actually inhaled three martinis each.

Even so, when at last the looming figure of Vincent Hull appeared near the maître d', Sabine managed to rise and meet him halfway as he strode toward them. To Jenna's booze-addled eyes, Hull's wife wobbled a bit, and she cursed herself for not getting out of there in time to avoid the man himself. Tasha had somehow made her way to the ladies' room, and now she and the Hulls occupied the same table alone together.

"Have I missed the party?" Vincent boomed out at them, looking remarkably fresh after his transatlantic journey as he ran a hand through his thick hair. His tanned, expressive face seemed to welcome her, despite the potentially dire situation, and he looked full on at her, no hesitation at all. Instantly Jenna had the feeling of a giant, collective stare directed at herself from every other person in the room.

"You've missed only the beginning," Jenna said too quickly. She wanted to get the talking part over with so she could leave.

Within minutes Tasha strode back their way, so commanding, always as if she marched toward her own future, this evening in a sleek, dark green dress, her hair hanging in a long braid, and around her neck a hammered bronze Maltese cross necklace. Hull stood, pulling out her chair, then sat down again. In the midst of all their drinking, it seemed they already had ordered dinner, which Sabine explained to her husband, but as yet no food beyond the hors d'oeuvres had appeared, and now the maître d' returned to their table to apologize. "Unfortunately, well, this is unprecedented for us"—he pronounced it as "unpreecedented"—"The chef has quit."

Vincent threw up his hands in mock horror. "They love to quit. It's their only option."

Tasha interrupted, "But we're starving to death. We've been sitting here for three hours."

"Waiting for you, Vincenzo." Sabine Hull rubbed her hand with her napkin, as if polishing something. "Always late. It's a disease, but I can't think of what it might be called."

"Your English isn't good enough." Hull sipped his wine. "This isn't any good either."

The maître d' still stood nearby, embarrassed for every reason in the world. "Some of the waiters have stepped in and are cooking the food, so please just wait for a few more minutes."

"Are you serious?" Hull said loudly. "I doubt they can cook anything edible."

"Vincent!" Sabine socked his arm, and Jenna giggled, then hid her face in her napkin, while images of his body parts rolled through her head. Oh god, she had to get out of there.

At this moment, Vincent pulled out his chair, every eye in the place upon him, and marched toward the kitchen. "What's he doing?" Jenna by now felt stuck in a bad dream.

"It wouldn't surprise me if he tried to cook the dinner himself." Under the gaze of the multitudes, Sabine pulled out a cigarette and lit up. At this the maître d' ran over.

"No, no, miss. Sorry Madame Hull, no smoking at the Plaza."

The Madame looked about to slap the man, and now Jenna knew she had to take action. Where was her purse and where the inventory binder? She stuck her hand beneath her chair, flapping it about trying to hit something. Staring down again, bending down, she wanted to crawl onto the floor, but finally these fat objects let themselves be felt right next to her left leg. "I must go," she said stiffly.

"No, no, you can't," a chorus of drunken cries came up from Tasha and Sabine. "We need you."

Even in her stupor, Jenna recognized a seriously bad idea when she saw one, and just as Vince marched their way, followed by a waiter pushing the roast beef cart, she managed to stand, her purse and the binder giving her welcome ballast. "Thank you, thank you all so much," she intoned like the hostess at a charity ball. How she got out of there, in later years she couldn't ever remember. The lighting so dim, herself completely hammered, she prayed that almost everybody at that table forgave her or didn't notice, and Vincent of course, would understand what she had done. She had, in fact, taken one for the team, that's how she wanted to think of it in the end, despite the fact that very stupidly, she'd forgotten to hand him the blasted art inventory.

Outside she spotted Angelo and the car, but leaned in through the window to wave him off. "I have to walk. Just forget about me."

"How could I do that?" He threw out his hands dolefully.

But Jenna refused the temptation to enjoy yet more luxury and congratulated herself that at least she had gotten out before the bill came. From Central Park South all the way down to 20th, she actually made it on her own steam, and it helped that she still wore her work shoes, nothing pointy or high, just patent leather flats. Her head began to clear. When she saw the familiar Gramercy Park Hotel on the corner, for the first time since she had moved here to New York, she felt herself at home. It was late now, almost midnight, and Jenna wondered if she would find her roommates anywhere about.

Tiptoeing into the apartment, in the darkness she could see that their two doors were open, so Allyson and Vera were off doing a Friday night thing themselves. She flopped down on her futon. This night, how awful, how drunken and right in front of Sabine Hull and Tasha. Had she said anything terrible or outrageous? Would the two other women have been able to read the signs, the shifting body moves that meant yes, she and her boss had made love recently and a lot. Jenna couldn't even look at herself in the mirror as she brushed her hair. Unfolding what passed for her bed and climbing into it, she snuggled herself into the blankets, the newly purchased air-conditioner blasting out at her as if she crouched in a high wind. God, she hated this stuff, this artificial air.

The little cell phone Vincent had given her chirped, and for about ten seconds she thought of not answering it. Maybe he would believe her fast asleep. Unnerved, as it was after one in the morning, at first she couldn't find it, finally knocking it off the table. By the time she'd fingered her way toward it, then figured out the buttons, only silence came through from the other end. She put it back on the table beside the bed and got up to grab a ginger ale out of the fridge, trying to stare down the phone. Maybe it had been a wrong number? It pinged again, and this time she pressed the tiny button, pulling it up to her ear. "Hello?"

At once she heard Vincent Hull's deep voice. "Where are you, Jenna?"

"At home in bed."

"I want to see you."

"You did see me."

"I want to see more of you than that. Besides, we couldn't talk."

Since when did they ever talk much, but she didn't want a fight, and after all, how could she refuse, even though it was late and she was in recovery mode? "I've finished the inventory, in fact it's in a binder right here." She sought some semblance of normalcy amid the weirdness.

"Maybe you could bring it to me?"

"Now?"

"Why not now?" Jenna looked down at the shiny hands of the clock on the floor next to her bed: 1:20. Okay, so how was this going to happen? "I'll send Angelo."

"No," she said sharply, startling herself.

"He'll be there in ten minutes, and he'll bring you back to the townhouse on 57th Street." What was this, another residence? She hadn't even known about this one. A secret office, perhaps one he used for his charitable foundation? Worse yet, two blocks from the Plaza.

By now halfway toward sober, Jenna jumped out of bed and pulled on some black slacks, a red T-shirt, dressy though, with a slash of lace at the collar, and piled her binder into her black leather tote bag. The binder looked sleek and professional. Angelo, Angelo, a fellow sufferer in the land of filthy lucre, what would she say to him? In a few moments she heard the discreet toot of a horn, and outside in the shadows the Lincoln hummed. She jumped in as if escaping someone or something. Angelo gazed at her in the rear view mirror, at first silent. Since she didn't know what to say, she stared down at her purse, fumbling with the clasp compulsively. He wheeled the big car around the block and headed uptown, still without a word.

"Angelo, I'm sorry, I mean, I don't know what to say—"

"Not necessary."

"It is necessary. This, I don't know how it happened."

"No one ever does." Angelo adjusted the mirror, tilting it slightly to get a better view of her. "You know, I worry, I really do. If you don't mind me saying so, you're not like the other people—girls or women or—"

"Don't tell me, I can just imagine."

"Not sure that you can, actually."

"I can't explain it to myself, but I'm alone in the

world, no one to live for or look up to or really even get close to. These New York people are not so friendly, and here I am in that incredible office. Everyone's afraid to say hello to me."

"True, but I thought you had that writer who went up to Rye, you know, more your age. I drove him a couple of times when he first started at the magazine. He seemed like a nice guy."

"We're friends." They left it at that, in part because there was no more to say, but also now Hull had positioned her somewhere ambiguously above Angelo, no longer strictly an employee, but a lover and therefore in a position of power herself, not that she had any sense it could be used, but still, it was too much. She had left the ground and floated upwards into a social stratum she neither deserved nor knew anything about.

At East 57th Street, Angelo stopped the car in front of a stately townhouse that looked to be from the Art Deco period, iron scrollwork curving over the stained-glass doorway. Jenna stepped out of the car, glad that Angelo stood beside her, as it was now close to two in the morning, no one about. She ascended the front steps, pressed the bell, which sounded like a gong in the silent night, and right away a soft buzzer hummed as she pushed the door forward. Into the extraordinary hallway she walked, its walls covered in green damask, geometrically carved wooden ceilings above. Before her hung a chandelier of iron and glass curlicues, and at the far end of the hallway, there loomed an elaborate gated elevator.

It was very old, and it creaked upwards slowly, its menacing metal bars giving her a glimpse of the ancient mottled wood that made up the interior of the building. At the second floor, where it jolted to a stop, Jenna just stood there, not really knowing how to get out. Finally she wrestled the grillwork door aside and entered a room unlike any other she had seen. She glimpsed mahogany-lined bookshelves, probably a Chardin still life, what appeared to be a Van Gogh, and finally, on a green couch, Vincent Hull himself, dressed casually now in blue jeans and one of his black T-shirts. Drink in hand, he leapt up, trying to sweep her into his arms, as he planted his drink on the table. "I waited so long for you." His voice sounded hoarse and unnatural.

"No. I won't do it." She hugged the thick binder to her breasts. He took it gently from her hand and set it on a nearby table.

"Do what?"

"I don't know." She really had no words for whatever conversation she thought she had planned. Looking up into those deep-set eyes that spoke to her always, she felt drugged. He covered her mouth with his own, harshly, not waiting at all for her to respond, but of course she did, and what happened next she could never forget. He moved her forward as if to go to another room, but she grabbed his arm and pulled him down toward her. "Here."

"Here?"

"Yes, on the floor."

"What?" He let her pull off his shirt, then slide her hands over his hips and unbutton his jeans, but he swept off the rest while she waited. She did not let her gaze waver. She took off her own clothes slowly, as he sank down and watched without a word. Once completely naked, she stood over him as he grabbed a pillow for his head and looked up at her. Except for that one really hostile moment she had ravaged him in his bed, normally he had dominated her so absolutely that she might have been a captive lady in the castle keep. Now he took the place of captive.

She sank down onto his chest and began to kiss him gently from the forehead down to his throat, his chest, to his belly, and finally to his sex. He groaned and closed his eyes, while she whispered into his ear, "I want you to beg."

Even in the midst of this, he laughed. "Never. I don't beg."

Once again, she moved slowly over his body, her lips resting for a moment in his secret places, in places she had never touched before, and then she caressed with her mouth the very center of the man until he started moving hotly to touch her. "No touch," she whispered again. "Just beg me."

"For what?"

"To fuck you."

"No, no, you've lost your mind, I don't—" But her fluttering tongue had him gasping now, and though he tried to touch her, too, she flicked away his hand.

"Just say please. Do you know how to say please?"

"Okay, fuck me." He breathed heavily against her breasts and seemed about to explode.

"Say please." Jenna herself was about to scream with pleasure, but she held herself in so tightly, bottled up with her rage against this man she wanted but didn't even know.

"Please." As he got this out, she sank down upon him and the sound that came out of his mouth she had never heard before, but at the same moment, she herself let out a cry. Hot, sweating, still inside her, Vince curled his arms around her and rolled her onto the floor next to him, wanting to hold her there against him, but she struggled and slid away. He pulled a throw rug around them, drawing them together. Almost but not quite, Jenna drifted into sleep. After some moments, she pulled herself up, aware somehow that these postures, this attitude, could not exist where she currently lay. While the man watched, silent, she pulled on her clothes and then, before she could leave, drew the inventory binder off the couch and flipped through it quickly. Fat as a Russian novel, it looked professional, consequential, a careful record of size, date, and provenance of artworks that, taken together, she had valued in the hundreds of millions of dollars. This was her work, the only solid piece of anything meaningful she had done for him. She laid the book carefully down next to him. Vincent still said nothing, though at last, "You're going?"

"Yes."

"Don't"

But Jenna fled into the hall of this singular abode, more appropriate for an eighteenth-century magnate or country gentleman, yet stuck right here in New York City. She wasn't sure Angelo had waited, but as she peered around her, there the car purred like a panther after a feed. She climbed aboard and lost herself in its leathery darkness. She did not speak at all.

SEVEN

For the whole of the next week, Vincent Hull did not come into the office and, according to Jorge, the man had once more decamped to Paris. "What does he do there?" Jenna was unsure how much to ask, but she fully expected to get fired and wanted to be prepared.

"Drinks coffee, scouts paintings, eats croissants, I don't know. Lives the charmed life."

"What about his family?"

"The wife goes with him sometimes, and the girls stay with Mrs. Hull's parents."

One of her phone lights turned red. It was Inti, busy, stressed, anxious to get the photos. "Where have you been? I've been trying to reach you."

She fished the photos guiltily out of her desk. "Actually, I have them right here."

"Messenger them, I'm not kidding. This could be a big story, at least for Rye and could be for a lot of other towns. Time passes. What the hell are you doing?"

"I'm sorry, I just got busy. It's not that easy with the Leica. I couldn't go to a regular photo processing place." Jorge listened to all this, trying not to stare. "The pictures are really good. I think you'll like them." In one, she had caught the glazed, fiery eyes of the coyote looking at them helplessly. In another the retreating rear ends of the pack lined up almost symmetrically, and in one of the saddest, a coyote lay dead, fallen down before them in exhaustion.

"This could be serious. Get them to me right away."

He sounded truly angry, and she could see why. Inti hung up without making any sort of plan to see her again. Within minutes, Jenna enlisted Jorge to package up the photos, and out the door they went with the messenger.

Her roommates, who up until this point had alternately ignored her or laughed at her, for the first time in a long time invited her out for a drink and a hamburger at their favorite pub in Gramercy Park. Ten days after Jenna had ravished Vincent Hull on the floor, there they all sat. The irony of it made Jenna stare solemnly into her second martini. *What do you know, and when did you know it*, she almost wanted to shout above the din, like some demented television reporter. Of course they must know nothing, but maybe they just felt her changed for the better. Sounds of Ricky Martin's "La Vida Loca" streamed loudly through the room and Jenna couldn't stop herself from swaying her shoulders as if dancing, whether fearful or nuts she wasn't sure. Allyson looked at her strangely, while Vera swiveled her head right and left to see who was around, especially her errant boyfriend, Ed Delong. They didn't talk much to her, and so she was left to watch the TV up behind the bar. Without warning, the imposing figure of Vincent Hull appeared, being interviewed, it seemed, in a building distinctly Parisian. "Quiet," she said to Allyson and Vera, and then shoved her way closer to the bar to hear what the man said. Vera snickered, and Allyson tossed back a tequila shooter, making strange faces all the while.

By the time she had pushed through the people, Hull was off the screen, but there before her stood the Rothko that had so transfixed her in his New York townhouse. Had he taken it to Paris? She couldn't imagine such a thing, but then she really couldn't fathom his life at all. Maybe he had put it in his plane? When she got back to the table, her roommates both started to interrogate her. "All right, come clean, Jenna. We know what's going on, I do anyway." Allyson flicked a cigarette ash into a glass dish before her.

Vera leaned far forward, poking at her with a French fry. "You'd better be careful, missy. Whatever you're doing, you don't know what you're doing, that's for sure."

"How do you know that? How do the two of you know anything?"

"Come on," Allyson crooned. "We've tried to make friends, but you're never around or you're out, god knows where."

"You're out all the time too. Besides, I thought you didn't like me."

Vera shook her head. "You're the one who never talks to either of us. We thought you hated us, maybe for sticking you with the futon?"

"No, no, not at all. I'm just too flustered to know what I'm doing." Jenna had decided to play dumb. Her roommates didn't buy any of this, and had taken to speculating daily about whatever salacious business Jenna was up to, but she was younger than they by at least five years, so they were unsure how deeply she might have gotten herself into trouble.

Late on a blustery hot August night in the city, many days after her curiously satisfying erotic frenzy with her boss, Jenna awoke from a sound sleep startled by the phone. She grabbed it right away so as not to awaken Allyson and Vera. It was, of all people, Tasha, screaming, "You've got to come to the office, oh please right away!" She gasped and sobbed as she spoke.

"What's wrong . . . what's happened?"

"Just come, please. If you really care about Vincent."

How did Tasha know what she felt for her boss? But

the latter was too hysterical for her to ask. "Has something happened to him?"

"Just come to the office and bring some good clothes, or some sexy little touches, no, that's wrong, something conservative, office-like."

"It's two in the morning, Tasha. I don't understand, what's going on?"

"Stop talking, please. Maybe it doesn't matter what you wear. We can switch clothes or something. Come as fast as you can. It's a matter of life and death."

This was all nuts, but she obeyed and dressed hurriedly in one of her work outfits, pulling on black stockings somehow to fulfill Tasha's wishes. Her hands shook, and she smeared her mascara, but she made it out to the pavement in close to five minutes. No one was about. The eerie quiet scared her, and she turned uncertainly until out of the darkness a cab swerved her way, and she flagged it down. As the taxi shot along, free of any obstacles, Jenna searched obsessively in her purse, checking for her money, her lipstick, her brush, her cell phone. In the midst of an anxiety attack, she needed an outlet in the certainty of her stuff. Once she shouted out, "Slow down!" then caught her breath and added, "please." The driver slowed down just a bit, then swung around the corner of 41st Street and hurtled along even faster, slamming on the brakes at last when they reached Vincent Hull's office building at 54th and Fifth Avenue. Jenna leaned forward, gave the man a ten-dollar bill, and leapt out of the cab.

She raced up to the heavy doors, waiting nervously, shifting from one foot to the other. New York was always strange, but never stranger than in the early morning hours, the near-total silence heavy with menace. The shadowy figure of the security guard appeared behind the door, and he opened it immediately; walking with her to the elevator, he turned his key to let her go up. This was her world, familiar, and by now, almost homey, but she felt disoriented in the stillness. At the fourteenth floor, she stepped out to an empty hallway. Turning left, she walked fast to Vincent's office, but before she got there, Tasha, strangely dressed in a long black velvet caftan, came running down the hall to meet her. At this moment her friend looked not at all like an employee, more like an African princess attending a ritual dance.

"What are we doing here? What are you doing here?" Jenna whispered as she followed along behind her stupidly.

"Come to Vince's office, but I want to warn you. You'll see things."

"What things?"

The woman didn't answer her.

Once inside the suite of offices, Tasha shoved her into the small, very private inner sanctum that existed behind where Hull normally worked, a secret place Jenna had only glimpsed once before. There Vincent Hull lay, pants down, passed out or possibly dead on the floor. Tasha looked up and faced her. "His lawyer is calling right away."

"His lawyer? We need EMTs. Maybe they can still do something. Oh my god!" She started to wring her hands.

"I already tried CPR." Tasha looked haggard, confused.

"How long ago did this happen?"

Tasha looked at her watch, and then shook her head. "I don't know. I've lost track of time." She reached out to Jenna and held her arm. "We were making love, and he rose up like this," and she reared back grasping at her own chest. "He made a terrible sound and flopped forward right on top of me. It's been about an hour, total, I think."

An hour? Realizing now that a woman she barely knew had been making love to the same person she was, and on the floor of this office at somewhere near two in the morning, Jenna shifted her mind to a new, horrible place. Why had she never considered that if Vincent made love to her, betraying children and wife alike, he could do anything, he could have anyone? Ruefully, at least out of all of this, she realized that one question did get answered: by what means Tasha had acquired her fantastic wardrobe.

Tasha bent down now and rubbed her hand along Vincent's naked back, that beautiful strong back. Jenna looked straight at it now and remembered how he had encircled her own in the shower. She could taste that moment still. The phone rang, and in the silence sounded as loud and out of place as a gong. "Here, talk to the lawyer."

"No!" Jenna cried instinctively, clapping her hands over her face, but Tasha calmly answered, murmuring "Yes," nodding her head.

"Me?" Jenna shook her head violently. "No, no!" but Tasha shoved the phone into her hand.

At the other end, a deep male voice introduced himself. "Miss McCann, I am Rudolph Hayes, of Hayes, Rudinksy, and Baugh. This is a very unfortunate situation, as you can see. "

"Unfortunate? We have to get him to a hospital."

"Yes, of course, we understand how you might feel about what you're seeing, but for the good of the family and yourself, I'd like to make an arrangement with you. It's to spare the Hulls even more grief. As yet, you see, they have no idea what has happened."

"I want nothing to do with this, absolutely nothing."

"Yes, well, it's a particularly delicate matter because clearly, they, or rather the world will ultimately know that the man died while performing an intimate act. We won't be able to hide that fact. The question will be, who was that act with? Do you understand me?"

"No."

"We would like you to substitute yourself for Miss Clark."

"But why?" There was blank space through the phone line. "Because she's black? This is the modern age. Who cares?" Jenna was afraid to look at Tasha.

"There are other considerations, related to the family, his children in particular. Of course you will be amply compensated, and when I say amply I mean handsomely. It should be enough to allow you an opulent lifestyle for the duration."

"For the duration of what?"

"For your lifetime, if I might put it that way. We would manage the publicity, and after the initial storm, you, of course, would leave the country, again at our expense and with all the resources of the Hull network at your command. You are only twenty-four years old, with your whole future ahead of you. This is a significant proposal that could make your life."

"Am I getting this right? You want me to be a decoy, so the family and everybody else won't know that he was making love to Tasha?"

"That's it exactly."

"They will think he was making love with me?"

"You were having sex with him, weren't you?"

Even in this grotesque moment, Jenna did not want to admit to any relationship with the man. It was bottled up inside her like one of his precious wines. As much as it hurt her to say it out loud, though, finally she did. "Yes, but briefly," then wanted to take this back, because it sounded as if she wanted to diminish what they had done together.

"If I may point out, now that Mr. Hull is no longer alive, your temporary position at his company will evaporate, and you will be looking for work. You have no real prospects. If you accept our offer, think how your future would change. You would be helping his family immeasurably, saving his reputation, helping them deal with their grief. Ms. Clark is also a long-time employee, so let's try to maintain dignity for everyone involved. No one will know, no one outside the other lawyer involved, not even his wife. This is a disaster control operation, but there is only so much we can fix."

"So you mean his wife would never know her friend was sleeping with her husband?"

"That's the idea." The man went on to describe in detail what she might have for her future, anything really, everything except her own destiny. Her future would vanish into a fraudulent life, lived elsewhere, as a very rich young woman. He even indicated how she should place herself under the dead man.

"I have to think about this. I can't just do it, right here, right now, can I?"

"You can, and if you don't mind my saying so, you must."

Tasha watched her carefully, then stood up and began to pace the room. She looked so strange, like a model just stepping out of the pages of a magazine, the caftan was that extraordinary. Jenna moved toward her and grasped her hand, and the two stood at the window watching the empty street below. Only a taxi now and then, one limousine, a man in a dirty jacket weaving slightly. "How did you know about us?" Jenna said.

"We know everything around here. It's our job." Tasha hugged her close. Jenna thought of the neat little housekeeper in Water Mill who seemed to vanish at just the right moment, and then return with silent grace.

"How long have you been seeing him?" But as she

spoke she pictured those two in the exact same postures she herself had enjoyed with him, more than enjoyed, passionately, ecstatically engaged in with him, with that body that now rested on the floor. Finally she asked, "Did you love him?"

"I don't know. He was amazing, but he could be mean, truly mean, cruel. Yet what a lover." Tasha managed a laugh.

"But how long have you been involved?"

"A year and two months." Tasha and she had overlapped, so to speak.

Like it or not, Jenna still had the smell of him, the taste of him, all that made him part of her flesh. About the need for the lawyer and the failure to call emergency services, she had only dim inklings. Could he have been saved? Did Tasha just sit there and wait for him to die? Jenna looked over now at Vince in that grotesque position. Oh god, how she had loved to touch that body, but now, how horrible even to think about it. Without him, what would her future be? She had nothing and no one on this earth. She would have to leave New York, which wouldn't in itself be bad, but where to go? Back to the awful, bleak, depressed countryside of northern Ohio, not an interesting job in sight and nothing but painful memories.

Truly, was it because of the children and the wife? Did this plot really have to do with protecting their notion that Tasha was a friend to the whole family? Certainly, to them Jenna was invisible, so would this lessen their care about his sexual sins? The lawyer had laid out a specific scenario. First Jenna would place herself underneath the man, where Tasha had been located earlier, and then she would call 911. Once his body left for the hospital—and she would have to accompany him—she could take refuge in her own apartment, where there would be security. A week or two after that, depending on the level of journalistic fury, a flight to a foreign country, to a temporary place of her own choosing, at least until she decided where to live permanently. She would have to change her last name and several fundamental aspects of her appearance. "Think of it as sort of a witness-protection kind of thing," the man had said.

Dazed, uncertain, her head pounding, now she wished for a parent, a cousin, someone, anyone who would advise her except the well-dressed sinner Tasha, and the curse of her aloneness came upon her now in all its meaning. Could she call Inti? A mad thought, and she rejected it right away.

Jenna thought of her grandmother in death, so beautiful, an unlined face even after all those years, but the turnout at her funeral had been tiny, only her caregiver and her doctor, such that Jenna cursed her family for its disarray, for its shameful emptiness. The Hull funeral would probably fill several city blocks. She stared down at him. Vince Hull didn't look waxy, he still had vitality, though splayed on the floor, and that made it hard to think of him as dead, but of course the eyes told all. "'When you're dead, you're dead, as dead as Kelsey's nuts,' Granny used to say."

Tasha gave a harsh laugh. Walking over to the window, Jenna searched for a way to open it. At last she found a small safety latch, tripped it, and the window slid open a crack, to let his spirit escape the room. She plucked the turquoise cashmere throw off the couch and draped the mirror with it, "out of respect," she said to Tasha, and then knelt down beside the body. Reaching for his hand, which had grown cold now, she bowed her head. "Thank you for every moment you gave to me, Vincent Hull," and then she rose up to face Tasha. "I'll do it. I'll do everything the lawyer requested." In that instant, she felt a single breath of pure panic, as if she had jumped off a building.

"They've bribed the security guard." Tasha wouldn't look back at her and sobbed into a Kleenex, which she had torn into shreds. "I think I have to leave now. Will you be okay?"

"Yes." But, of course, she did not know at all. Years after this event, Jenna still tried to suppress the recurring nightmare of what happened immediately thereafter. She had to stage things to look as if the last hour and a half had evaporated, and the death had taken place at that instant.

EIGHT

I n death, Vincent looked puzzled, shocked was it? The shock that life had stopped right that instant? Maybe he had seen it coming, in the midst of his own ecstasy. Soon the EMTs would be here, and she started to cry again. That would be a nice touch and a true one too as the grave import of what she now did came upon her. She struggled to get herself beneath him.

She heard footsteps and increased her sobbing. Into the front office burst a gaggle of males, and suddenly she felt ashamed of her exposed, unkempt body. Maybe she should try to get up, but no, her instructions had been clear. She lay there still weeping, and these were true tears. Four paramedics, intent on resuscitation, release, information, but restrained somehow, now intruded on the man and the woman in their idyll. From behind, one of them clutched her arms and slid her slowly up and out from beneath the dead man. Jenna gasped and clung to him. "It was horrible, horrible. His mouth just opened, and then he stopped breathing."

"It's fine, we're here now. We'll see what we can do." She straightened her blouse, as he hung onto her while the others ministered to the fallen titan. Even they were in awe, and she could see that from the careful way they cut his clothes and rolled him over. Jenna still had her hand to her mouth to keep from screaming.

A man who appeared to be in charge said, "Would you be a part of the immediate family?"

"No, a friend."

"Ah." The man paused at the significance of her words. "Please make a report to Morris here."

Jenna relayed a story of their having a private meeting in another part of the building, then going up to his office for a drink. She didn't get much beyond the drink before the man called Morris gave her a warning. "As soon as the press finds out your name—and they will— you need to be prepared."

"Yes." She knew this already, but what could she tell anyone? That for money she had replaced her friend underneath the body of a dead man so that his august, prejudiced family would avoid scandal around the man's affair with a black woman? The family demanded this new story that would name Jenna as the guilty, horrible woman at the heart of the matter.

The ride to the hospital in the ambulance, more than anything, gave her the first moments of her altered future, the instant crossing she had made into another world. She sat on a jump seat beside the prone man on a stretcher, calculating how soon the doctors would realize he had died hours before, rather than just minutes. Watching the paramedics work with oxygen and IVs and violent chest-thumping made her hyper-conscious of her task, to feign hysteria. It was all such a terrible lie, and yet her own heart pounded, and she kept wringing her hands in despair, because she was in despair.

Jenna followed the gurney as it rolled off the ambulance and rushed straight into the emergency room with what remained of Vincent Hull. Perhaps because of his status in life, the hospital personnel did not stop for one moment in their attempts to resuscitate him, and Jenna found herself ignored. As they sprinted away from her with the body, she stood awkwardly in the waiting area, not knowing what to do, conscious that the state of her clothing rendered her guilty, if anyone cared to look. Her role had only partially been explained to her, but within minutes she saw Hull's wife, and then Jorge, her comrade-in-arms, enter the emergency room. She shrank back, she thought of flight, but then knew she could not and so huddled with her purse clutched to her chest near the vending machines. Whatever was going on in this strange play, she had no idea of her lines. Alone and frightened, she watched Jorge talking with hospital personnel. When he looked her way, he cocked his head to one side and eyed her strangely. She wanted to reach out, to communicate with him somehow, but at once an older man in a suit approached her, and from the sound of his voice, she recognized him as the lawyer who had issued instructions over the phone. He led her to a corner, but not before Sabine Hull glared her way and then pointed her out to Tasha, who now wore slacks and a T-shirt. These two women huddled together, as if they found themselves in a high wind.

"His wife saw me!" Jenna moaned, ashamed.

"Of course she did. That's the whole idea," the lawyer, Rudolf Hayes, whispered and held her arm to shove her slightly forward. "From even a cursory examination, they will know he was with a woman, it will be obvious on his body. We're controlling which woman he appears to have been with."

"I understand," but she did not, really. Jenna was so bewildered by the evening's events she had left off thinking altogether.

Sabine Hull continued to watch Jenna closely, and even managed a cautious, pained nod in her direction. Jenna kept her head down, fearful that the woman might attack her or worse, start shouting and make a scene, but

shortly thereafter two other men in suits took her by the
arm and ushered her out into the lobby, and thence into a
waiting black SUV, as if hustling away a fugitive. They all
waited together in the car—for what, Jenna had no idea
—until at last the lawyer appeared and got into the back
seat. "We're going to take you to your apartment."

"What about my roommates?"

"They've been moved."

"So fast? To where?" Horrible idea, that Vera and
Allyson would be thrown out of the apartment because of
her. They would be outraged, probably never speak to
her again. With a start she realized that it wouldn't matter what they thought because she would never live with
them again, probably never even see them again.

Gramercy Park was deserted at this hour of the
morning. "Great address, crummy apartment," she muttered stupidly, as the lawyer hustled her to her front
door, up the elevator, to their small place, which now,
oddly, seemed huge, as she was the only one in it. The
bedrooms had been cleared of everything, and in the wee
hours, somehow or other, even their eccentric furniture
had disappeared. The two roommates had vanished, so
had their stuff, and in their place reigned a bleak mod-
ernism, a dining room table and four chairs, and several
brand new lamps. It had been transformed into the
apartment of nobody she knew. "Where is everything?"
She felt distracted, trying not to panic.

"Their furniture moved with them. Don't worry, they
replaced this with a three-bedroom on, oh, you don't
need to know that now. I may say, they are two very
happy, very rich women now."

"They're lost to me, right?" Jenna had heard the
terms of the agreement surprisingly well, considering the
circumstances, but she still couldn't believe any of it. Five

hours ago she inhabited her own life; now she had stepped behind the mirror into an altogether different one. She wanted badly to wash, though, conscious of Vincent Hull still on her body. "I need some time alone," she managed to say, embarrassed. Rudolph Hayes bowed his head and nodded.

"The press will find you by tomorrow, so you'll have to stay inside much of the time."

"For how long?"

"For a decent interval, but we will decide that. Then we'll let them get several good looks at you, but after that it's off to, where is it now?"

"I haven't had time to figure that out."

Such was the plan, that after the press had had a field day with "the other woman," and Jenna had been photographed and stalked and whatever else, her identity firmly sealed in their gullible little minds, she would disappear to some village in Europe or Fiji or Australia, or anywhere her heart desired, because she would have the money to do so, because she would be rich beyond the dreams of avarice, certainly beyond any of her dreams.

That night, as she sank into the new bed these people had bought for her, she couldn't stop thinking of the face of Vincent Hull, his jaw slack, in a perpetual gasp, as the paramedics hovered about him. And the look on Jorge's face when he saw her, that grimace, appalled, horrified, confounded. She wished, she wanted so much to tell him the truth of all this and vowed to ask the lawyer about it the next day.

"Are you mad? You can't call him," the lawyer said when she rushed out her intentions as soon as she got up in the morning. "The deal is to hole up, talk to no one. Your phone number has changed anyway. Despite the speed of all this, I did think you understood."

"But at least if Jorge knew the truth. . . ."

The somber man interrupted her. "He could tell other people."

"He's been keeping Vincent Hull's secrets for years."

"In the modern world, nobody keeps any secrets, except lawyers, and they can certainly be bought. You know what the deal is, and I dare say you are capable of fulfilling it. If you weren't, Tasha would never have enlisted your aid." He made it sound as if Jenna were almost religiously anointed.

The death of Vincent Hull in such circumstances was bound to whip the press into a frenzy, and it did. Ensconced in vans and camp chairs, they waited and watched at the Gramercy Park apartment house, annoying dog walkers and residents alike. Collectively they had discovered Jenna's address in about three hours, and now she was a prisoner and did not even dare to part the curtains. Her first visitor, a hair stylist and makeup artist, almost broke a leg trying to get through the free-for-all, but once inside, she proved the only rational person Jenna had talked to since Vincent's death. An employee of some relation to Rudolph Hayes, she turned Jenna into a hot-looking, full-on New Yorker, with shapely hair that damped down her curls and made her look truly dazzling, even while still ridiculously young. If she was the guilty temptress, she had to look the part.

The first time she ventured outside, as the lawyers instructed, was just to get her picture taken posting a fake letter, wading through screaming lady reporters in chic suits, guys with baseball caps and boom microphones held perilously over her head, shouting photographers shoving competitors out of the way with heavy cameras. She faced down this scrum in a white shirt, black pants, a heavy jacket, and sunglasses, and it had taken every bit of nerve she possessed to open her door and descend one step and one step alone, before she rushed back inside. The next morning she adorned the front pages of the *New York Post* and the *New York Daily News*. Of course, *The New York Times* ran an extensive article on Vincent Hull's demise, briefly mentioning the presence of one of his assistants at the death scene. Its placement on page four made it even more conspicuous, at least to Jenna's eyes. Soon enough every press outlet used that first photo, a front view of her holding open the apartment door, in glasses, with that dazzling hair. She had an uneven grin on her face, highly inappropriate considering the circumstances, making her appear indifferent to his death, downright moronic. The next two times she braved the crowd, at the lawyer's request, she wore a dark coat and a large hat, sort of like a Russian oligarch's wife off to shop at Bergdorf's.

Now, while alone so much, she began really to think about her life, and more particularly about Vincent Hull. The worst of it, the very worst of it, was how awful it had been to see her lover in death. She had loved him, she had, she told herself, and to prove it, or to make her tears flow even harder, she listened over and over again to her cherished Prince CD, "Nothing Compares to U," nothing compares to you. Her most ordinary thoughts now turned to some version of the apocalypse, and she would never recover. All had changed; she had agreed to that change.

Another baffling element in the evolving complexity was Inti, a journalist no less, even if off in Rye. Would he believe this trumped up story? He had always seemed to know her, by the look in his eyes, but he wouldn't understand this. She would be cast as a betrayer, a liar, and a cheat. Unbearable, these thoughts, and she wanted to wish them away, but she could never see him again, it seemed, and for the first time she began to feel the heavy burden of a decision made so quickly. The job, the affair, all to betray everyone for riches? How despicable. She felt such a deep shame that she wanted just to close her eyes and disappear. Could she communicate with him somehow and tell him this was all a lie?

Her phone rang constantly, despite the new number, but she didn't answer, as instructed. She had no family left, though doubtless her astounded roommates would wonder at seeing her depicted as "the other woman," since they hardly seemed to think her a woman at all, pathetically in lust after her impossible boss. Would they believe any of this? From time to time she longed to see, just for a moment, their faces. But the one she really couldn't get out of her mind was Jorge, and she vowed, somehow or other, to let him know enough not to hate her.

PART THREE

Winter, 2000

Former Ohio resident, Jenna McCann is no stranger to her fellow students at Ohio University. Sources called her "pushy, very competitive." She told her friends one day she would be famous. "Basically, she was something of a slut."

—Athens Mirror, January 3, 2000

Mark Rothko's painting, "Untitled," 1969, from the estate of Vincent Macklin Hull, broke records last night, reaching the 22 million dollar mark. Curiously, his widow, Sabine Hull remarked at the auction that "the painting was so dull," and she "wanted to get rid of it as soon as possible."

—Artful, February 10, 2000

I believe in reincarnation. May Vincent Hull come back as two Asian sex slaves.

—JORGE GARZA TO HIS MOTHER

ONE

Nothing in this life could have prepared Inti Weill for what happened to his erstwhile girlfriend. Two months ago, seeing her face on all the major New York papers, her obvious new look in hair and makeup, hiding herself in the oversized collar of a white blouse, had him confused and outraged, and he still had not recovered. Who the hell was she, really? Though in the major papers, descriptions of her actual position underneath Vincent Hull were restrained, he got the picture all too well. Filthy, disgusting images had roiled his mind each night ever since, and he couldn't sleep. It outraged him that he could have been so wrong, deluded about her, more particularly about her supposed interest in him. Up until this point in his romantic life, he had been confident of his powers of seduction, having succeeded many times where others had failed. Then too he really liked women; his mother he regarded as his very best friend. About Jenna he had felt smug, priding himself in his compassion for her, stuck as she was in a chaotic big world she didn't seem to understand. But now, of all the people known to him on earth, she struck him as least likely to be tabloid fodder, least likely to have done what was asserted. Could she possibly have been the mistress of this aged man at more or less the same time she huddled with him in a tent in Rye, New York?

He had, however, a more immediate concern. When the coyote story came out in the *Rye Register,* he had credited Jenna, "Photos by J. McCann," a name that he now regretted using. It had been generous of him, he thought, to name her. Much as Inti realized his coyote alert was up against some stiff competition from the 86th birthday of the owner of the town hardware store, also a party for women who wore purple hats and gave to charity, still, people had read it and reacted strongly to the pictures, though so far no one had connected this minute reference (did anyone read photo attributions in the newspaper?) to the young woman at the heart of a major scandal—as yet. But they might, and then what?

Predictably, the *New York Post* had raised questions regarding the timeline of the tycoon's death and had named "his assistant, Jenna McCann," as the woman who had called the EMTs and been found in a highly compromised position in the room with him. *The New York Times* discussed these details days later, in terms that could only heighten suspicions. "The mysterious timeline of Vincent Macklin Hull's death grows even more murky. According to the family spokesman, the man collapsed at approximately 9:30 p.m. but was actually spotted in the emergency room at midnight, physicians still attempting to resuscitate him. The medical examiner's report has yet to be unsealed, but apparently no autopsy was performed, and the man who lived in something like an imperial court was reportedly cremated and buried within two days at the family cemetery in Chicago." To Inti's way of thinking, the story given out to the press made no sense, and adding to his suspicions, during the next few weeks a "family spokesman" kept trying to reconfigure all this through a series of revised statements.

Once again, Inti looked through the photographs Jenna had taken, admiringly. In the first one, a skinny, wretched-looking coyote hung down its face at the entrance to their tent. Jenna had caught her, clearly a female because the teats were still full, in a moment of surprise and curiosity. Unlike a healthily skittish animal, this one seemed desperate and dazed. Some of her fellows appeared in the background, guarded, glittering eyes visible through the foliage. Another pictured just the scrawny back end of the creature as it moved slowly off into the trees, and in yet another image, a coyote lay dead in the grass.

He really needed more photos, as the story had become a sensation. On the very day he filed and shortly thereafter, the pictures had fanned out over the airwaves and across twenty other unexpected venues. Fliers up all over Rye detailed how to wave off the creatures, and "make yourself big" became a mantra, while zealous pet owners organized nightly hunts to scare the animals away, if not kill them. It solved a local mystery, and the story got picked up elsewhere, even so far as *The New York Times*. Rye had whole teams of midnight watchers in tents now, and Inti had caused it. Seriously, how many coyotes were wandering right now around Central Park, snatching up Fluffy and Fido? Zoologists had told him that coyotes really were everywhere—the stealth beneficiaries of a civilization discarding a tremendous amount of edible trash. He expected to hear from Jenna, though he chided himself for even wanting to. A fraud and a liar, that woman, using him as her beard in front of the family. He had tried every single phone number he could think of, even down to her roommates, but all had been cut off. With a shudder he recalled all the nasty things he had said about Hull, and yet he could remember no reaction whatsoever from Jenna, maybe a smile or two, and he had thought she was just being discreet about her boss. He tried briefly to reach Tasha and got nowhere, though he had little faith in a woman who basically worked for *NewsLink* as a professional liar.

After his third coyote article—spinning it out for months at the behest of his editor—Inti heard from the regional New York editor at the *Times* with an offer to work on the "New York" section of the country's paper of record. Out of the darkness and into the light, ecstatic to be back in the game, as he put it. Once ensconced in a new apartment and a slightly bigger desk, Inti had every intention of learning a great deal more about Vincent Hull's death and now was positioned to do so.

Unfortunately, he had had no idea how ridiculously similar this new job would be to his old beat at the *Rye Register* until, during what seemed like a long lead up to actual snow, he attended four or five zoning meetings in Westfield, New York, near Lake Erie, boring to the point of stupefaction. From there he worked up something on the wineries nearby, those that supplied grapes to the Canandaigua Wine Company, more interesting certainly, also tasty. Next he went on to write about Amish life and found himself amid a quantity of buggies and quilts, some of which had won prizes at the county fair, all of this because his editor thought him adept at "local color." Despite being employed by a much bigger paper, he seemed even farther away from the major news of the world than ever, and these three months seemed like forever.

Also during this time, news had died down about Vincent Hull's death. Nevertheless, recently more facts dribbled out: his immense art collection, the many gifts to charity, random bits meant to convey his good character, and the astonishing news that he had left Tasha money to buy a co-op on Park Avenue. She certainly didn't live there because Inti had researched the residents of the building many times, looking always for notice of a new tenant. There didn't seem to be one. He even tried to chat up the doorman, who stared him down and remained silent.

Inti feared that his own vanity kept forcing him to question Jenna's actually having sex with the great man, but his instincts cried out that the story was doctored. Who had actually screwed the man to death? This question haunted him, but the principals had disappeared, and no one was talking. Even Mrs. Hull had returned to France with her children, and all mention of the family remained respectful and discreet. Someone had put a lid on it, difficult to do in the year 2000 but still doable, especially considering the reach of the family and their great wealth. For his own part, Inti felt, oddly, as if he held the keys to the kingdom. Whatever his misgivings, he had the wit to understand that potentially he sat on a big story. The girl with Vincent Hull in his death throes, he knew her, though not where she was. He could make something of this, he could use her to further his career at the *Times*, but during these days he was too conflicted and angry to do any serious searching.

Inti even found it painful to try to remember whether Jenna had ever talked of favorite vacation spots or places she wanted to visit. Her horizons seemed to involve Manhattan and Mecox Bay in Water Mill. Vainly, proudly, he considered that he absolutely should not pursue this, even though she had materially furthered his great coyote success. Then again there remained a greater gift from the eccentric world of the Weill family. They had not fostered that rabid hunger that demanded devotion to career above all else. About work his mother and father affected a nonchalant reluctance to struggle, and they hadn't had to, living off the very tolerant students of Evergreen College in Olympia, Washington.

"There's been an art theft in Tarrytown," the *Times* deputy editor announced to him over the phone. "Get up there and see what's going on."

At least Tarrytown was closer to Manhattan than the hinterlands he had of late been visiting, Inti thought as he pulled on his heavy coat. After a ride on the Metro-North Hudson line, then a trip by taxi up to the immense front door of a Tudor revival pile of bricks that sat on twelve acres, he found himself inside a mansion only Dracula could love. The harried housekeeper, a woman in her sixties who kept picking nervously at her pockets, dragged him from one large room to another, and finally to a sitting room with shimmering yellow raw silk on the walls and two empty squares where the paintings had once rested, one small, the other enormous. "See, see, they are not where they should be. Disappeared."

"Do you know what happened?"

"Two men were working here on the house, repairs, loose chandeliers and lights, all those things. When they first came, I couldn't get hold of the missus to see or ask anything, but they had been here before so I just let them in. I kept on working, but when I went back they were gone, and so were two of the paintings." The woman started to cry and hung onto Inti's jacket. "Is it my fault, do you think? Oh no, so much money!" She began to moan and blew her nose into a large, white handkerchief.

"Don't worry, I'm sure your employer will understand," though he was not sure of any such thing. "Do you have the names of the paintings?"

"No, but they were beautiful, so nice. I used to love to look at them."

The woman did fill in information on her boss, a Mrs. Regina Pittman, wife of a big-time hedge fund manager, Jack Pittman, with a home in St. Croix and a chateau in the Loire Valley, in addition to this place. Once back at his tiny desk in the city, he phoned the woman at each, only to be told that no one could reach her at the moment, though they had tried. Finally one minion gave him a lawyer's name, and Inti called the man.

"Yes, Mrs. Pittman knows about this already. One was a Fragonard, quite small, the other a large Bartholomeus Spranger, the very best of his work, both worth together, maybe ten million dollars."

"Incredible, and the two guys just walked out with them?"

"Apparently so, though these thefts are almost always inside jobs. We'll have to depose everybody there, because no doubt they got help. Unfortunately the works might even be overseas by now."

Inti instantly spotted this one as a story he could pursue, as did his editor. "So many rich people read the *Times* or wannabe rich, it's perfect. And an inside job? 'Did the servants know?' I can see the headline now. In fact, write that down." The NY region section of the paper adopted a slightly more hysterical tone than one the managing editor might adopt, but they were tolerant. "It's not a coyote, Weill, but it's damn close. And Jack Pittman is a very big deal, must be dirt there you can use."

Inti tracked down every known art theft in the New York area for the last ten years, but found, to his dismay, that there really was no identifiable tribe of known thieves, just a hodgepodge of greedy housepainters, small-time crooks who didn't know what they were stealing, even some distraught political activists with knives. Occasionally a crime syndicate would use stolen paintings as collateral in a drug deal, but a fair number of these people dumped the art wherever they could because well-known pieces couldn't be sold. At last he found Mrs. Pittman herself at her home near Amboise, predictably hysterical about the theft and eager to talk.

The Fragonard involved a rosy young aristocrat clad in crinolines on a swing, while a comely young man in blue pushed her forward. It all sounded charming to Inti, in a gooey sort of way, but the Spranger sounded positively horrendous. From her account, Venus and Mars were canoodling, the woman's breasts completely naked over a red swath of silk, while Cupid played nearby and even seemed to bless the two as they snuggled together, more difficult because Mars wore a suit of armor and would not have been very snuggable. These details the Pittman woman relayed, giggling all the while, seeming to revel in the subject matter. Oddly chirpy, almost flirtatious, Reggie, as she had instructed him to call her, had several theories about who had done the deed but didn't want to talk about them on the phone. "Send me an email," Inti suggested, "with photos if you have them," but she refused.

"Oh, I never do email, besides, they're not secure."

These absurd notions must have furthered the ease with which people stole from her, Inti thought, but then, on impulse he suggested that he might be doing some reporting in Europe soon and could possibly interview her in person. Loudly she encouraged this idea. "Publicity is the only way art gets returned, Mr. Weill. They can't sell any of these famous paintings on the open market."

Inti wasn't totally sure how famous the works were, and to his mind the nutty woman would probably have to give them away or fling them toward some innocent passerby on the Bois de Boulogne, but he was prepared to sell the hell out of this "go interview the wife" idea to his editor, even if he had to pay for the flights himself. Given the spin Inti put on this art theft story and the fact that Jack Pittman had recently been investigated by the SEC, his editor agreed to pay for three days only in France to extract some semblance of a story. "Maybe the husband stole them himself? I've heard worse."

Not that Inti had much understanding of his own intensity about the business. Nothing for him had clarity at this time in his life. It was cold in the city, empty and dead in a way he had never experienced. Why Jenna's betrayal, less than that really, her unaccountable role in such a mysterious drama, hurt him so, he wasn't sure, but on the flip side he had that itch, that ambitious curiosity regarding a great story, and the urge to know more prompted him to calculate the timeline over and over again, especially late at night while he listened to the screech of cabs navigating through the latest snowfall. He finally settled on the fact that basically he wanted to get out of town, number one, but also he had finally remembered something Jenna had said regarding Vincent Hull. "He loves France, reveres it, and says I will never really understand the painterly impulse until I go there myself."

"On fait de la chasse ici?" became Jenna's first inquiry of the young woman at the front desk. At least she knew that she had landed in a region of grapes and the hunt, the Champagne region of France.

"Mais oui, Mademoiselle," the delighted girl had answered, shocked that an American who could afford to stay in this hotel actually spoke some decent French. Alas, though, the young woman proceeded to describe the hunt in great detail, rolling forward with so much of the French language that Jenna lost the thread entirely and was left to mutter, "ooh," and "oui," and "magnifique," at comical intervals in her speech.

Jenna now resided in an exotic, ornate hotel that contained layers upon layers of French history. The newer building, completed in 1856, was surrounded in a semicircle by the ruins of a twelfth-century castle. Its arches bowed, sliced in half, some stones lying on the ground, the older castle displayed the authentic cast of an ancient world, so much so that visitors could feel the weight and the power of those who actually managed to have such structures built. In these first few months of her exile, Jenna took to wandering through the arches, especially in the late afternoon. January now and freezing cold, she couldn't do much but obsessively go over the sequence of events that had led her here, and the people; they haunted her thoughts. What did Jorge do now, still at NewsLink? He had worked there forever, impossible to think of him anywhere else. And where was Tasha, at a new job? Mrs. Hull, what of her and the girls? Of an age to read the newspapers and hear about their father, his children too must hate her, though not even knowing who she was.

Only a few months prior, holed up in her New York apartment, stuck in something like a *tableau vivant* of a fake event and before the powers-that-be disconnected her land line, she had had to stop herself from listening to her old voicemail messages, Inti yelling into the phone, "They're fantastic, the best photos. I'll let you know when they appear. Call me. Where the hell are you?" He mentioned her current notoriety not at all, and that in itself was quite mysterious.

Jorge had left her three messages, shock filling his voice, and question after question. "Can you see me somehow and talk?" "Why didn't you come to me for help?" Finally, plaintively, "There's still some of your stuff at the office. Don't you want it?" And then at last, "Listen, I completely understand. I told my mother Vincent Hull was going to get reincarnated as twin Asian sex slaves." At this she had to laugh, but she wasn't allowed to respond in any way, and she hated being hated, that much she knew and felt it almost as a physical pain in her chest.

Her anguish from that time could only be allayed by exercise and vigorous attempts to master the French language, two current obsessions that kept her mind full, engorged even. Under her newly stage-managed surroundings, this proved stranger, more alien than she expected, living at this extraordinary hotel outside the small market town of Fère-en-Tardenois. All meals took place in a gilt-edged fairy-tale dining room that felt like a perpetual holiday gathering with relatives she either didn't like or didn't know. Having to eat with people much older than herself made her shy, and especially the huge amounts of food, even for breakfast, had her aching for a small cup of yogurt and an apple. At one particularly fattening lunch, she heard the whir of helicopter propellers, her heart sinking for a moment at the thought of more Hull minions arriving with some terrible new demand. When she took herself to the lobby, with its gothic arches and massive blue urns standing watch over those who entered, she saw that the well-dressed foreigners, Germans as it turned out, couldn't possibly be the paparazzi, just rich people who had arrived for lunch by air.

One of the most confounding elements in her present life involved her new appearance. Every time she caught her image in one of the carved wooden mirrors, she gave a start. Bobbed dark hair, darkened eyebrows, conservative slacks, jackets, even suits sometimes for dinner, this was a woman she did not recognize—an older woman. And her name, now there had come a sticking point, the only time she had balked at the commands of the Hull attorney. He had presented her with a list: Barbara, Karen, Sarah, all of which she found too old-timey. In the end, she'd chosen Catherine, acceptably French, though of course she couldn't completely pass for that nationality, last name Myatt. Cate, or Catherine Myatt, she could relate to her, whoever she might actually be, and she could tell people her mother had loved France and had given her a French name. Vincent had loved it too, and his raptures on the subject had led her to flee to the only country he spoke well of.

Another result of her flight and the only consolation during these early months of her new life involved the high level of luxury she currently enjoyed: shimmering soft bedding, a quilt that mimicked an antique French tapestry, the enormous suite with a set of table and chairs that no doubt would have cost what she would have earned in a year as Hull's assistant, even a stone fireplace. Foreign, baroque design, full of puffs and embroidered stools and stuffed velvet pillows, so unlike anything she had ever had, but she loved their goofy unreality.

And then there was the larger weight of her money. Hitherto having never had any, she now possessed what she called "absolute piles of the green stuff." She didn't like to number for herself the actual dollar amount, as it frightened her even to think of it, and besides, someone might take it away as quickly as those murky powers had given it to her. At first all had been handled by Rudolph Hayes, including the sending of a large sum to a French bank to cover her residence here. He made it clear that she must familiarize herself personally with the financial advisors he supplied, as no information about her fortune could seep out into the larger world. They weren't even allowed to communicate by email, only phone, but she hadn't gone to see these ephemeral managers, only just managing to call them when she needed to replenish her account in the tiny local bank.

Even on sleeping pills though, she still couldn't sleep, often waking up at two or three in the morning, restless, overheated under the heavy comforter, tormented with the awful weight of Vincent Hull's dead body on top of her, so alive at one time in her arms, so loved. Had she loved him? Yes, she had, surely, though before meeting him, she had never known much about what sexual love really meant. What about Tasha? Had she loved Vince too? Once Jenna had admired her point of view, her very realistic assessment of things, whereas she herself lived in the land of what she hoped or what she fantasized. She had wondered at the sophistication, the personality able to fit into whatever world she encountered; in truth she had wanted to be like Tasha, but unanswered questions tormented her. Tasha and Mrs. Hull had seemed to be friends, even close friends, so why had she betrayed her? Jenna remembered all the cautionary tales she had told her regarding certain New York norms of behavior, warning her off Hull, it had seemed. So Tasha was preparing her for something? But she couldn't have known the man would die in such circumstances, could she? Had Sabine and Tasha collaborated and killed him? A grotesque thought, but somehow she felt caught up in real evil, the origins of which she did not understand.

In this pained mental state, Jenna found herself in the French countryside, where the rosy pink morning sun, the regularity, the neatness, the fixed square shapes of the land had her transfixed. If nothing else, this order comforted a most rattled visitor. She hadn't jumped off her old life, she'd been thrown out of it, and during this time she felt herself falling into a psychological nowhere, though at the very least, geographically, this nowhere had a landscape, which despite her sad state, she liked.

Jenna had promised to remain here for at least six months, unless someone got wind of her residence before that time. As the dead months of January and February wore on, it grew colder, freezing at night, and in the morning a sheen of white frost glazed every structure and all the surrounding hills, like a snow globe that never settled to the bottom. This was weather as awful as northern Ohio, made worse because she could find no one of interest to talk to and had nothing to do except relive the past, this at age twenty-four. The terms of her agreement resembled almost exactly the requirements of someone in the witness protection program. She could not get in touch with any of her friends, nor let them know where she was. She had to get serious about her personal transformation, buy contact lenses, and have her hair colored in a more professional way, all the while remaining silent on what she had done and her knowledge of the circumstances surrounding Vincent Hull's death.

Thus Cate Myatt, of great wealth, no family, no friends, no associates, resided alone at a hotel. She drove a rented Renault and didn't talk to many people, only the staff. There was some curiosity about her, but the Hull officials had sufficiently covered her tracks to prevent any real detection from the jaded French press. A discarded mistress, a daughter in hiding—it meant little to anyone in this part of the world. The only thing she really wanted to do was let both Jorge and Inti know. But what? That she wasn't Hull's mistress? Not quite, but she had had an affair, no, merely encounters. How sordid was that? Therein lay the central secret of her life, and she could think of no words to craft more lies, worse yet, to let them know the truth. She had gained a great deal, but at the same time seemed to have lost everything.

By chance one day the friendly, even concerned concierge pointed out to her that the surrounding tracts of land near the chateau actually contained a vast cemetery for American victims of World War I. "Very beautiful there, peaceful, as if for them there was no war." The small dark man lifted his eyebrows and smiled in a sad, resigned way.

Jenna took to driving out to the Oise-Aisne memorial and walking the lonely fields of white crosses. The wind swept over this land of the dead in broad, cold sighs. She moved slowly, reading each name on each cross, and as she made her way from one field after another, she developed a strong sense that she must repeat to herself the names of as many soldiers as she could. "In Sacred Sleep

They Rest," yes, such sacred sleep. There were 6,012 souls beneath the ground, and 597 of them nameless. "Here Rests in Honored Glory an American Soldier Known But to God." Attention must be paid, she the witness, and her actions had a soothing effect, as if she were worshipping at a kind of church.

Where was Vincent buried? It would have been a huge funeral, and must have taken place while she was hiding out in her transformed apartment. Deliberately she had avoided reading any newspaper whatsoever, afraid of the horrible pictures of herself and the hideous speculations. She also never responded to a single email. Not that she had any family, but some old school friends back in Ohio wondered and wrote, and even had questions in the subject line. "Was this really you?" "Hey, old friend, how are you holding up?" "I can't believe this. They must have the wrong girl."

Yes, the wrong girl, but still the actual one found underneath the dead body of someone she had cared for. Everyone else in her field of vision seemed to dislike him, even hate him. In reality, was it a silly crush, loaded up with meaning because she had been forced to lie beneath the man? Maybe. Why had she done what Tasha asked? She should have reacted in outrage, told her to get some older, more desperate employee to become rich, disappear, and lose whatever future had been her destiny to live out instead of becoming another human being altogether. Here the true fear lurked. She had evaded her own future. She didn't know anything about this mythical Miss Myatt, a young woman with no past and certainly no present, the future looming as a blank.

Exhausted with the cemetery, she changed her driving ritual. After an early morning walk around the crumbling castle ruins that surrounded her own luxurious abode, she mounted her Renault and vowed to follow whichever sign on the road she saw first, and on this frosty day it led her deep into the countryside of vineyards and wineries. Not too far distant resided Euro Disney, so today she caught sight of tourists and their children in buses and rental cars, like home really, or somewhat like. It breathed America, its openness, its fun. She envied the tourists and would have liked to take one of the rides, but of course couldn't join them.

Undeterred, she drove with more purpose, this time following the signs to Villeneuve-sur-Fère, where the doomed sculptor Camille Claudel had lived for a time, before her hateful mother and brother had her locked up in an insane asylum for thirty years, even after the authorities had told the family that she was most definitely not mad. Armed with her treasured Leica, the only Hull item she had actually stolen, she drove an hour to the small, square village perched atop a flat hill. The whole town seemed to consist of just this public square and perhaps ten houses surrounding it. Beyond that, fields swept out as far as one could see, glistening with a light sheen of frost.

After a trek around the square, she could find no notice at all of the famous artist except a small plaque on a nondescript house just like every other one in the town. Yet another one of these houses appeared to be a restaurant. Inside were plain wooden communal tables, no menus, only men recently come in from the fields eating the dish of the day, *blanquette de veau*. But it was so cold, and Jenna wanted to eat somewhere smaller than a castle, so she stayed and in her passable French ordered what everyone else was eating, trying to look nonchalant while every pair of eyes in the place stared at her. Had they read *The New York Times*? Were they addicted to page six of the *New York Post*? Impossible, ridiculous, she thought. Stolid, grim fingers heavy with work, why on earth would they know or care about a New York City drama?

The aggressive staring made her anxious to go. After all, with a population of 231 people, one more would excite major interest. She drove home quickly through the winding roads, nothing in sight except vast empty fields. She could feel the panic rising like a wave in her chest, and for a moment she gasped and had trouble breathing. Was it a heart attack? She clutched the wheel and gripped it until her hands shook. Where was the chateau? The signs were so small she had to lean out of the car to see them, but at last she spotted Fère-en-Tardenois, her village, and with three thousand people it seemed positively crowded. She had only to make her way through the tiny streets of this market town, and then she would know how to get home from here. Home, her hotel, part of a lost medieval world. No one had discovered her, no press people. There weren't even any American guests, only Germans and Italians, it seemed, well-heeled, talkative, completely engaged with each other as they sat under the glass chandeliers of the dining room near a roaring fire. Outside everything else had frozen solid.

She stopped her car and went into the local coffee bar where she often had an espresso. Steamy, smelling of cigarette smoke, it typified everything foreign about her new home but also its potential warmth, if only she could choose that, or choose some sort of life here. Maybe get a job? What a strange thought, and as she sat alone at her tiny table, looking out at the villagers mushing about shopping, she paused again to reflect on the oddity of what she had seen in the private office of Vincent Macklin Hull. Nothing about it made any sense, and yet all those authoritative New Yorkers had explained and explained. They counted on her, they had entrusted her with a stunning secret, and she held their future within her hands, sort of, but if she told the "true" story, what would they do? Had they done something to Vincent? "Something's wrong that isn't right," her granny whispered from the grave.

As she walked into the hotel out of the cold and heard her boot heels click and clack on the marble hotel floor, the perpetually worried concierge motioned her over to him. "I have a small package for you." He handed her a box with an elaborate French crest on the outside. Champagne, Veuve Clicquot Ponsardin, Maison Fondée en 1772, à Reims France.

"Thank you." She carried the heavy box up to her rooms, secretive, wondering who on earth would send her such a gift.

THREE

Two days later, in the early twilight, she set out for the Veuve Clicquot cellars with a firm purpose, to find out how this lovely bottle of bubbly might have made its way to her. Even if she learned nothing, drunkenness seemed pretty appealing, and Champagne had always made her tiddly after only one glass, but as she drove, she became more and more wary. Such investigation seemed too weighted with the unknown. Someone had found her or knew about her or wanted to tell her something, or maybe it was a handsome local, wooing with a bottle. If only. Jorge Garza would have loved its golden yellow label.

Thinking better of this quest, instead of toward Reims, she headed south toward Épernay, the landscape still unvarying, field after field covered in snow, not a house in sight, until at last she spotted a farmhouse with a dangling sign that read Galerie Legard. She pulled her car over to the side of the road and made her way to the front door. Inside was a French version of a curio shop, small paintings resting on even smaller wooden easels as a way to display them. The artwork, though, was lovely, and Jenna bent down to look at one particularly charming still life, just a bowl filled with lemons and a rose in a small brass vase next to it. It reminded her, for a moment, of all the paintings she had seen at Vincent Hull's house, with just that sort of immediacy and force.

"*Bonjour, Mademoiselle.*" An elderly man came out of a small, side office. Dressed in paint-spattered blue jeans and a Cleveland Indians sweatshirt, he wiped his hand on a piece of cloth. He was tall, with long gray hair tied back in a ponytail and bushy eyebrows, but handsome, even with his deeply tan, wrinkled face. "Are you looking for a painting?"

"I am, as a matter of fact." She could buy things, though she hadn't done any of that until now. "I like the one with the lemons. How much is it?" His dark eyes surveyed her closely, squinting. The man named a price in francs, and though not too good at computing back and forth into dollars, suddenly she didn't care how much it cost. She had to have it. "Yes, that will be fine." She handed him a wad of French money, acquiring the first thing all her own that she had bought with what she thought of as the Hull legacy.

The man smiled at her in a knowing, almost flirtatious manner and threaded through the bills, taking up a number of them. She imagined that the painting cost about two hundred dollars, but wasn't sure. "Are you an artist, by any chance?"

"No, no, far from it, but I do know a little bit about art."

"What does anyone know, young lady, a little bit? That's all. I have a studio in the back. Would you like to see it?" Hesitant a moment, because in some respects, though older, he was still a man, but finally Jenna followed him as they wound through shelves and shelves of cups and plates and platters. He had an enormous kiln, and she could see the work of his hands in vivid blue and green pots in playful shapes, and into each one he had traced the name, M. Legard. On the far side of the studio, oil paintings rested upright against more wooden shelves, and about the room stood several more easels that displayed works in progress. Jenna stood close to each one, trying to see what he was up to. "Did you do these?"

"Yes, but don't look. They're not at all ready."

"Don't worry. I just want to see how you work the colors."

"Are you sure you don't want to paint yourself?"

"Absolutely not, but I'm interested in the process. I have no vision."

"But you have an eye," he said, all the while pulling more canvases out of the racks. "Here, I have one that's not mine. I'm restoring it, a different kind of work altogether, like taking something back to what it once was. A bit of plastic surgery." He laughed. "Or chemistry." The painting was of a large field populated by scattered cows, a furious, threatening black sky above the tranquil scene below. Dwarf beech trees lined the upper right-hand corner, and they twisted peculiarly around themselves.

"I studied art history in college."

"So you know about all this."

"I couldn't find a job, nothing decent. I went to New York and became," but she stopped, remembering the words of her contract, "a caterer," she said, thinking that mixing up a few boxties might make this vaguely true.

"Then you know food. Please, come and eat a bit. I'm tired of eating alone." She searched his face for signs of lust behind the invitation, but saw none; besides he was way too old, and so she agreed. Like two country neighbors, they sat at a small table sharing wine, which the old man poured out of one of his ceramic pitchers, and cheese and bread. He told her of his art, his dead wife, and his two sons, who never came to visit. "They live in Paris and think I'm a hermit in a shack. The artistic life is not for them. Where are your parents?"

"Long dead, I'm afraid. I was raised by my grandmother, Margaret Grace McCann."

"An Irishwoman?"

"Through and through, though she never had anything good to say about the Irish."

"They never do, a self-hating race, I'm afraid, like the Americans. Not that you are, my dear." The old man and the young woman drank the evening away until at last he gave her two cups of strong French coffee to prepare her for the road. As they walked out to her car, Legard stopped and then leaned against the trunk, studying her carefully. "Why don't you come and watch me begin to restore the painting? I'll teach you about it, as you know something of art already. Not a good painting, I'm afraid, but the rich man who owns the chateau down the way, he likes it. Unfortunately the painting is cracked. Done by some Italian, and you know how they are."

"No, I don't."

"Cracked," he opened the car door for her. "I'm Matthieu, and please call me that."

"Matthieu," she said loudly, pleased at how much better her pronunciation had become. "*Je suis* Cate. When could I come?"

"Why not tomorrow?" And just like that it was arranged.

At last Jenna had a purpose, and so the next morning, after yet another paralyzing hour-long breakfast with the high flyers at the hotel, she arrived at Monsieur Legard's studio prepared simply to watch. He worked at cleaning the cow picture, in particular the beech trees, the stream, and several dogs leaping up in the background. Over the next three hours, she sat quietly as he removed dirt and grime from the outermost layer of the painting, the varnish layer, using small brushes dipped in several watery-looking substances. Her neck began to hurt, and she moved closer to follow his exact movements. He stood in front of her, but finally he let her stand right beside him.

This close to the painting, it took on an entirely different look, more precious, deeper, despite the mundane subject matter. After all, it was no longer a cow but a chipped slab of brown and white paint irregularly aging, like the record of some forgotten past.

"Look here. Someone has retouched the painting, from a long time ago, in oil and imitation resins."

She could see small marks and scratches but nothing very big. Such painstaking work, it made her eyes glaze over. However could he have the concentration? "I'm amazed that you can do this."

"The owner pays me big money, and that helps in a hard time. He loves it, merde, thinks it has historical value."

"When was it painted?"

"In the early twentieth century, but he pretends it's older."

Matthieu leaned away from the painting, sitting on a stool, and grasped onto his coffee cup. "It gives me nerves to work on it for so long. You know, you might help. I could pay you a little, and then do my own painting. It would be worth it to me."

"But I wouldn't know what to do."

"I'll teach you, you'll be here beside me." For one ridiculous moment Jenna thought this man was actually infatuated with her and just wanted her around, making up a silly reason, but no, this couldn't be. He was old, seventy-five at least. He must be quite sincere, but given the levels of duplicity she had seen before, she had lost faith in what she knew or thought she knew. Nevertheless, she agreed.

These frigid days found Jenna in the Legard studio, and under Matthiu's tutelage she had restored the losses in the paint and ground layers of *The Summer Storm*, filling them and texturing them to match the surrounding original paint layers. She felt like a painter herself, working with the tiny brushes to inpaint any of the remaining cracks or discolorations. Inching over the canvas focused her mind, made her forget her loneliness, and made her wish that she had looked much more carefully at the Hull works she inventoried. All the while, she and her maître had become fast friends, laughing and gossiping about the locals, none of whom, of course, she knew. Who was sleeping with his neighbor's wife, which one dodged taxes, who had shot a stag illegally small or out of season—it was grist for her mental wanderings and made her feel somewhat more at home. After a month the painting had been fully restored, its cows and dogs and trees glowing with brilliant color, and her new employer wanted her to go with him to the chateau of the owner to present the work in a formal setting. "I don't want to, Matthieu. You do it. He hired you, after all."

"But he'll love the beautiful assistant, and perhaps he has more such paintings, and we could continue to work."

Startled at the word "beautiful," she wanted to please the man who had uttered it and allowed herself to be persuaded, in part out of loneliness, in part out of curiosity. Her status in life had changed so dramatically that she hardly knew where she fit in the social world, the problem more acute because her bank balance seemed to belong to somebody else. "You're rich, a millionaire many times over, so act like it," she said to herself. But act like what? She didn't like what she'd seen of the rich acting rich. Guests at the hotel, for instance, were curt, clannish, overdressed, overly demanding, whatever the nationality. Only occasionally did she spot an act of kindness or courtesy to the staff, hence she went out of her way to behave so. Her best friends had become a bellboy and a maid.

Jenna insisted on driving the two of them, because,

considering all the wine Matthieu drank on any given day, she didn't imagine him too steady at the wheel. Over the vast countryside they rolled, the painting carefully tied in the trunk. "What's the owner like?" She suddenly worried that she would be encountering someone who resembled Vince, maybe even someone who knew him, since he had traveled to France all the time.

"He's a nice man, yes, with a big family and lots of very bad art. He gets his money from Champagne, and it flows and flows all over the world. Maybe it will flow toward you and me?" The old man patted her on the arm.

They wound up a cobblestone driveway and found themselves before an enormous, crenellated chateau made of gray limestone. Flanking the heavy wooden doors stood a row of structured shrubs, almost like bonsai plants but large, sporting rounded tops with skirt-like growths at the bottom. Matthieu guided the painting out of the trunk and carried it proudly, as they ascended the steps. "Oh dear," Jenna whispered. "Designer shrubs?"

"Yes, a magic castle," Matthieu whispered back.

Once inside, though, they found little magic and much domesticity. The count's children, all four of them, were running about in various states of excitement. A nanny or some such, followed a toddler, cooing and begging in French at his naked behind, trying to get the little one into some pants, while the boy rushed forward pushing a plastic toy with wheels in front of him. Two older boys tossed a Frisbee to a Weimaraner dog in an ornate formal dining room nearby, and a young girl, maybe eleven or twelve, danced her way through the front hall with a Walkman on her head, singing in English. She barely looked up when Matthieu and Jenna entered, toting the painting. The girl pointed them toward another room down a long hallway.

The count, a short, trim man in his forties with dark hair, wearing a sweatshirt and blue jeans, talked loudly into his cell phone, waving airily as they entered the room. Bookshelves lined the walls, with ladders running up to them, and here and there marble busts in the Roman or Greek mode glowered down at them from above. Another dog, a black-and-white spaniel, raised its head as they entered and wagged his way over to Jenna, while Matthieu unwrapped the painting and placed it on the floor next to the couch. The count gestured toward them again happily but kept on talking into his phone. Jenna noticed a number of other paintings that hung about the room, mostly involving hunting or horses or dogs.

"*Ma peinture*," the count cried, shoving his phone into his pocket. He rushed toward them with open arms. "*Magnifique*," he cried again and sought to embrace the two of them in his arms. Then he stood back, assessing their work and finally bent down to examine the details, even touching the surface several times.

"*Maintenant*, Monsieur le Comte, my assistant is American, so we should speak in English. Please, don't touch the painting yet."

"I know, Matthieu," the man said in unaccented English. "I mustn't but I love it so." The toddler, still without pants, rushed back into the room, and the count swept him up in his arms. "Hello, my boy, you should learn English too so you can be a man of the world or maybe an airline pilot." The count laughed at his joke and motioned them to sit. "We'll have Champagne and drink to my cows."

The word "Champagne" caught Jenna off guard, and she had the mad thought that the count himself had sent her the bottle, but then realized this was nuts since she hadn't even met him when she got the thing. Anyway, he had his own *cave* or label or something like that, his own business, and wouldn't have sent the Clicquot brand. Normally she would have refused a drink at what she now called "work," but today seemed like the first festive time she had had since Vincent Hull died, and she was so eager to have some friends, or at least acquaintances with whom to share a laugh. They were having such good fun, and the count made so many jokes about Americans that she felt suddenly at home, even though he certainly didn't think much of her countrymen. "I have another American coming here today," he seemed to remember and then consulted his watch. "A little journalist. He's writing about the French aristocracy, whatever that is, and wanted to visit a real chateau. Poor fellow must be desperate if he wants to talk to me. My neighbors are vastly more aristocratic."

At this Jenna took alarm and wondered how fast she could get Matthieu out of there. She had her instructions, and journalists perched atop the list of people she could not associate with. One of them might recognize her. "Matthieu, shall we go and leave the count to his interview?"

Their host, who was still bouncing his son on his knee, jumped up and surveyed his pictures. "No, no, I need more paintings fixed." He took down a small portrait of a prancing horse. "Unfortunately everything is falling apart here, it always is. It's a fight against breakdown and dirt. My house is dead, and the land is alive. Take this one and make it shine. Oh, but I may have some others." He proceeded to lead the two of them down a winding stone staircase into an enormous climate-controlled cellar, where hundreds of bottles of Champagne and wine rested neatly in exact order, one upon another. The cave smelled musty, like a grave, and Jenna became more and more anxious as she followed the others deeper into the darkness. At last they reached a storage room filled with paintings, rugs, lamps perched oddly here and there—the count's treasures, at least that's what he called them. He pulled at several canvases, surveying them, shaking his head until he finally hauled out a very large piece with a voluptuous redheaded woman and a man in a suit of armor clasping each other—according to the count, Aries and Aphrodite in adulterous love. To Jenna it looked pretty awful, but in her self-deprecating way, she immediately assumed her own ignorance, although she managed to say, "I'm an Aries." The two men stared at her. "You know, my astrological sign."

"Oh." Matthieu laughed, and the count patted him on the arm in some sort of agreement or understanding.

"Here is one you might fix, brighten it up. It would fit nicely in the grand salon."

Her maître stopped talking now, taking in the unwieldy canvas, possibly an important work to his eyes, and he nodded toward her as the two men carried it and its heavy frame upstairs. "We will see," Matthieu said as even the count pitched in to help them load it into the car. Just as they were trying to figure out how to close the hatchback without damaging the painting, another Renault swung into the driveway. Jenna assumed this was the journalist come for his interview, and she tried to hurry Matthieu into his side of the car. She turned around and saw the retreating figure of a young man with a backpack, wearing a puffy down jacket. Thank goodness they had missed him.

On the drive to his studio, Matthieu swore and muttered to himself, shaking his pipe out over the side of the open window, glowering at the landscape. "*Bâtard.*" He seemed very unhappy about something, enraged almost, but Jenna asked him nothing.

FOUR

Because of her sort-of job, Jenna had given up on the endless breakfast ritual at her hotel and had taken to having *café au lait* and a *pain au chocolat* at the tiny coffee bar in Fère-en-Tardenois. This was her major pleasure in life, along with surfing her way through France on a wave of butter, cheese, and wine. She found the early morning swishing and squirting sounds of the coffee machines comforting—the smell transported her, and since she had become a regular, the thirty or so odd men and women who frequented the place barely looked up now whenever she appeared. They were mostly shopkeepers, a few local farmers, a lawyer or two, and many of them liked to smoke, so the misty, pungent ambience fit her cloudy state of mind. As she nibbled on her pastry, contemplating the milky coffee in her cup, she noticed the back of a youngish man standing at the bar, looking almost nattily, if casually, dressed. That back looked familiar. Could she possibly know anyone here? She turned her chair slightly away toward the window, not wanting to show her face to anyone from the outside world. It was cold, really cold this morning, and the grass across from the road had frozen solid. It would probably be cold in Legard's studio, so she had worn a thick sweater under her coat, just in case.

As she began to pull on all her layers, a hand tapped her on the shoulder. She started. In this current life not that many people touched her at all. She turned her head, and there stood Inti Weill. She couldn't breathe and didn't know what to do, and after a moment, rose to leave, knocking against the table. Inti gently pushed her back down into her chair.

"Stop that!" Jenna cried out, and now those who watched were concerned and whispered. Rather than make a scene by racing out, Jenna faced him, motioning him to sit down.

Awkwardly he saluted her with his own cup of coffee and the collective onlookers seemed to relax, no drama after all, and they returned to their newspapers. "What the hell?" he finally managed to get out, apparently as astonished as she was. "I didn't recognize you at first, but no one else has that perfect skin."

"What the hell indeed? How did you find me?" She burned her tongue on a big gulp of coffee.

"I didn't find you. You found me by walking into this café." He rubbed his forehead with his napkin, flustered.

For a moment Jenna registered anew the wonderful looks of this man, his dark shining eyes, his Roman nose, and the soft, almost fleshy cheeks. He looked like an Arab or someone from the Middle East, with his black hair curling at his ears. He seemed to her larger physically than when she had encountered him in New York, slightly heavier but also muscled up, at least from what she could see of his body. "You mean you just happened to be wandering around the French countryside in the nasty month of March and chanced upon me?"

"After what you were up to in New York, it may appear that this great big world is all about you, but in fact I was interviewing a French count and trying to get a look at his paintings."

"That was you?"

"What was me?"

"The guy walking up the count's steps."

"I'm following a story, and I work for the *New York Times* now, just the regional section, but still." He felt proud but also a bit stupid and boastful in front of her.

"Oh my god, the *Times*. And what story would that be?"

"I can't tell you. It's an undercover sort of thing."

Jenna looked around the smoke-filled café, suddenly wondering who or what else was about to come upon her. She had no words for this man, certainly no explanation. At last she muttered, "It's hard for me to think about what happened in New York."

"I'll bet it is." Inti sounded sardonic and angry. Around them the men and women began to head off to work. "Want to tell me what you were doing at the count's house?"

"I'm learning how to be an art restorer."

"Out in Bumblefuck with that old man?" "That old man" came out too loudly.

"He's not an old man," but then she blushed at the other older man who had once occupied her life. "Anyway, now you just magically show up here."

"The whole world doesn't follow you around, you know. It's all forgotten, disappeared, your own private drama, or maybe I should say very, very public. They must have put a lid on it, somehow, one of the few families in the world who can actually do that. And what's with the hair? I would barely have recognized you."

"Just, I don't know, a bit of a change. I don't like to think about it."

"I'll bet you don't."

At this Jenna stood, grabbing her scarf and wrapping it around her neck. Outside, she ran to her car and drove way too fast over the hills and across the empty, winding road. The lawyer had discussed with her how to handle any potential meeting with someone who might recognize her and had counseled her the way one would an alcoholic: "Never get too tired or too lonely or too hungry. Then you'll be unable to resist the urge to talk." She hadn't talked. But how had she agreed to this fantastic subterfuge? She, who couldn't tell a lie to save herself. And this young man had been a prospective lover, maybe was even a lover still.

In fact, she still couldn't accept what she had actually done, and she could feel herself pick and pry at this wound until she bled out. Was it purely for money? She had never even been that interested in money. Her grandmother, a school cafeteria worker, had considered rich people exactly like poor people except they had a wider field for bad behavior, and whether rich or poor, they all came to the same end. Jenna had tried hard to block out the face of the heavy, very dead Vincent Hull on top of her, but now, thinking of her grandmother in her own beautiful deathly repose, the whole awful scene came back to her. Whatever his motives, though, she presumed Inti would just leave the area once his story was finished, but she checked carefully every time she went to Monsieur Legard's studio. She didn't want to be ambushed again.

No, the "Here I am out of the blue" journalist didn't turn up at the café again either, but to her horror he appeared at her own hotel three days later. She was eating yet another scrumptious breakfast in that intimidating dining room, when she saw Inti's face as he passed by the giant urn of flowers in the lobby. No time to flee. He sauntered up to the table, and the ever-present waiter simply pulled out a chair. "How did you get in here?"

"I just walked right in. Apparently if you can find the place, you must be a guest because nobody in reception even looked up. *Un café, s'il vous plaît,*" he said to the waiter.

Jenna broke off a piece of her chocolaty croissant, dipping it into the warm coffee. "I've gotten used to deliciousness every single morning." She watched his face carefully. His brown eyes, animated, curious, too curious, no doubt, surveyed her. "You know," she said, "you have some inner core of happiness, a quietness you hold onto. Not self-involved the way all those other manic writers were in New York."

"Thank you," he smiled and lit up like a youngster.

"Everything French is delicious, I'm convinced of it. I have to get out of here before I get too fat. So why are you visiting me today?"

"To find out why you're here."

"I live here."

"On what?" Inti tried not to strike a prosecutorial note with her, though he felt bitter that she'd been sleeping with the older man, and very very angry. He couldn't even count the number of lies she must have told him. "You live in this incredibly expensive hotel, out in the middle of nowhere. It doesn't compute. Oh wait, I guess it does. The mistress gets a pay-off. Am I close? And now you're in hiding. That explains the whole hair change and general new look, less Fairyland, more French."

"Fairyland was what I looked like then? What the hell? Anyway, 'a change is as good as a rest.' Just ask my granny, she'll tell you that, well, she would tell you that if she were alive." Jenna sighed. "I've taken up art restoration, and I study with Monsieur Legard. He feels I have an eye, as you said."

"Not exactly a world famous art restorer."

"How do you know?" She sipped her coffee.

Inti Weill shrugged his shoulders and swiveled his head around, surveying the grandiose room they inhabited. Only two other guests sat at the far corner. "I know things. It's a gift. But you're right, you do have an eye. I brought along more of your coyote shots." He reached for his backpack. "The whole story was, and in some ways still is, important. Coyotes are the secret watchers of all of us." He tried to hand her the newspaper clippings.

"I've seen them already." Jenna stood up. "I have to get to the studio."

"Don't leave me." Inti jumped up to follow her out into the lobby. "Please, I'm sorry. I'm a snooper. I can dial this giant brain down any time I want."

"Maybe you should just turn it off altogether."

"Have dinner with me tonight. There's a cool little restaurant in Fère-en-Tardenois. I've gotten to know the owners."

She turned to appraise him now and was startled at the sudden, visceral reaction she had to his smile, his person, his deep attractiveness. "Yes, let's do that."

Later that day, working on a sliver of canvas, she tried to rationalize why she'd agreed to the date. She had lived alone now at a hotel for almost five months, as if on perpetual vacation. The guests changed every three or four days, small families, big families, and the current residents included two silent Czechs who often sat stolidly lapping up Champagne, also a single elderly male who spoke Spanish but turned out to be from Argentina. He had been gracious to her. Most of the other guests ignored her existence. A quantity of Germans, several Austrians, one of whom suggested she move to Vienna, visited as well. She had become a fixture of the place, along with the employees. It was so odd that she thought of moving, but then there was only one small *pension* nearby, and it would have been horrible living as the lone long-term resident in such a tiny place.

Months had gone by, and here she stayed, a friend to

maids and bellmen, very friendly with the man at the front desk, who seemed to pity her. Whenever new guests showed up, he watched Jenna as she peered out of the immense windows to get a look, as if she were waiting for someone in particular. She was not, instead just making up stories in her head about who they were and why they had come to this particular hotel. Soon enough she would have to shrug off this paralysis and decide where and how to live. The first step would be to recognize herself as a lively, healthy young woman wanting everything young women need. She wasn't some old dowager with piles of dough. Yes, that's why she'd said yes to Inti, despite the danger.

FIVE

nti and Jenna were to meet at La Courte Échelle, a tiny restaurant up a narrow street in Fère-en-Tardenois, everything about it absurdly small, at least by New York standards, but the life therein was personal and known to all, not unlike where Jenna had grown up in northeast Ohio. On this frigid evening, she had trouble parking her Renault, so finally she just pulled it up on the sidewalk the way every other resident did when pressed. She had to steady herself as she got out, to pull down her skirt and straighten her sweater, which was now one of an astonishing number. When she actually had the energy to shop, there was no place to do so unless she travelled to Reims, and so with map in hand, careening about on the small roads, she bought the best because she could. Happily, the price no longer filtered through her brain like an accusation of her own worthlessness, as money meant nothing to her now, and there was nobody to stop her.

In the glittering light of white candles and the pungent scent of beef simmering and potatoes roasting, Inti waited for her, sipping a glass of red wine. He wore dark pants and a well-cut sport jacket and looked to her so much older than when she had known him in New York. This dangerous activity of hers had ratcheted up the naughty effect, and she felt a slight glow begin to warm her. He too seemed genuinely affected and wanted to please her that evening, but their secrets floated about like unwieldy phantoms. In simpler times Jenna had been a stranger to self-hatred, but now it plagued her, especially at night when, unable to fall asleep, all she could remember was that startled picture of herself on the front of the *New York Post*. Now she had changed her appearance, drastically she thought, but Inti had recognized her right away. She worried over this and drank more red wine than she should. For a long time neither of them spoke.

At last Inti tipped his glass to her. "Thank you again for the photographs. They were very good. Because of the story I got a job at *The New York Times*."

Uh-oh, her nemesis, the nation's paper of record, with her ridiculous face on page four, messy hair, the look of idiot-girl at the scene of a crime. "I don't like them."

"At the moment I'm not sure I like them either. They've got me running all over the state, 'Regional section,' that's me. But the coyote stuff, it made a sensation. Did you know the Navajos called them God's dog?"

"Alas, no." She decided to take a breath.

"They exist everywhere in the United States, but they're like ghosts. If you see one, you'll know that maybe two thousand are there, even in New York City."

"Like me. I'm a ghost, but God had nothing to do with it."

Inti stared down into his wine. "I gave you a credit for the photos. Just J. McCann for the *Rye Register*." Jenna made a face and looked around as if someone from the press, other than the man she sat across from, could be stalking her right now. "Don't worry, no one reads the photo credits."

"I've never even noticed them."

"What are your plans?" he said. "You look so different."

"I'm giving myself the opportunity to figure this all out."

"Obviously you're not starving to death."

Here was a subject she knew would come up, but she could reveal very little. "It wasn't what you thought."

"Really?"

"I can't talk about it."

"Or you won't?"

"Either way."

"Frankly, Hull was famous for his general rutting in the bins of *NewsLink*. One girl, in advertising I think, a real bombshell, curvy, not too bright, he paid her a year's salary after the affair was over. Told her to go save the rain forest or something. Everybody knew about it." But at once Inti flushed at his own meanness, wanting to take it all back, especially when he saw Jenna tear up. "I'm sorry, I don't know what—"

"You think he picked me out of a bin?" She stood up and grabbed her coat off the back of her chair. "Now I know why I'm in France."

Outside, stars shown through the heavy, lowering clouds, and ice tipped the trees, bending them toward the ground. Though they'd had a fight of sorts, Inti followed her out of the restaurant, and the two kept walking together, wandering nowhere at all, just around, until at last he put his arm through hers. "Really, please forgive me. I felt dumped, an unusual occurrence," he said, looking embarrassed. "It was good for me, in a way."

They passed by a small pharmacy with gold lettering on the front window, J. Fournier. "That man gave me a bottle of his special, homemade perfume." She had dabbed a bit on her wrists this evening and held one up for him to smell.

"Very nice." Just as she told Inti about this gift he bent down and reached for her, kissing her softly on her beautiful mouth. Afterwards, with no urgency but also no hesitation, they walked to his little hotel, the lopsided stucco pension. The night clerk didn't even look up as the two Americans climbed the stairs.

His room was small but cozy, and a fire had been lit in the grate. "This is actually a suite, as you can see, a hot plate, a table big enough for two mice, big enough if those mice have a close relationship. And Champagne. We have all we'll ever need." Jenna laughed but stopped the minute she saw the bottle he pulled from the fridge. "Veuve Clicquot, the best, I think. I've been making a study of Champagne around here. It's purely personal, of course, but I bring to it a certain journalistic fervor."

Immediately she was on her guard. Was this some sort of signal? Had he sent her the bottle of that very same Champagne that stood on the desk in her own, much more sumptuous suite? "How do you know about this Champagne?"

"Everyone knows about it. It's not a secret."

"Were you really at the count's just to do an article on the French aristocracy? Why would anyone care about him in the greater New York region?"

Inti popped the cork expertly, with little more than a snap of his hand. "Can you keep a secret?"

She stared at him a moment, and then they both broke into laughter. "I'm trying to, but I'm not really cut out for secrecy."

"I was there to check out his art. There was a robbery of two important paintings in Tarrytown, and it involved the collection of a big deal hedge fund guy, so I coaxed, well, exaggerated, or maybe just lied to my editor, even paid my own airfare, just to get here. After all, keeping our captains of industry happy can be a full-time job, even for a guy as low as me on the totem pole." Inti blushed at the implications of his speech. "Damn, every time I say something, it comes out wrong. Maybe I just wanted to get out of town, since everything reminded me of you and what had happened. I couldn't figure it all out."

"What would the count have to do with it?"

"Certain associations. I have my sources, you know." He leaned in and put his warm hand on hers. "If somehow they made their way here, it's a story."

"And are they here?"

"I don't want to commit myself right away, not being an expert, and I only saw one of them, but it certainly looked like the picture in a photo the owner sent me."

Jenna didn't want to hear about which paintings, because if she did, yet another worry would barrel into her world, another disreputable person crossing her path, about which she could do nothing anyway. Legard and their work together were too much a part of her "getting well" plan, and more info might destroy what she wanted to walk toward, not back away from. Worse still, this theft business sounded a lot like the convoluted machinations of overprivileged New Yorkers. She hadn't understood those folks, still didn't, as she was pretty sure she had been duped in a fashion she couldn't face right now. But she did want to know about the Veuve Clicquot sender. "Someone sent me a bottle of this stuff, out of the blue, to the hotel. Very mysterious. It wasn't you, was it?"

"Of course not. I didn't even know you were here."

"It freaked me out, and now the bottle just looks at me accusingly. 'Drink me, drink me, if you dare,' it seems to say. I thought I'd go to the caves and see if I could find a clue."

"The widow Clicquot was one of the first female owners of a Champagne winery, developed new methods supposedly, all kinds of good stuff. She was important in the industry."

"The count makes wine, or Champagne, at least he

says he does. He sure does have a lot of the stuff piled up."

"Too weird. Too nineteenth-century, if you know what I mean."

"I don't know. I'm suspicious of everybody, and I see plots everywhere." As she sat there now, she began to reflect on the word "widow." Could the mysterious sender be Sabine Hull, the only widow she knew?

They sat quietly, sipping on the golden Champagne, watching the fire, as the whole room steadily warmed. Inti cranked open one of the windows, pulling his sweater over his head, flinging it down on the couch. Jenna stood to take off her own heavy scarf and then, like falling into a warm embrace of maleness and heat, she moved into his arms. She had had no love for so long and had nothing now that protected her at all from his warmth and passion. He was an ardent lover, and he touched every part of her as if meeting a woman's body for the first time. She adored his youthful kindliness and vigor, and it encouraged in her a wildness that had only come out before in her riotous lovemaking with Vincent Hull. This time it came out with a rush.

She wanted to take the lead and did so by keeping control of herself despite every touch of his hand in any soft spot having an almost instant orgasmic effect. Instead, she pushed him onto his back and began to slide slowly down his chest with her breasts brushing down across his skin softly, as he stared up at her, sometimes eyes closed, sometimes wide open, smiling, laughing even. When she reached his sex and his thighs, he wanted to move into her, but she held him back, taking up the condom in its little package by the bed and ripping a corner with her mouth. "I saw this on TV."

"Watching porn again, are we?" Inti managed to get out.

"Just one of those late night things. Two girls who sell sex toys and stuff. This time they used a banana." She pulled the thin condom out of the package and slid it into her mouth, bending down over him, and then she rolled it with her tongue onto his penis. By this time he could stand it no longer and turned her over, moving into her, and at the end they made enough noise to wake everyone in the hotel. Fortunately, there were no other guests.

"The staff will have to suck it up," Inti said, sweating and laughing but suddenly, without waiting at all, he wanted more. "So to speak."

"No, no, I have to rest a moment."

"That's my line, isn't it?" They lay alongside each other, his arms encircling her from behind, as she fell into a happy, grateful sleep. Not much time must have passed, though, because she awoke with an anxious start. Birds had begun to sing in the darkness, and she looked down at Inti's comely face. He opened his eyes and pulled her toward him, and this time she let him touch every secret, wet inch of her body, passive, until at the last, when he entered her and brought her as close to ecstasy as possible, she held on, held out, and squeezed him hard deep within her groin muscles just as he had his climax. He cried out, and only then did she succumb to her own pleasure.

When the sun shone through the shutters, Jenna arose before he did and watched as he slept. She felt wonderful, alive after all, not like a dead person crushed under the body of someone else, also dead. Creeping into the minuscule bathroom, she splashed water on her face, still flushed and overheated, dressing quickly, for no good reason she could discern, not having any plan. It was a Sunday, after all, but for a moment she sat down in a chair and watched as Inti turned away from her, the covers falling slightly off his back to reveal a couple of moles and a remarkably straight spine. She could see out of the window a few families walking to Mass, always the grandmas in the lead. Just as her own had been, she remembered. Maybe she needed to find a French granny, someone to advise her on her future. Jenna leaned forward to press on Inti's shoulder, and he rolled over immediately, drawing her toward him, but she pulled back. "I have to go."

"To where? It's Sunday."

"Back home," she said, laughing a bit.

"Right. The hotel. You're running away from me. And after last night."

"No, no, I'm just not used to so much . . . I don't know . . . contact. We'll see each other soon."

"I'm supposed to leave in three days."

She struggled now. "Then we'll make a plan." She got her jacket and purse off the chair.

"Okay, be a woman of mystery. But I can find things out." He rolled over on his stomach and put a pillow on top of his head.

"Idle threats." But she wasn't so sure, and she worried about Inti's parting shot. It would be a big story, and he needed one of those. It wasn't just a slim little one-line scandal. It was the kind of story with edges, depths, about race and sex and betrayal, with greatness in it somehow. Trying to switch off these sickening thoughts, she drove the Renault through what were by now familiar fields, at last coming to her "home." Hurrying inside, she sat on her bed trying to think of someone to call. Could she confide in someone? Oh how she wished she could speak to Jorge, just to go through all that had happened, just to laugh and cry and explain it all somehow. Did Tasha regret the plot she had concocted with the lawyers? How had she gotten them to agree to it, and why would they have? The African-American angle still didn't work for Jenna, and she pictured her now in a Park Avenue apartment, elegant and rich, bought off just as she had been.

What time was it in New York? Probably not too early to call. She dialed Rudoph Hayes and waited until finally a woman answered, sounding quizzical as to her identity, but then the lawyer picked up. "Jenna, or should I say Cate? I'm surprised to hear from you on a Sunday." He sounded sarcastic and not happy.

"I just, I've got no one to talk to, so I had to speak with someone who actually knows what happened."

"You want to vent or something like that?"

"Not quite," but she caught the edge in his voice.

"So, you're unhappy in some way?"

"I live in a hotel, I have no friends, only an old man who restores paintings." She hesitated, but said finally, "I met a young man, he's great, a journalist," not admitting that she'd known him before.

"What?"

"He wrote about coyotes up in Rye."

"Could you have picked anyone worse?"

"I couldn't pick anyone else at all. Everybody in this town is over seventy."

"You can move. You can do anything you want. The world's your oyster." She grimaced at the cliché.

"I don't want to move. I don't know where to go, since I've never been anywhere except, now, France. I'm like a prisoner."

"Stop right there. You're richer than anyone you know, richer than most people have ever dreamed of. You're lovely and bright, and if I may say so, spoiled. You need to comprehend reality and get a grip. People are starving. They've lost their parents and at ten years of age have to work digging through garbage. Look around carefully at that world and then call me up again, and we'll discuss your problems."

"Oh, well. . . ." She broke down into loud sobs.

"Get a book called *Urn Burial* by Sir Thomas Browne, the finest prose writer in the English language. He talks about being dead. Think about that. Vincent died, you know, and he left behind a wife and children and many who actually loved him, me for one."

"I'm sorry, really."

"You were just a blank girl with no particular identity who worked for Vince and did . . . I don't know what else. Now you have millions of dollars and can do anything you want. My heart aches for you."

That Sunday slowed way down after this conversation. She had to get away somewhere, somehow, but she didn't have any ideas, and the length of her sojourn here was part of her contract. For a time, she circled the old chateau wall, thinking furiously about what she should do next. Buy a house? She could. Buy a farm and raise chickens? She could. Buy a large chateau like this one, she could do that too, but it would be ridiculous. She would totter around like a character in a romantic novel, lighting candles, drinking brandy, taking young lovers. "My god," she cried out loud, "you're only twenty-five!"

SIX

On Monday morning she drove to Monsieur Legard's studio, though she wasn't sure whether to be relieved that Inti hadn't gotten in touch with her yet or worried. At least she had a place to go, and her maître had a big new job awaiting her. The count's Bartholomeus Spranger, for that was the painter of the awful Aries–Aphrodite work, stood propped up on an easel. When she had a chance to look at it more closely, she caught a resemblance between herself and Aphrodite, curly blond-red hair, widely spaced eyes, breasts and shoulders exposed, embracing the god with thick hairy thighs, his sex hidden behind a shield. Did she spot a freckle? Hardly, but she gazed up at the portrait and thought, goddess of love indeed. What lay beneath the lawyer's hatred of her surely involved an image exactly like this one of an old man and a young girl frolicking, naked and unrepentant. Legard seemed to note the resemblance as well and stole a look at her several times to gauge her reaction, but she refused to meet his eyes. Without talking of any of this, they shared a coffee in silence and then got to work.

In the afternoon, her day was ruined. Legard had a copy of the *International Herald Tribune* on his desk, and despite previous vows, she paged through it. Until now she had avoided newspapers altogether, fearing any mention of Vincent Hull's name, perhaps even more frightened that the story the-powers-that-be had concocted would unravel or be revealed as impossible or worse. The story she looked at today involved a memorial service held over six months later, awfully long, it seemed to her, after his death. Even given his status and worth in the world, the story didn't occupy the first page, but appeared deep in the paper, and it revealed tidbits from the will about disposition of the Hull property. His wife and assorted foundations got mostly everything, but there was a bequest for Tasha, forgiving her loan on a large co-op apartment, and its address. Sure enough, Park Avenue. In and of itself, the gift was not too extraordinary, since he had forgiven other loans as well, but several shadow trusts had aroused press suspicions, and Jenna suspected hers to be the largest.

Old questions were rehashed, especially the fact that when the EMTs found Jenna awaiting them, the dead man had been splayed out on the floor in a most exposed condition. She had given the police a timeline, but the *Tribune* reporter questioned this because his research suggested the death had happened much earlier, though he could not confirm this with hospital records. No autopsy had been done or been requested, and the Medical Examiner signed off on the cause of death as a "myocardial infarction." Away and gone and quick. The family could have arranged anything they wanted, so maybe they were just so embarrassed as to what had happened that he had to disappear immediately. It made her sad, all this, since the Irish worshipped their dead, and they hung out with them until the last moment before they went underground. That's what Jenna would have done for him, if she could have.

As she paged through *Urn Burial*—the lawyer had thoughtfully overnighted it to her—she wondered how long it would take the reporters to find out that she too had received a bequest. She didn't know the steps Hull's moneymen had taken, since it had all happened so fast, but she assumed they hid her name carefully, perhaps under some corporate heading? Had they backdated the will and stuck something in there, or perhaps her money had not come directly from him but from some other corporate entity, of which there were many, so she wouldn't appear in the will at all? Then again, wouldn't they have wanted her name in there and not Tasha's, since wasn't her job to deflect attention away from Tasha?

Drinking yet another cup of Legard's strong coffee, Jenna read from the lawyer's favorite book: "But who knows the fate of his bones, or how often he is to be buried? Who hath the oracle of his ashes, or whither they are to be scattered?" Alas, the book actually did involve dead bodies. Before seeing this, she had thought the title a metaphor or something, not a book about real human beings no longer with us. Where was Vincent Hull buried? Perhaps in an urn like this old Renaissance person? Someday, somehow she would find out.

"What are you doing, Cate?" He pronounced it "cat" and shook his index finger at her, frowning.

"Reading a book about the ashes of dead people and where they end up." She put the slim volume down near a can of linseed oil.

"But why, you poor thing? Get busy and clean this little spot here, where these flowers are, right down here at the bottom." Of course he never would let her do any inpainting of this supposed masterpiece, certainly not at the center.

She closed her mind off with such detail work, dabbing at the sweeping calendulas at the bottom right of the canvas with a cotton ball dipped in ammonia, trying not to consider all the dark thoughts crowding her mind. More than once she stood back to survey the entire erotic landscape of the piece. Much trouble with it, areas blackened, paint cracking around what once must have been a pink nipple, now turned brown. Aphrodite, languid in the embrace of an older but muscled-up man, showing off her body and her desires to the world. The worst, the blackest of her own thoughts: she would have to leave here altogether. She hadn't figured out who had sent the bottle of Champagne, but somebody knew where she lived for sure. Was that what the bottle meant? "I know about you, and now you have to figure out who I am?" Or did it have some other meaning that she couldn't fathom. Both Legard and Inti denied sending it, but maybe one of them was lying. She had never really believed Inti had appeared by chance in her current hiding place, but she couldn't figure out how he had worked it out. She also didn't know how completely the Hull minions had embroidered her story, her college history, her made up past life. If any other journalist picked up on these falsehoods, that person might be on her trail.

In the evening, she invited Inti to come have a drink with her, to question him, and she sat drinking a glass of Champagne in the lobby of the hotel, to get the ball rolling. Staring down at a nice pair of dove gray high heels she had picked up in Reims, she wiggled her feet, the best part of her really, and she often thought Vincent had seduced her poolside that extraordinary night because he thought them beautiful. If only people would look down when they first met her, things might go better. Soon enough the very man she awaited appeared at the golden door of the hotel and sauntered over to her, yes, a confident young man, especially about love. "Can you order me some of that Champagne?"

"Of course," she said, and she spoke to the waiter in her now excellent French.

They sat looking at each other, shyly, given their intimacy. When the drink arrived, Inti saluted her with his glass. "You, you. What will I do with you?"

"I'm not yours to do anything with, except maybe lovemaking. There I am obviously your slave."

"Clearly, and I'm going to encourage that, but we may have to postpone our ramblings for the moment, sadly."

"Why?"

"Work. I have to get back to New York. Listen, I need to warn you. The stolen paintings are a Fragonard and—"

"We're not working on anything like that," she interrupted. "I would recognize one right away, at least I hope I would."

"Okay, well, the other one is a Bartholomeus Spranger, a big god and goddess thing. Looks hideous, but valuable, seventeenth-century." He stuck out a color photo of the piece. Jenna coughed and then drank a big gulp of Champagne. The exact same painting she had just worked on, the one that sat at this very moment in the Legard studio. "What? Do you know it?"

"I've seen reproductions of it. Sexy looking," she choked out. "Ach, it went down the wrong pipe." No revelations about stolen paintings would issue from her lips, she was sure of that.

"I've got to get to Paris for my flight, tonight actually." He reached out his hand and pulled her up. "Let's go outside."

"Why do you have to go so soon?"

"Stories breaking all the time."

"You're always so mysterious. I don't like mystery. Even trying to find out who sent me that bottle of Champagne is driving me crazy."

"But it's you who are at the heart of a mystery."

"Real heroes often act in secret." Inti looked at her, startled, but said nothing. "Ignore me. I don't know why I said that. You're not pursuing all this, are you, journalistically?"

"No. Your particular enigma I have decided to let go." The moon shone over the jagged walls of the ancient castle, like a romantic painting in and of itself.

"It's so beautiful here," she whispered, and he enclosed her in his arms, but she hid her face from him, and her eyes filled with tears. Like many people in their early twenties who make a bad mistake, she knew she would have to lie for the rest of her life.

"Can you stay in touch with me somehow? You don't even have a cell phone."

"I'm not allowed to have one."

"You're in something like the Witness Protection Program, is that it?"

"You can't use any of this, you mustn't."

"I know, I know." She didn't necessarily believe him, but she kissed him deeply and firmly on the lips and let him go away with the wave of her hand into the glistening, frozen night.

At the end of the next day Jenna and Matthieu shared yet another glass of wine, and she broached the subject of the Spranger painting. "Do you know anything about how the count got it? It's extraordinary in its own awful sort of way."

"It's very strange. It's got a lot of layers, and maybe there's even something else beneath, another image altogether. Why should we care? He pays me big." Nevertheless, he looked away when he said this and fingered the rim of his glass nervously. "I don't like to think of people as criminals. Do you know something?"

"No, no, not really, but the world is full of fakes. They say possibly forty percent of all museum collections are fake."

"That can't be. Only Americans say things like that, but then who really cares? Is a beautiful fake worth less than the beautiful real thing? Originality is overrated. And so what if he stole it? *The gift must always move,* no? So said the famous Lewis Hyde in a book I just read."

Jenna didn't understand quite what he meant but didn't want to press him, as she was grateful and loyal to him, reminding her of the too forgiving people she knew in Ohio, closing off painful discussions, wanting everything ugly to go away. Or maybe he was just being French, surrendering the world of morality to those who actually cared about it. After he calmed down, she delicately broached the subject of fellow art restorers. "The best are in Italy," he said, "though they eat that terrible food. How many ways can you cook a tomato? I do know someone in Ventimiglia. He is quite the gentleman, but the town has its drawbacks. Tourists, people from the Riviera go there to shop, and there's a train back to Nice every day. My competition, but why do you ask?"

"I might have to leave here."

"Don't leave me. You're the nicest American I've ever met. You must not." He stood up suddenly, moved and confused.

"I must, Matthieu. There are things you don't know about me—"

"I do know."

"What do you know?" She felt sick, worse though, ashamed.

"I see you're hiding yourself. It's obvious. And why do you live at the hotel?"

"I might buy a house."

"How can you? You're a child. But you don't have to tell me anything. I'm content with the hidden thing. It's in every one of the paintings I work with. You can tell it in the layers: who first painted it, who then reworked it, when, with what skill, with what understanding, even perhaps what year. It's a record of each hand that has touched it, so you see, I'm familiar with what is behind. The history of the world submerged under resin."

"Would the man you know take me on, do you think?"

"No, I won't have it." But when she left the studio that night he hugged her hard. "Think more about this, but don't think too fast."

That night, as she sipped her wine at dinner, she sat ramrod straight in her chair. Behold another stupefying evening watching three wealthy Londoners laugh loudly and drink quantities of Scotch, Vincent's favorite drink. They swirled before her in a gaudy tableau, and she marveled at her newfound ability to deal with loss, as if she had participated in training for some massive loss contest like a runner for a reverse marathon. She had lost her only family in Ohio, and then her work in New York, her friends there, her boss and her lover, also a new lover. And now the only other person with any real interest in her at all, Matthieu—she would have to lose him, too. She had developed a new muscle, that was how she thought of it, the "I'm losing you" muscle, which, despite all her wishes, had grown taut and strong.

Two weeks later, after another long and painful conversation, Matthieu finally agreed to help her get a place in the studio of the Ventimiglia restorer. Rather than buy a house for herself in the Champagne region, she bought Matthieu a new car and the six hectares adjacent to his studio. All this she managed in Fère-en-Tardenois, to the amazement of the local real estate man. He couldn't understand a secret transaction of this magnitude; he couldn't understand such a rich young lady, nor why she would want to help a seventy-five-year-old artist and art restorer of limited future, but she had her way. He recommended an agent in Ventimiglia who could help her find somewhere to live there. "Though it's a shopping place, for the French to save tax. At least it's on the water."

No matter to Jenna. She wanted out of the hotel, and the date was fast approaching when she could leave. By the looks on their faces, the staff couldn't believe it when days later they finally got to say good-bye to someone they called "their perpetual guest." They seemed tremendously eager to help her with her belongings, perhaps because the spectacle of someone like her moldering in what they, more than any others, experienced as an unbelievable old heap of a building, made no sense to them. Her bill had reached magnificent sums, the highest anyone had run up, though she had paid it off by the month. Nevertheless, the tip she left them, collectively at the front desk, was unprecedented, the largest in their history. At her departure in her car piled high with her bags, maids, bellmen, the gardener even, all lined up and waved her off. She was to them "*la petite Americaine sans patrie.*"

SEVEN

Jenna and her Renault drove down toward Troyes, thence through the Loire Valley until it intersected with the Rhone River, past Lyon, and then east over toward Antibes on the French Riviera. It was a very long drive, and very beautiful, the great yellow fields of rapeseed flowers, starting out small and growing bigger and bigger as she moved south, and at this time of year there weren't even many tour buses. But there were post offices. She had written a list of suspects regarding the Champagne bottle, and right at the top stood Jorge, who studied and collected wine and always boasted he could find anyone, anywhere, so why not herself? Had he wanted to tell her something specific?

At the beginning of her journey, not far from Tours, she mailed a label she had collected from G. H. Mumm, a golden label with a red sash across the front, to the Hull offices, addressed to Jorge. Nothing else, but what she meant was Sabine, a "mum" all right, also silent. If it was he who had indicated the widow to her, she would indicate the same back, as if she understood him. Any more direct communication would reveal too much, since the lawyer knew her movements and probably, at the very least, would have told Jorge her first location.

Not many miles from Monaco, she crossed the Italian border into Ventimiglia, winding down the tiny roads along the cliffs. Like many villages in the region, the town rose up from the port stepwise, and Matthieu's

friend had arranged for her to rent a penthouse apartment looking out over the newer part of town. Though
thirty minutes from France, and the train came bearing
shoppers every single day, especially for the market on
Friday, Jenna felt herself very much in Italy. Each
evening she could smell tomatoes and garlic roasting in a
pan from the apartments nearby, and she would sit out on
the balcony, glass of red wine in hand, breathing in all
things Italian, especially now in late April, when the
nights grew softer and warmer.

For days after she first arrived in her new country,
the freedom from constraint, the frequent laughter of her
neighbors, the wonderful obsession with eating, eating,
eating enchanted her, until she was living solely on gelato
and pasta and could no longer close the buttons on her
skirt. This had to stop, and she had to work, which she
soon began to do in the atelier of Maestro Pietro Sarani.
Her way had been made easy with Matthieu's letter of
introduction, and she found herself, without much fan-
fare, learning to restore Italian Renaissance paintings that
had, over time, turned brown.

Signor Sarani was a handsome, gray-haired man in
his fifties, with a high forehead and a distinctive, aquiline
nose who, even in the jumble of the studio, wore silk
shirts and soft woolen slacks, smoking incessantly and
tipping the ashes anywhere he liked with his long, thin
fingers. Abrupt, businesslike, he had first been titillated
by Jenna's beauty, but very shortly thereafter considered her an asset and set her to work with two of his
other assistants, brothers Gianni and Paolo, who laughed
constantly and poked each other like schoolboys but
were careful over the canvases. The atmosphere was entirely unlike that of Monsieur Legard's studio, church-
like in its cool silence and intensity. Here life figured as

a joke, a joke and a mess, and the boys—*i ragazzi*—teased Sarani forever about his clothes, his whole elegant manner, aping it both in front of him and behind his back. They existed for fun and often tried to rope Jenna into their doings. She resisted their antics, feeling some days as if she were back in high school, and besides, she wanted to impress Sarani.

So far she had heard nothing more from Jorge, because she now figured him as absolutely the first Champagne sender, but maybe he would choose some auspicious time to send more info or clues? About Inti she had done nothing and heard nothing. She returned to her old trick of avoiding newspapers, but at last she got up the courage to thumb through the *Herald Tribune* while sipping espresso at an outdoor café in the old part of town. Nothing at all about the Hulls, thank goodness, nothing to suggest there was any mystery about the will. This was the year 2000, and people concerned themselves with the millennium, the thought that every digital link might unexpectedly come crashing down. Cell phones certainly existed, and those who owned one felt heavily dependent on it, but the lines of international gossip had not yet reached celestial proportions.

Unfortunately, the one person who could do her real harm did at last get in touch with her again. The hotel forwarded to her a typewritten note from Inti. Back now in New York, he informed her that he was working on an exposé of kickbacks in the giving out of airport concessions. She disliked the investigative sound but even more so his cold tone. With no real explanation for his hasty exit from the French countryside, he also did not say when his piece on the art-loving or art-stealing count would appear, if ever. At the very bottom he had scrawled, "You had me, and you still have me." All in all, the note made her even more anxious than before, but she could do nothing really, unless she wanted to communicate with him, and she could think of no good way to do that.

For the next year Jenna worked in the Sarani atelier without incident, learning everything she could about the restoration of Italian Renaissance oil painting. Matthieu wrote to her that the so-called Spranger had been restored and duly returned to the count, and that as a result he labored away on a host of the man's new paintings, delighted with the flow of work and money. By late August of 2001, everyone had gone off on holiday except crazed tourists. Jenna spent these hot days in the temperature-controlled studio where she meticulously restored a still life of dubious value, but it was very bright and appealing, a modern piece that one of Sarani's best clients insisted needed to be "refreshed," the apples perhaps "*molto più rossas.*"

One evening, exhausted from her work, as she sat sipping a glass of red wine on her balcony, her phone rang. On the line was Matthieu, sputtering, shouting, "You cannot believe it, oh, I cannot. How could this have happened?"

"What, Matthieu? What has happened?"

"There is a newspaper, a friend told me, an article by a young man, Inti something, what kind of name is that? I never heard of such a thing. He writes that there was an art theft in New York, and it all happened with the possible 'collusion' of a certain French art restorer in Fère-en-Tardenois. Who is that—me and nobody else, but he doesn't say my name, according to my friend. Or you maybe, no, how could that be?" Jenna's heart stopped, and her mind went blank. "Cate?"

"I don't know anything about this. When did the article appear?"

"My friend said a few days ago. I've been trying to find a copy, but it seems impossible. What can we do?"

"I do actually know that person, Inti Weill."

Matthieu interrupted, shouting, "What, you?"

"I don't know him well, but we met at the little restaurant—" Her voice floated into empty air. He had hung up on her. That night she slept not at all, frantic to get hold of the article, but where, an international news-stand maybe? In a frenzy, her mind went back to the literal, but the digital was the answer. She got on her computer and found the article itself from the *Times*, and it read pretty much as Matthieu had said. Still, it was buried in the metro section, a very short piece on the continuing investigation of an art theft in Tarrytown, a work by Fragonard and one by Bartholomeus Spranger, both owned by Mrs. Regina Pittman, though the investigation had been subsumed into the recent divorce filing of Mr. Pittman. Neither Jenna nor Legard were mentioned by name. Did that make the count a thief or just the buyer of a stolen work of art?

She called Matthieu back. "What? I don't want to talk to you."

"Please, Matthieu. Listen to me. If we did work on this particular Bartholomeus Spranger, the count has something to do with the theft. How much do you really know about him?"

"He has a big house and many paintings, coming from where I don't know. He seems a rich man without much taste. Will we go to prison? *Dieu me protège.*"

"We're not going to prison, Matthieu," but Jenna felt terrified of what this might mean in terms of public exposure. She had to get in touch with Inti somehow and warn him off or beg him or bribe him, and contacting him would be easy enough to do on the *New York Times* Web site, but dangerously public as well. She should wait a bit to see if he wrote another story, since there was nothing they could do now about whatever he was up to. Perhaps he had no more information or was waiting to expose the count? All speculation amid emptiness, and Jenna needed to stand back a bit from the dimensions of this potential disaster. God forbid she herself should be named in succeeding stories. That would send the lawyers down upon her head, even given her pseudonym. Could they take away the money? The contract said so, but that would pose difficulties for them as well, unfortunate ones that might lead to their public exposure.

While she watched and waited, the rattling general mess of the Sarani atelier comforted her, and Jenna now worked alone on a piece of sculpture that had sat outside in its owner's garden for way too long. The twisted limbs and the dancing feet of the Three Graces, Beauty, Mirth, and Abundance, were covered in solidified green mold, and she had to sand every piece of tiny drapery and each minuscule corner to get it clean. This was a bad job, a big job, and amid her panic over Matthieu and the Spranger, she had the gloomy thought that possibly Sarani had demoted her.

On the upside, when she worked so painstakingly like this, with three sets of toothbrushes in descending order of size, she lost herself in the focus on the small, on the minuscule, its out-of-the-way-ness seemingly a parallel to her own removal from all familiar life. She knew what others did not, but this knowledge did not help her because there appeared to be no outward-facing life attached to it. All flew inward and roosted beneath her weary mind. "Something's wrong that's not right," Margaret Grace McCann would say, and she began to think more and more that her substitution under the body of

Vincent Hull was no accident, but how or why it all went down remained a mystery.

During the three weeks from the time Matthieu discovered the newspaper article, energy fields in the world began to shift and rearrange themselves. Security agents at a small Maine airport pulled aside one suspicious passenger, but he managed to get through. Two other passengers boarded in Washington, and within hours a hail of flame, ash, rubble, paper, and human body parts rained down upon the city of New York and a field in rural Pennsylvania, while Jenna sat before her television in a state of breathlessness and tears. She watched over and over again as the planes crashed into the Twin Towers at the World Trade Center, and stared unbelieving at the tsunami-like plumes of the buildings as they rolled through the streets and over people fleeing. Nothing terrified her so much as seeing human beings jump from that immense height to certain death. Her own exile had lopped her off from much sense of place, but she realized now she had wandered around rootlessly, as if in a postcard. In spite of everything, she did have a home, a place she had left behind and could lament for, that awesome, chaotic home, New York City.

Were her friends still alive? Gramercy Park was not all that far from the southern tip of the island. What of Jorge, he who had wanted her to take that wine tasting class with him at Windows on the World restaurant? She longed to get in touch with them all somehow, but she could hardly envision what she would say or how explain her new home and way of life. Inti loomed at the center of this tragedy, for he must be reporting on it, God willing if he lived. At this point, her own little sphere might be spared an investigation because nothing else mattered now, since the world, and her world too had come to a stop.

But of course it did not truly stop. It stopped for several days, during which time Italy fell into mournful hiatus. At last Sarani called them back to the atelier, and in a more somber mode, work continued. Whenever she had the chance, Jenna combed the newspaper for any and all New York news, not sure whether self-interest was a suitable motive. She saw nothing else about any supposed art theft, but instead read many pieces by Inti about the terror and chaos in New York after the planes hit. At least he hadn't been hurt. Could she go back, would she ever? She thought of the words of her granny's favorite psalm, "Better dwell in the midst of alarms than reign in this horrible place." A tale of two alternatives, this she could understand even if both seemed bad and impossible.

After a mournfully quiet month, with nothing but work and worry, Jenna resolved to visit Matthieu. She went by train, with a box of his favorite candies, Calissons d'Aix, little sticky sweet cookie-like triangles covered in icing, and a bottle of single malt Scotch, The Balvenie, one of Vincent Hull's favorites, absurdly expensive in France due to tariffs. The old man didn't want to let her in, just peered out at her from his door. "Please, Matthieu. I come bearing gifts," she said in her still excellent French. During this past year her Italian had become passable, but the French language remained embedded in her heart.

"Go away, you traitor." He closed the door, but she was already out of the car, marching toward him waving the Scotch. He peered out again, recognizing the bottle and simply could not refuse her. The kind of drunk that ensued, Jenna had never experienced before in her life. Even though Matthieu covered the table in dishes of olives, cheese, and thick country bread, mainly they drank. It was all Scotch for hours afterwards. What had tasted like medicine at first began to warm and excite her until she swam in good cheer and a kind of preternatural sense of power, as if drugged.

"He's a thief, he must be," she leaned in to Matthieu proclaiming over the count.

"International criminal or moron, who can say? Whenever I ask him about one of those paintings, he says he's not sure where it comes from. I still have some in the studio. Yet more cows."

Jenna fell over laughing, thinking about the long days she had spent perfecting the brown on those animals, so tiny in the background. "But he could be anyone. Why is he a count, or maybe we should investigate him?"

"How?"

"I might hire someone."

"You could hire me."

"Don't be ridiculous."

"But I must thank you again and again for the wonderful gift you gave me, all that land. You must be very, very rich. I know you are, I know you are. Don't tell me how much."

"Don't worry, I won't."

"Don't. Have a piece of cheese, no, no *un calisson*."

"Maybe one more Scotch."

"Oh yes." As night fell the two of them ceased to speak. They drank water now and watched the land around them, Matthieu's land, in the darkness. She slept on the couch, the fluffy comforter over her head and snuggling into it.

Jenna did not hire anyone to investigate the count. She resolved to do something that she had never managed before, to forget. Inti and everyone else in New York were preoccupied with what had happened and had no doubt passed quickly over an article on some small-time art theft. A rich hedge fund divorcée's problems with two paintings would slide off into nowhere. Of her own involvement with Vincent Hull, probably no one cared anymore except a small cadre of people, and no more Champagne showed up in the mail.

EIGHT

Over the next two years she became a confirmed, if highly critical, Italian, mired in the present and in the material. Each morning she had espresso for breakfast at the café, along with a hard roll and quantities of butter. Sarani did not allow the usual Italian long lunch, so they had French baguettes with ham and cheese and a carafe of red wine. The biggest meal was dinner, pasta to start, a steak or piece of veal, and then perhaps a little gelato, only enough to satisfy her craving. She developed a small circle of friends—one writer, another, a young woman who worked in her mother's tailoring establishment, the owner of a T-shirt shop, and a man with a guided tour business of the Roman ruins in the area. They met every Thursday night for dinner, and the two who had spouses refused to include them, since they all liked to drink and swap scandalous stories. Jenna adopted a jogging course through the hills and over onto the beach, so her weight never became quite the problem she expected. In fact, she grew much leaner, and she became a student of Italian style. She dressed with significantly more flair, always wearing silver bangles on her arm, and even while price was no longer an object, she stuck to dark skirts, slim pants, fitted tops that showed off her breasts and shoulders.

Finally Jenna's hair began to make sense to her, and she no longer stared unbelieving into the mirror. She liked this young woman who looked back at her; she had a different personality altogether. Her life resembled a masquerade party at which she was the only guest. Other people thought it all real, while she could feel the thrill of being hidden. In some respects, anything she wanted to do was fine, since she was no longer her real self. Perhaps the best, most promising aspect of her life was that she learned to laugh, a lot. Watching Italian women day after day, she saw that they had a quality of joy that came from within. It was aggressive, relentless charm, and she decided to imitate them. They smiled all the time and laughed at the silliest things. It seemed like a system to live by, to pretend to be some way, and then she would become that way. To a certain extent, she did.

Inevitably romance entered her life, first in the form of a young professor of mathematics in Turin who came often to visit his aging parents. He spoke beautiful English because he had taught for some years at UCLA, quite the brilliant young man, and she enjoyed him very much, enjoyed the unfettered sex too, but he was occasionally unfaithful, and she did not like that. He talked endlessly about *Mama*, which bored her, then infuriated her. She could see the fat grandmas always presiding over their broods of grandchildren, especially at the beach. Older women would sit in a round heap of clothes, parceling out bread and sweets to the humming little bodies plopping toward them, until at last corralling them for an even bigger lunch. When did the eating stop? The grown sons would hover there, and she grew to detest the infantilizing process going on all around her.

If there was one thing she became expert on, it was the juvenile Italian male, led first and foremost by the boys at the atelier, who schemed endlessly over their pranks. One day they strung a tarp across the door to the studio, and because they knew Sarani walked always with his head straight toward the ceiling as if thinking higher thoughts, never really looking where he was going. He ran straight into the thing and almost fell down. No angel himself, Sarani lied to his wife and his mistress and was always trolling for women on the side, to whom he lied as well. None of this ever fazed him and when caught out in one of these lies, he began to lie some more, often in front of Jenna. Then he would wink at her in complicity and light up another cigarette.

Jenna's more important affair began with a lawyer in town, Stefano, who also had a *Mama*, but he kept her in check somehow. In his late forties, he was really too old for her, at least that's how she thought of him, but he had the fatal Italian charm, seemed faithful, and told her every piece of gossip worth knowing in the town. At some point marriage became an issue, but Jenna couldn't even contemplate such a move. Though she spoke good Italian and lived an entirely Italian life, still in her penthouse apartment in the hills looking down at the Mediterranean, she hungered for all things American, not the least of which was a hamburger. Her one extravagant habit became many a weekend jaunt to Venice to eat at Harry's Bar, specifically to consume their hamburgers and drink their martinis. She loved that meal, the perfect juicy burger with cheese and lettuce and tomato and the straight up icy cold vodka. Weird how it satisfied her, as if a bit of her life in New York existed right here in her adopted country. She took Stefano with her often on these jaunts, and he seemed amazingly content to be kept in such style at the Gritti Palace, continuous meals at Harry's. Another manifestation of *Mama*, she knew, and one that would no doubt worsen the longer they stayed together.

The four years she'd been absent from her native

country had passed by quickly. Though her life in Italy had a routine, a smoothness, without many worries, only small ones, still, the larger ones loomed. She very much perceived herself as a person in hiding. Even though she visited Matthieu once every few months, and he continued to do work for the count, nothing further was said regarding art theft, no investigators from either France or the US appeared, undoubtedly consumed with bigger international worries. In the dark as to Inti's doings, Jenna was nevertheless grateful that more serious issues must now occupy him.

In the later days of December, just before Christmas of 2003, Jenna and Sarani sat before a late nineteenth-century oil painting by a minor painter, Giametto, but the beauty of the piece enthralled them both. A young woman sat at a small table, her head bent down as if in sorrow. On the table rested a teacup and a bowl of flowers, red and yellow. The girl's hand brushed her cheek, and the other clutched at an astonishing blue robe, deep, dark blue with tiny flecks of golden paint. Therein lay the problem, the texture of the robe. Small bumps, like grains of sand, popped up all over the blue paint, a texture not evident in any other part of the work and obviously not intentional.

"I just saw a paper on this. It's the lead soaps, a reaction of the paint to fatty acids in the oil binder," Sarani said.

"Not altogether unattractive though." Jenna and her "maestro" talked often about the chemistry of oil painting, and by now she had mastered a number of aspects of the subject, but this new intersection between art and science posed a problem for both of them.

"Shall we try to change what's happening? There are many things that happen to a work over time, and the cracks and bruises and movement of the paint, they constitute the life of the piece. What we call 'inherent vice.'" He smiled over at her. "A facelift is nice, but should we do it?"

"I need one of those."

"You're young, you're beautiful," and at this he placed his hand lightly on her back and rubbed it slowly in small circles. Out of the cool darkness of the studio, Sarani's wife advanced upon them. "Oh, Sylvia," he started and jumped up. "*Ciao, Bella, mi amore.*" He rushed to kiss her, but the tall, elegant, black-haired woman had already frowned at her husband and glared at Jenna.

Jenna stood up, feeling helpless and ridiculous in a situation made, of course, much worse since the man beside her engaged in chronic philandering, how much known to the wife she had no idea. But she tried to smile several times at the irate older woman, getting nothing but a cold stare in return. Sarani gathered up his coat and moved as if to guide his wife away, but Jenna stepped in front of him. She took the angry woman by the arm and led her onto the patio outside. "Please, Signora Sarani."

"What do you want?" The woman looked down at her watch and then shook her wrist at her. "I am late."

"Please, what you saw, there was nothing to it. We were only looking at the painting. I'm just a student here, and he was trying to make me feel better about my work. I need you to know this. There is nothing else going on." Jenna spoke in excellent Italian.

The still flustered older woman softened, and a smile broke across her face. "Oh, thank you, my dear. I worry, you know, I worry."

"Yes, we all worry." Signora Sarani bent down and kissed her first on the left, then on the right cheek, and this was what the Maestro saw as he walked outside to find them. He wondered if his assistant, his best student so far, had actually told his wife something of his doings, but when he saw the smiles all around, he thought no, neither one would betray him, not ever. It was the first article of faith in his own private canon without which all restoration would stop, including the personal.

NINE

At the end of 2003 change came to Jenna's small, self-contained world. She received three Champagne labels, but no more actual bottles. The labels arrived at the doorstep of her Ventimiglia penthouse, wrapped in a purple box, a gold lace ribbon tied around the outside, no shipping stamps, as if dropped off by a mystery messenger. Each label rested one on top of the other, surrounded by a cascade of purple tissue. The first, another Veuve Clicquot exactly like the one Jenna had saved, the second from G. H. Mumm, Reims, just like the label she herself had sent to Jorge, the third read Champagne, Taittinger, Nocturne Sec, identified as in Reims yet again, this one with a purple background and gold letters that matched the packaging. Jenna sat on the floor, placing the labels in a row to puzzle them out.

Okay, so whoever sent these, and this time it certainly had to be Jorge, already knew she had once lived near Reims but had moved south to this specific address. What was he trying to tell her? "The widow was mum," a very bad pun but just like him, and she herself had meant something like that when she'd sent him the same clue. But now perhaps it referred to herself. "Mum" Jenna certainly was and would remain so for the duration. She was one of those "if it's written down" people. Anything in writing was sacred and true, right down to the instructions on the side of her vacuum cleaner, and she had signed an astonishingly thorough agreement with the lawyer, listing every possible contingency. Taittinger, a sec nocturne, dry dreamy nighttime something? Sex accompanied by slow music? No idea about any of this, though this last label suggested florid, mysterious sexuality.

A dry night would be a bad one, in her view, sexually speaking, but she couldn't picture Jorge ever alluding to something so personal. He had always been a wink-wink, nudge-nudge kind of guy, even in the face of Vincent Hull's depredations. How to get in touch with her old time buddy became the immediate problem. She could just call him, but this absolutely did violate her contract. Could she speak to him without there being any trail or record? She now possessed a cell phone, sleek, just the right size for her pocket.

Not knowing what else to do, she opened a bottle of local white wine, straight from a nearby vineyard, very raw and fresh, and wandered out to her balcony to contemplate the meaning of the labels. But her mind wandered. A young mother hauled her basket full of vegetables up the steep steps, while her son skipped beside her, sometimes tugging at her skirt. Having grown up alone in the house of an old woman, without any brothers and sisters, Jenna had no experience of children running around and did not know whether she wanted any. Still, as she watched the little family below, she felt that at least she could think of wanting them.

Jenna fingered her new little phone. What a shock it would be to call him. The time in New York, six hours behind her, so she'd have to pick the moment carefully. Who had taken over for Vincent Hull? What would it be like to work near a room where that extraordinary man had actually expired? Ghostly, macabre, his soul must fill every corner of one very tall building. In the end, Jenna did nothing, too depressed at her options and wanting to be absolutely one thousand percent sure that what she did would accomplish the goal. But what was that, to find out who sent the Champagne labels and what they meant? A trifling mystery and one she probably could live with. After all, she lived at the very heart of a number of mysteries, not the least of which was herself.

Just after midnight two weeks later, after a long, hilarious New Year's dinner celebrating the advent of 2004 with her small group of Ventimiglia friends, Jenna arrived back at her doorstep to find a Federal Express envelope. She threw down her shawl and sat in a chair, holding onto it, looking out through the window onto the Gulf of Genoa. Blue and white yachts bobbled on the water, and their rigging tinkled all the way up to her perch. It was a cold night, and she wasn't warmly enough dressed, but still she sat without opening the envelope. At last she went into her small kitchen and pulled out a bottle of the local red wine. She poured herself a glass and went back to deal with whatever this was; she feared to open it, and since she had no more family members left alive, assumed that it had something to do with Hull.

Of course his New York lawyers knew where she lived, but they never liked any sort of paper trail, so they only phoned, but rarely. She tore open the tape and a heavy white envelope fell out. It resembled a wedding invitation and in bold black handwriting summoned her to New York. "Cate Myatt, please report to the New York Children's Hospital on February 15th of this year to meet with the head art curator for the conservation and restoration of Marc Bélange's *Diver*, 4 p.m. sharp." *Diver*, the name didn't mean anything to her, though it did sound sexy, at the very least. But then she thought back to her inventory and the large painting in Sag Harbor with just a small signature, Bélange, yes, that was indeed the name. The girl standing in water, holding her wet hair behind her head, the very picture of what she and Hull had done together, in the dark pool, in the warm night, and then more, later above him, beneath him, cold, gone.

So she was wanted to restore this painting that belonged to Vincent Hull, at a hospital for children? "They," whoever they truly were, needed her back in New York for some reason, and she suspected not really to fix it. The painting was not at all suitable for children, so why would it be there? Was this note a threat to take back the money, to kill her? To what?

But didn't they have bigger problems now? Surely the New York of 2004 would be utterly changed, since every person in that town who had experienced the terrorist attack would never recover. Those who had jumped; they rose up in her mind yet again. She could almost feel herself falling into the air just as they had. Of the sculpture *Tumbling Woman* by Eric Fischl, rejected by the authorities because of protests at its intensity, she was deeply aware. The Italians had sympathized with the American plight and had demonstrated in the streets in solidarity. But now, the horrors of the Iraq War ongoing, America had become like a vengeful, murderous friend off on a dangerous tear. From her own standpoint, nobody cared any more how Vincent Hull died; no one, perhaps, except Jorge, Tasha, and his family.

Later that night she rummaged through the chest of drawers in her bedroom, where underneath a gaudy blue-and-red scarf, she found the box holding the Champagne labels. Fingering the beautiful, archaic looking collection, little works of art on their own, she decided that once back in New York, no matter what her instructions or the dangers to her fortune, somehow she would meet up with the two important living men in her past, Jorge and Inti. Remembering that Manhattan was, in essence, a small town in which every street corner or bar or restaurant held the promise of a chance meeting, still she would take charge to make absolutely sure these meetings happened.

"When will you come back?" the two boys at Sarani's cried in Italian. "We cannot live without you."

"Somehow I think you're going to make it," she laughed. Twenty-seven and yet complete children, as she herself had been. At twenty-nine she felt old enough to be their mother.

PART FOUR

Winter, 2004

Tasha Clark, our esteemed leader and favorite kvetcher, has presided over us now for four years. We wish her good luck in the New Year and thank her for every kind note (and every nasty one) she has sent out on that distinctive stationery of hers. Here's to four more years.

—Newsletter of the Chicago Foundation for the Betterment of the Lives and Health of Children, January 12, 2004

Thank you all for coming to Jorge Garza's retirement party at Le Bernardin. Asked what he will miss most around here, he said, "Letters to the Editor." About Vincent Hull Jorge remarked, "He was a great man trying to be a good man, even an ordinary one. This was not possible."

—Retirement party for Jorge Garza, group email, *NewsLink*, February 10, 2004

ONE

nside the dark, warm leather of the Lincoln Town Car, rolling through the dreary landscape of Queens, Jenna felt, in her woozy, jet-lagged way, that this looked a lot like the poorer districts of Ventimiglia, but without the red ochre and the brightly colored towels hanging off balconies. Instead front porch doors hung open, even in the cold. She needed a plan for this momentous visit, but couldn't think about it and spent the ride into town compulsively rooting around in her purse to check for her cell phone, her lipstick, then the keys to her Italian apartment, the card naming the woman she was to meet at the hospital, all as if to avoid meeting the eye of the city. She had developed this nervous habit when she lived here, fingering crucial items about her in case she landed on the street or had to escape the place altogether, taking her worldly possessions with her, New York seemed that threatening. Who knew where her body might end up?

Who indeed? She tried to read the lawyer's instructions again, but the movements of the car and the noise level of the big city outside made it difficult. She had read the letter several times in Italy, but now she reconfirmed that she had exactly twenty days here, no contact with anyone associated with *NewsLink*, no contact with the press, no activity that would call her identity into question with any living person, maintaining "Cate Myatt" as her only name. Upon arrival, she was to go immediately to her hotel, the next day to the Children's

Hospital on the Upper East Side, get her assignment, and set to work.

Exhausted, startled, like a fugitive who might be recognized any minute, Jenna hugged her knees while the livery car crawled through the clogged streets toward The Lowell Hotel at East 63rd Street. It was six hours earlier here, cocktail time, and she considered for a moment jumping out and just walking to some watering hole, like the old days when she abandoned cabs that went too slowly. But now she had her suitcase, and a cold, clear rain pounded the car's metal roof. Yes, the worst time to get a cab, as she remembered from former days. Those days had not at all included The Lowell, an elegant, discreet venue, and as she waited to register, she noted a baggage trolley piled high with monogrammed brown suede luggage. A rock star, she was informed, had arrived.

Inside her suite, replete with blue silk and white lace pillows, she plopped straight down onto the bed, this after dismissing Robert, her personal valet for her sojourn. The bedclothes were heavy, covered in rich damask, comfy and deeply soothing. It was like sleeping in a stylish bank vault, as she snuggled beneath the pile and promptly fell asleep.

An hour later she awoke to shouts drifting up from 63rd Street. Harsh Bronx-accented tones blasted their way even through her closed window, and she rose to peer out. A cab driver and a truck driver stood beside their vehicles, screaming at each other. "Move the fuckin' truck, move it now."

"I can't move forward or backwards, you asshole. Can't you see that?"

"I can't see nothin' up ahead of you because your fuckin' truck is in my fuckin' way." The two men dodged back and forth toward each other, gesturing, pointing fingers wildly, even while turning to avoid random vehicles trying to get around them, also honking.

Jenna perched on the banquette at the window, entranced by the drama. Everyone was so loud here; she herself had gotten loud, almost without realizing it. Once while trying to cross at the light on Lexington Avenue and 87th, she had spotted a big truck turning toward her. Instead of jumping out of the way, she had planted her feet and screamed at the driver, "What the hell do you think you're doing, asshole?" People walking near her were startled. She had startled herself, and thinking of it now, she felt real shame at how distorted her personality had become while living here.

It was definitely time for her to eat, better yet to drink and forget all these regrets. She got up out of bed, changed her clothes, and then walked quickly south to the King Cole bar at the St. Regis hotel. The bartender noticed the delicious-looking woman in the black jersey dress, and so did several others. She warmed to the attention. She wasn't dead yet, she reminded herself as she took a seat at the famous bar, and male lust could still change her mood. She requested a dry martini and watched as the bartender artfully handled the thin metal rod in the snifter. "I like your technique. No shaking or stirring."

"That's for amateurs. You have to twirl." He handed her the frosty glass and stood back again to smile at her.

At this time of night, soft conversations circulated through the bar, steamy and subdued, and many bar-goers appeared as exhausted as she. She had that fuzzy, off-kilter buzz from jet travel and sipped her martini slowly, resolving not to go over and over in her mind the painful past. No one approached her, though a range of appealing men looked, they watched, but unlike Europeans in a bar, they did not enjoy easy camaraderie with women. An approach would signal intention, and in a certain sense this was a relief. Italian men had worn out their welcome with her, their boyish randiness ever present—"*Si, Madonna, come stai, Madonna?*" The winks, the nods, the too close flick of the hand so inappropriately used to signal interest, as if her availability were obvious and up-for-grabs. Where at first she found it encouraging, thrilling even, given what she had suffered in her home country, she now found it absurd, a way for men to expend their charms while wasting her time.

Not for nothing had these five years passed, and Jenna was now richer than before because she rarely spent much money, also more courageous because she had expertise in something, the restoration of fabulously valuable paintings. Whatever was going on with the survivors of the Hull family mess, somewhere over the cold, dark sea she had recently traversed, she resolved to find out what had really happened to Mr. Vincent Hull, and why she had been dragged into it. Her addled twenty-four-year-old self had just agreed to everything the powers-that-be said, but now in this more mature life of hers, she had prepared for the visit with an email address for Jorge, the *New York Times* contact for Inti, two home addresses, which of course she already had, for Sabine Hull, and the Chicago address of a children's foundation Tasha apparently worked for. Jenna folded up her little Moleskine notebook and sighed, staring at the Old King Cole mural. It too had an antic leer in almost every face, and she felt a little antic herself. First off, she would get in touch with Jorge. A note through his personal email might work. Next, she would probably have to go to Chicago to talk to Tasha. Then Sabine Hull, whom she might encounter at the hospital. Finally, and as a big, fat gift to herself, she would arrange to meet up with Inti, he of the wonderful body and the strength to use it—coyote man indeed.

On a clean page of her little blue notebook she scribbled questions that needed answers. So Tasha was having an affair with Vincent while she was friendly with Mrs. Hull? Not that that was so evil, but it was pretty evil, even by New York standards. Jenna's own affair she preferred right now to find accidental, because it was. Just a swimming incident, followed by a shower, and a bed, not much more than that. There was, of course, the night of the Plaza debacle, with Vince playing chef, and for one moment she teared up. He was wonderful in his way, so worldly, so entitled, and yet gentle and sympathetic when he wanted to be. Despite herself, she envied a man who could walk upon the earth as if he owned it. Of course, he did own a chunk of it, but still. He had given megalomania a good name.

Jorge must have sent her the wine labels, so he knew where Jenna currently lived and presumably wanted to tell her something. When she did see him, of course, she would have to tell him that she had been sleeping with Vincent Hull, though he probably knew that already. Still, she would have to come clean in order to keep faith with him. No innocent in the midst of the carnage, but innocent in her heart, she thought, staring down into the olives at the bottom of the glass. As for Inti, she wanted to ambush him somewhere, somehow, so unlike her to do such a thing, and he would appreciate the irony. She knew his haunts, and she could always just hang around the door of *The New York Times* building. Were they watching her, evil lawyers every one? Could she manage all this on the sly? Whatever else happened, she'd gotten used to being rich, she liked it, and she didn't plan on giving up a cent. Not one cent.

The hospital soared up between a dark red armory and a low flat row of expensive clothing shops on Madison and 89th Street. Jenna stopped at the front door, seeing through the glass a packed waiting room, suddenly uneasy at the thought of moaning children. She wasn't good with this sort of thing. Happily, before she could even approach the front desk, a determined-looking woman in a brown suit strode toward her. "Ms. Myatt, I'm Holly Cavanaugh, the curator of our collection. I say collection—it's a small one, but special, meant to cheer and educate our young patients." She clapped her hands together and smiled.

"Art for the sick," is what Jenna thought, but she stopped herself. It sounded so cold.

This woman, of that curious indeterminate New York age, thirty to sixty, coiffed and heavily made up, took her by the arm. She didn't know anything about the person in front of her except that the patrons of the collection had insisted on her, "Cate Myatt," and her qualifications seemed sound. While she guided Jenna through white doors, along a glassed-in hallway with a thick blue arrow pointing the way forward, she chattered on. "We take art seriously here and always have. Just keep going this way, yes that's it, oops, where is my file?"

Instead of blank white walls and yellowing vinyl tile on the floor, the place was full of brightly colored murals, goofy faces from cartoons clustered together near certain departments, and the nurses wore green and yellow scrubs with happy faces on them. No hospital smell, and, momentarily heartened, Jenna wondered where all the really sick children were. After a few more twists and turns, during which they passed a child on a gurney and then a young boy making his way slowly down the hall, hooked up to an IV, Jenna encountered a door with a gold plaque on the wall beside it that read Hull Library and Art Collection. There it was, in print right before her. They, that amorphous, infinitely mysterious "they" had demanded that she return. She shuddered and turned as if to back away.

"Anything wrong?" The curator pushed on the heavy door before them.

Jenna gathered herself up and shook her head. No matter what the lawyers had told her five years ago while explaining the original contract—"You are explicitly forbidden from entering the United States for the next twenty-five years and then only with permission"—here she stood. Inside this little library, someone with distinctive taste had created a special world, a cozy one, with deep velvet banquettes for reading and mahogany shelves up to the ceiling. Perched on a round table was a sign, "Books of the Day," before a pile of leather-bound volumes. A teenaged girl with a bandaged right arm lounged on a banquette and, with some difficulty, thumbed through a heavy picture book.

The curator turned toward the wall behind them, hung with four symmetrically arranged paintings, collectively worth maybe thirty million dollars or more. Jenna stepped forward to take a look, one original Andy Warhol Campbell's soup can, a magnificent orange-and-red Mark Rothko, a Jim Dine heart painting in throbbing black, magenta, and green, and finally an exquisite old Dutch work by a painter whose name she didn't recognize—a still life with a wine jug, two apples and a pomegranate. Despite all her cataloguing of the Hull collection, she had never seen any of these pictures. "These all look beautiful. I don't see a problem."

"No, I've put the one in need inside here, because it looked so awful."

The Cavanaugh woman shoved her forward into what was basically a closet, dim and cool, where Jenna found herself looking at that one picture, during her long exile, that she had come to love more than any other in Vincent's possession—*Diver*, the girl in a pool of water, shoulders wet, as she gripped her hair at the nape of her neck. That same pool had cradled her in its soft wet blue. How well she remembered the night she had seen it in Water Mill, had lived it out even while she herself swam naked, but the picture was horribly altered, like a grotesque caricature of the one she had seen years ago. The girl's neck looked odd, and her hand had changed in shape. The hair, so beautifully modulated in thin strands now looked blurred and fluffy, as if clouds puffed out around her ears. The thick oils almost appeared to slide down off the painting, the edges blurred, the colors mixed, gooey. When she had catalogued the painting before, it had certainly not looked like this.

"It's been this way for months. The paint just won't dry or started to run or something like that. At first it looked lush and beautiful, such a perfect work, although a bit sexy for these children here, but the Hulls insisted. Mrs. Hull said she felt it represented what she called a 'healthy sense of the female body.' She's French, you know. Naturally, I never worried about the surface until things began to slip a few weeks after we got it two years ago. As time went on, this. . . ."

Jenna leaned in to observe it more closely. "May I?"

"Of course."

Steadying herself to pretend detachment, she got out her small magnifying glass to examine the painting, tapping the sticky surface, and then she rubbed her finger over it gently. Yes, indeed, it was still wet.

"Bummer," someone said beside her, the teenaged girl

who had gotten up off the banquette to study the problem as well. "Looks like someone poured soup on it."

"That's a good way to describe it. We should take it out of the frame and inspect it more closely. I'm not really sure that it can be saved. It may be a corrupted medium, something we call inherent vice."

"Sounds evil," the girl said.

"Evil and not very fixable." Jenna sighed. "The underlying medium used to meld the paints onto the canvas may have been infected somehow with another substance."

"Call up the artist. He'll fix it for you."

"Good idea, except he's no longer with us. Marc Bélange, that is." Jenna knew that much about the work's creator.

"Then why don't you just leave it like that, make it sort of a performance piece?" The girl cocked her head. "We could watch it slide."

Jenna smiled. "Hmm, not really what I would do. I'm here to fix something, stop time, if you want to call it that. Tidy it up. I'm a good tidier."

The curator had grown impatient. "Come on, Sarabeth, don't you have some school work or something? We've got a studio space set up for Miss Myatt down the hall, along with some supplies, and she needs to get started. But not until tomorrow. You must be exhausted from your flight."

"Yes, I am." Jenna patted her rumpled tweed skirt self-consciously, noticing her beautiful Italian shoes now dirty from the New York streets.

TWO

Having heard nothing yet from her email to Jorge, Jenna took fate by the neck and messengered a note over to him at the Hull building the very next morning, and now she awaited some word from him. She and Jorge had been somehow in cahoots, not quite knowing about what, nevertheless often conspiring like disgruntled subjects of the king. It was their bond, and she had broken it, so she expected outrage on that front, as well as on every other one, or maybe he would refuse to respond. Possibly it was dangerous, for him, too. But those labels—she had never exactly figured out what they meant.

As she walked up Madison from 63rd Street, aiming for the hospital at 89th Street, she felt as if on a journey through her past. Most of the shops had just begun to open. She stared in at the textured velvets and brocades at Etro, where she had once spent a month's salary on a skirt, the mannequins lounging in suggestive, impossible postures. Though the cold cut through her, she kept on, head down, until she passed by the famously elaborate drug store, its window consumed with a doll collection of impressive bling and shine, the very one where once she had picked up Mrs. Hull's bath oil. On impulse, she went inside, knowing right where to find the stuff. Yes, Huile D'Automne, still there. She hadn't even smelled it that day, but now she opened the top of the tester and inhaled a vibrant spicy scent, grassy, not sweet at all.

Quickly she bought a bottle and stuck it in her purse—

to do what with? It had figured in the first real Hull drama she was forced to witness, Vincent's wife no doubt crying over his affair, Tasha two-timing her with her husband, if she knew it was in fact Tasha, or just her husband cheating on her, period. Would a Frenchwoman have expected fidelity? She hadn't seen much of that in France. Having a rich sexual history herself now, she saw these goings-on in the hazy, unfocused way that real life involved. No absolutes, no judgments without knowledge, and even then, sparingly. To herself she planned to be especially kind.

The curator had allotted her a good-sized corner hospital room as a studio, with big windows on each side, and only the nurse's station stood between her and the library. The woman had provided a lab coat, an easel, a basic restoration kit, a mask, gloves, and a number of scalpels, scrapers, and brushes. Logically, this should be enough. She sat herself down before the Bélange, examining it closely, keeping in mind as best she could the last time she had seen it on the wall at Water Mill, and without warning she teared up. That night, those things she did, they did. How she wished for it all back—the innocence of it, the not knowing what would come.

Jenna had no copy of her art inventory, but she remembered so well the moment when Vincent had run his hand over the thick leather covering on the book when she had handed it to him. What had she written about this painting in the past? Not a particularly valuable piece, but gorgeous then, luscious, sexy, now ironically, just plain wet everywhere. She couldn't remember a problem like the one she faced, but trying to assess it, she brought out the small digital camera she now used to photograph art, so much less impressive than her Leica but more serviceable. A moderate-sized work, the painting measured five feet by three feet. Photographing it from one side to the other, up on her laptop she could read several shadowy shapes in an underlayer behind the bathing girl, but their outlines had blurred to render them ghostly. Were they meant to be painted out altogether, but now revealed by the failing paint?

With a Q-tip dipped in water, beginning in the lower right-hand corner, she swabbed small bits of dirt and dust off the surface. Beneath this tiny spot she brushed a chemical solvent to reduce the synthetic resin varnish that had been applied. Finally, she came to the paint layer, composed of dry pigment ground, in this case, a linseed medium much like a paste. Bélange was known to grind his own paints and to layer them from "fat to lean," each new layer a bit oilier than the preceding one. He mixed his media, though, and Jenna thought perhaps he had used cold wax or an unusual resin to get the translucent effects so marvelous in the work she saw before her, even in this, its fallen state.

An oil painting can become dry to the touch anywhere from a day to two weeks and can be varnished in six months to a year. Still, when she thought back to her apprenticeship, she remembered folklore about one work still not considered dry after eighty years on the wall. Maybe she should take it to a tanning salon, Jenna laughed to herself. Had this painting been in the sun? That could help. She remembered that at the Water Mill house, all the Hulls' art had been carefully placed to avoid direct sunlight, even down to light canvas covers the housekeeper hung over selected works near a window in order to block out the afternoon glare. With good intentions, the hospital staff had instantly hidden this particular work, horrified at what they saw but confused too, as Bélange had told them, before his death two years previously, that they had only to put the thing on the wall and wait. The sun would "cure" it. But it was uncured, sicker, even, as Jenna examined earlier photographs the curator had religiously taken once every three months.

She didn't want to clean the rest of the painting as that might strip it of whatever remaining pigment it had. Instead, she cut out a large piece of tissue and laid it over the work's face, attaching it at the side with tape. It didn't touch the surface but protected it from getting dirt stuck on it when she turned the painting over to inspect its backside. The stretcher appeared normal, as did the actual canvas itself, no tears or defects. And then "Hello," a quiet voice said. She looked around to see a young black child of six or seven clad in a hospital gown staring solemnly at her.

"Hello," she smiled.

One hand holding an IV pole, the other outstretched, the boy shook hands solemnly. His fingers felt soft, almost papery in hers. He had a grown-up face, fine-boned, and at last he smiled, a shy little smile, and then looked down. "I'm not supposed to be here, I'm pretty sure. My mom might be looking for me."

"Should we go back to your room so you don't worry her?"

"No, they can miss me. It's good for them." He grinned. "Can I sit here and see what you're doing?"

"Sure." She pulled up a small stool for the boy. "I'm Cate."

"Hello, Cate. I'm Amon." He sat himself down gently, gathering his hospital gown around his thin little legs.

During the next hour the boy sat silent, watching her every move, a ghostly little presence, intense. Jenna didn't speak, but as she got out a magnifying glass and scanned the face of the painting inch by inch, the little boy crept closer. At last she handed the glass to him and positioned it in his delicate hand. For a child so young, he had the concentration of a much older person, looking up after a moment and shaking his head. "Dripping, looks like. Everything's mushed."

"That's what I think, too." Just then the door opened behind them and a heavyset white woman in blue jeans stood there with her hands on her hips. She had a fine head of curly light brown hair that flew out in all directions and a liveliness that scattered out all the somber quietness Jenna and the boy had created.

"So this is where you are, mister. We were really worried."

"Mom!"

"I'm very sorry," Jenna said. "He came by, and he and I got involved in working on the painting."

The woman looked harried, talking and scrolling through her calls on a cell phone all the while. The boy went up and put his arms around her ample waist, and they made an incongruous pair. She patted him on the head, distracted, and pulled him toward the door. "Bye. . . ." He turned toward Jenna. "See you soon, I hope."

"Oh, no you don't, mister," but the big woman stuck out her hand to Jenna. "I'm Lori, Amon's mother," she said emphatically as if expecting someone to deny it.

"He's no trouble." But then Jenna worried, would he become so, would he hang about too much? It wasn't really that large a room, and he was sick, worse than that, she now saw that fixing the painting would take a lot of time, more time than she probably even had, so she might have to give up the commission, but the mother and son were gone before she could say anything.

The young boy reappeared later that same afternoon. When Jenna entered the library, she spotted the small, recognizable face holding an oversized art book up in his hands, reading, supposedly, but glancing around, waiting for her. He lit up when she came through the door. No longer encumbered by the IV, he dropped the book and scooted over. "I'm here to help."

"Does your mother know about this?"

"She's not here. She won't be here for hours."

"What about the nurses?"

"Oh, they trust me. They let me do what I want."

Jenna wasn't so sure about this but didn't have the heart to turn him away. "Okay, but we'll have to let someone know you're here."

"No, no," he wailed. "It's so boring in my room."

Yes, it would be. She had tried not to look too closely at the children, but the inevitable glance proved they were bored witless, lying in bed all day watching television, that is, when they were not crying or screaming or trying to run away from some gruesome procedure, and run they did. She wished she could help every single one of them escape, so rather than call a nurse, she motioned Amon to follow her, and together they examined the painting once again. It looked even worse now, and she felt sure she would have to test every oil layer to see what was really going on. "You can hand me some of these vials, if you want, Amon." He perched himself on the stool again, gently picking one up each time she pointed toward another. He didn't say a word, though occasionally he bent forward to watch what she was doing, never getting in her way.

Jenna liked his delicate little hands, so gentle with everything. She wondered what was wrong with him, but of course could think of no way to ask. He seemed so grown up. Wasn't that always the way with sick children, old beyond their years, suffering what they never should have to and never knowing the reason why? Or perhaps blaming a malevolent being who, for reasons unknown, wanted them unwell, or worse. Disease made philosophers of them all.

The two worked like this for almost an hour. Amon said very little, only murmuring now and again when Jenna appeared particularly interested in something, so they were startled when the curator appeared, apparently shocked at the young boy's presence. "Back to the ward, young man. They probably think you're lost!"

Amon slowly moved from the stool and trotted out but waved to Jenna behind the older woman's back and stuck out his tongue.

"He's such a cutie. Why is he here?"

"Oh, we're not allowed to give out any information like that, but it must be serious. He's been here for weeks, from the Midwest, I think. What's the status of the picture? Any diagnosis on your end?"

"I feel almost sure it's inherent vice."

"You mentioned that before."

"Yes, corruption of the medium. Painters who work in oil strive for extreme effects in terms of depth and richness, the real world laid out flat on a canvas but round, three-dimensional. This is very difficult to do. Someone like Leonardo da Vinci experimented all the time with strange substances to enhance his colors, even while he had to get the thick oil paint to stick to the canvas, which actually he didn't always manage to do. Restoring the painting will take time and a lot of work. You might have to face that it can't be fixed at all."

The woman sighed, gripping her hands together tightly. "I wonder what I should tell the donors—or maybe we should give it back? No, that wouldn't be right. They'd be horribly offended. The Hulls aren't exactly the friendliest people in the world."

Jenna blushed at the name. Hearing it out loud set her heart racing, as if every piece of privileged knowledge would show on her face. "Yes, so I've heard." She looked down at the floor.

Before she left the hospital that day, it had started to rain, and now as she emerged into the open air, she put out her hand to catch the droplets. Just hearing "Hull," especially from the lips of someone ignorant of its significance for her, scared her. She didn't belong anywhere near them, but they had demanded it, why? To fix this painting? Any number of art restorers in New York would love to do it for them. Her phone pinged, but she didn't recognize the number. "Yes?" she said out into the void.

"Tonight, seven thirty, Columbiana restaurant, Astoria, Queens." It was Jorge.

THREE

When Jenna got back to the hotel, she just wanted to crawl under the bedcovers. Instead she found several voicemail messages from the full-throated Rudolph Hayes Esquire, of Hayes, Rudinsky, and Baugh, as he forcefully reminded her in the first one that there were specific terms for her visit. In the second message he enumerated them: no unauthorized contact with anyone in the Hull family, no unauthorized meetings with persons connected to *NewsLink*, and absolutely no contact with members of the press. He must have been reading her mind, or perhaps he was just a student of character. For the moment, Jenna settled on this explanation for the timing of the calls. "Should you have questions, here's my backline at the office, also my cell. Consider, Jenna, who you are and where you are."

On this otherwise lonesome evening, despite every single thing the lawyer had dictated, she decided to go to Columbiana for dinner with the esteemed Jorge. Or should she cancel? She looked at her watery eyes in the mirror in the bathroom, feeling tired, overwhelmed with the city and what she had to do in it. She had already laid out a beautiful rich blue Italian suit in the kind of wool that existed only in Milan, and it fit her perfectly. Enough, she thought. Did Hayes have spies roaming the streets, and what could they really do about this? She wasn't sure.

Jenna sat waiting in the noisy, family-filled restaurant, at an address she knew was close to Jorge's home. She stared down at the menu, trying to look occupied and ordered a milkshake-like concoction the waiter announced as Columbia's national drink. When it arrived it was green, frothy, and delicious. So nervous, she felt herself beginning to sweat. Moments later she spotted Jorge, who was thinner, just a little grayer at the temples, natty as always in a brown checked suit, a red scarf around his neck, squinting to see in the dark restaurant. She watched as his eyes swept over her with no recognition and then turned back again in her direction. She raised a hand slightly, and he focused on her now, staring. She tried for a smile as he made his way to the table. There he just stood for a moment, perplexed, and many at Columbiana watched with interest. "I can't believe it. Is that really you?"

"Of course."

He held out his hand in a formal manner and enfolded hers with it, still standing, until at last he shook his head again. "I didn't recognize you."

"I've changed."

Jorge found himself in front of a stylish, sophisticated brunette, definitely in the European vein, and he knew what Italian women looked like, bangles at the wrist, sleek, well-fitted clothing, an air of charm, maybe even delight, a real grown-up. "You've transformed yourself."

"I'm going to take that as a compliment. Sadly, I'm something of a fugitive, hence the change in appearance."

"Yes." He sat down, silent a moment, until finally he ordered himself a Columbian beer. To Jenna's eyes, he looked, as ever, the self-contained keeper of the secrets, a man not given to revelation of any kind, especially about his or anyone else's personal life. Always he had remained as stone compared to the talkative, gossip-obsessed staffers of *NewsLink*. "Here you are."

"I got your bottle of Champagne and the labels, at least I'm pretty sure you sent them." He looked down and laughed, taking another long swig of beer. "Veuve, widow, Mumm, 'mum's the word,' Taittinger's sexy purple night, someone having sex with Vince? That's what I've got so far."

Jorge winced at the casual use of their boss's first name, as if the guy wasn't really dead. "A little joke. I shouldn't have done it, but I didn't want you to feel so alone. Also, you needed something to go on. You've got the general idea, but you'll need specifics."

"Specifics?"

"At some point you'll figure out everything on your own, and then we can talk. Let's just say that it's totally appropriate he died *in flagrante delicto*, in blazing offence, a mental and physical space that bastard often occupied."

Jenna was shocked at what he said because she planned to avoid talking about her own in flagrante days and simply prayed he knew nothing more about them. For a time, they drank in silence amid the boisterous laughter of the restaurant crowd. Finally, Jorge spoke again. "Vincent Hull was in love."

Taken off guard, she could only nod.

"With someone highly inappropriate. . . ." And with that he launched into a tirade. "He risked everything— everything personal, that is. He could have had anyone. Frankly he did, but then to choose someone so *not* available, so wrong. . . ."

Could he possibly mean her? But then why did he talk about her in this dismissive, furious way? She felt herself begin to cry, ready to confess anything, but no, he must mean someone else, and she wiped her eyes in her napkin. A waiter dropped a tray of dishes, and this momentarily diverted them. Jorge did see her tears, though.

"I don't believe for one minute you were the one actually screwing him when he died. He was using you as a beard or something."

"Oh, my god."

"How much did they pay you?"

"I don't know."

"You don't know? Come on, Jenna, you didn't get that thousand dollar suit and those hammered gold bracelets on anything you made in that office, unless now you've risen up to become chief executive officer of an Italian conglomerate, and I can't really picture that."

She looked around in panic because at this moment the story seemed to have gotten bigger, even more confusing than what she knew. "I'm not supposed to talk about all this, but now I am, in fact, an art conservationist and restorer, gainfully employed and very well paid."

"She was such a schemer, and she made you call the police after what, an hour, maybe even more? Probably just sitting there on the sofa waiting for him to die. And then that whole charade at the hospital, as if they could actually revive him. He, deader than dead when he got there."

"Tasha?"

"Who else? I saw you palling around with her and wanted to warn you, but I didn't because of the prevailing code of silence, and I had hopes for you. That whole Hull universe was such a snake pit, and you seemed about to get bitten. Tasha Clark could read people and used them constantly. Seduction was her game, and everyone fell in love with her. The notion that Hull would ever be involved with someone like her—talk about birds of a feather. They would have clawed each other to death, not his type at all, but still he succumbed."

"I guess so." Vivid memories of their own lovemaking

flooded her with heat and embarrassment. What had she and Vincent not done together? And how she wished they had done even more. That time in her life had been like a tsunami, with herself standing on shore watching the surf recede way too far into the ocean, only to coil itself up and crash forward upon her. Now her current privileged circumstances made her feel like some weird, hidden family member, like the mad old relative in the attic whom everyone wants to forget.

"Whatever really was going on, Tasha knows the truth, not that she would tell any of us, though maybe she told you."

"No. I haven't talked to her since that night."

"She made a lot of dough off this thing, that's for sure." Jorge stood, apparently dismissing her, but then he sat down again, even more intense now. "And you're not telling me anything either. I get it, kind of, so typical of those terrible people, crushing the world between their teeth. They certainly tried to crush me . . . you too I'll bet."

"I'm sorry, Jorge. I know I haven't really explained anything."

"You will, though, someday."

She wanted so badly to plead her case, such as it was. Reaching across to him, she clasped his hands and began to summarize for him, in dry, sanitized terms, her romps with Vincent Hull in Water Mill and finally Tasha's request to substitute herself underneath the body of the dead man, thereby taking the rap. "So I was the decoy that night, though I still can't understand why I agreed to the whole plan. I signed papers."

Jorge let go of her and wiped his forehead with his napkin, upset and embarrassed. "They like people who will sign papers. I cannot believe you too got sucked in, and you were so young, so—"

"Gullible? Stupid?"

"He seduced everyone."

"Honestly, Tasha was beautiful, persuasive. I idolized her. And Mrs. Hull. Now she was the most exotic woman I'd ever seen. Mr. Hull, well Vincent—"

Jorge raised his hand. "Stop. You're worth fifty of those three."

"I keep thinking that the story they told me didn't make any sense, why I had to be there, not Tasha. Because she's black? Or that she was an employee, the supposed friend of Mrs. Hull? The cover-up was totally botched, yet the press didn't get into it at all. They just bought that I was the one, even given the screwed-up timeline."

"Triangulating was a specialty of theirs, an art form that they took to a very high level. Also, they have great control over the press. It's subtle and complete. Look at Tasha now, fat and happy in Chicago, well, maybe not fat." At this point, the two of them had eaten almost nothing, so now when the waiter appeared with two huge plates of bandeja paisa, steak, fried pork rinds atop red beans and rice, with a slice of avocado and sweet banana chips on top of all that, even a side of chorizo sausages, they dug into the food. "Speaking of fat, behold the national dish of Columbia."

"Listen, though, can you help me? I don't have much time, and I want to talk to Tasha."

Jorge took a big sip of wine. "You'll have to go to Chicago. She'll never come here."

"Right. I need to find out what was really going on. I've done everything the lawyers wanted, and, on the bright side, I'm rich, I'm living the life of someone else, or maybe I've become that person, I don't know. I have to get her to talk to me."

"Trust me, you can't figure them out, but also you have to watch yourself. They take no prisoners."

"You're not trying to say they'd kill me or something?"

"I don't know what I'm trying to say." He scribbled a number on the flip side of a business card he pulled from his pocket and handed it to her. "My cell. Let me know how it goes, or call for backup if need be." When she leaned in to kiss him good-bye, something she had never done before, he held on to her for a moment, whispering, "Seriously, be careful."

Despite the lateness of the hour, Jenna went back to the hospital, not quite sure why. Without a plan, she realized she wanted to see Amon again and went off in search of him. Of an age where she might have wanted children, she had prevented herself from even thinking along those lines, but now, despite the pileup of personal disasters in her life, she began to think of her future. She had always been comfortable around children, despite her personal only-child status. She liked their friendliness, their curiosity, their fearless laughter. Perhaps because of this little boy, the idea of having a child had taken up residence in her mind.

Eleven at night, late for such a place. She grabbed her lab coat out of her "office" and as quietly as she could, walked the length of the hallway, peeking briefly into each hospital room. In one a small baby slept while the mother sat nearby knitting. The woman looked up and smiled. Further down, she encountered a girl, maybe thirteen, pacing inside her room with her IV bag attached, talking on her cell phone. Several nurses glanced up at Jenna momentarily, not finding her presence odd, so she kept on in her search.

Around another corner she saw an open door and peeked in, ready to impersonate an official if the need arose, but this time she heard muffled cries, the sound of a wailing baby, and then a child really screaming, "You're not going to put that into me, you're not." More screaming was followed by soothing sounds coming from what must have been nurses. Jenna hurried along, peeking into the small glass windows of each room, until finally she spotted Amon. In the darkness she could just make him out; his stomach badly distended, he was curled around in a ball in his mother's arms. He cried and cowered into her, wailing, "Mom, Mom" in muffled tones. Right away Jenna drew back, ashamed of having seen him in such distress, fearing that he might have seen her.

His mother spotted her and waved her into the room. "I'm so sorry," Jenna murmured. "I just wondered where he was."

"He's been really sick. He's waiting for a kidney transplant, and you know, they just let the kids go down-hill until they're truly in trouble. He can't eat any food he likes and keeps getting his goddamned picc line fixed over and over again. It gets infected. So that's why he hasn't been to see you. The nurse doesn't like him to visit you either," the woman whispered.

"Why doesn't she like it?"

"It's something different, unexpected. Not what the other kids do. I don't know. "

"So . . . he's been in a lot of hospitals?"

"He was in Columbus Children's in Ohio for weeks last year. He still does have one sort of good kidney, and they've tried to keep it working. His mother smoked crack. That's what got us here. I adopted him when he was ten months old." Amon curled even more against his mother's belly, not acknowledging Jenna at all.

"I'm from Ohio too," Jenna said, and without quite knowing how it happened, she took the woman in her arms, the child as well, and held them both for a long time. More cries sounded about them, the nighttime anguish of children alone or in pain. No one deserved this place, an absolute rebuke to God.

In the wee hours, ensconced once more in her posh hotel suite, she arranged a flight to Chicago for the day after tomorrow. She had already created a whole scenario about giving money to the charity through Tasha's assistant, under her current phony name, mentioning a sum so large that any time she wanted to come, according to the young woman, would be fine. She barely slept, and right at ten the next morning, she raced to the Metropolitan Museum of Art just as it opened its doors. Headed for the museum store, she quickly found a mini artist's studio in a box, thirty colored pencils, twenty-four pastels, fourteen tubes each of oil, tempera, and acrylic paints, six brushes, a palette knife, sketch pencils, and a wooden palette. It even came with one stretched canvas and a small, foldable easel.

She had the present wrapped up in heavy paper and slung it into a cab on that drizzly gray day, determined to get it to Amon before she left town. Already his room was full of games and toys, so what would one more item matter? Because it looked like all the other gear she sometimes carried, security didn't stop her at the front door, and she lugged it up to her studio, fully prepared to surprise him somehow, even if she had to bulldoze through his hospital door. But he was waiting for her already in the library, again hiding behind an oversized book. He smiled solemnly, saying nothing, and pattered off with her to her workroom, the pain that had caused him to cry in the night apparently gone.

"This is for you."

The little boy didn't react at first, but then he balanced the large package on his knees, watching it with wide, dark eyes, waiting. At last, oh so carefully he peeled back several layers of paper. When he opened the easel and saw all the paints, he said nothing for a moment. Finally, "For me?"

She nodded. And then, without asking her, he set the easel on the table next to the Bélange, pulling out the drawers on either side, running his finger slowly along each of the pencils. At last he picked one up, poked himself slightly in the finger, smiling, and began to draw an entirely recognizable horse.

The door to their little sanctuary opened abruptly. "Now this is too much. Amon cannot be up here all the time working with you, instead of down in his room getting treatments and doing what the other children are doing." The Cavanaugh woman wrung her hands and folded them across her middle.

"And that would be nothing, right?" Jenna wasn't in the mood. The curator glared at her, and then took the boy's hand, pulling him up off his stool.

"No, I want to stay," he wailed.

But now she had hold of his arm and wouldn't let him go, though he tried to wriggle away. "Pack this stuff up again, and I'll get it put in his room."

Jenna removed the boy from the woman's grasp, gently though. "No need. I'll walk down with you." She placed the colored pencils back in their slots and folded up the box. As they walked single file down the hallway, Jenna watched Amon turn his head and stare back at her. Those eyes seemed to say, that's how things are. People get taken away from each other, their dreams crushed, and they are forbidden, inexplicably, to do what they want, even when in danger of losing their lives. Like every other injustice, this one had no explanation and no possible reaction except stoic silence, the same such charged acceptance Amon showed now, as the unhappy group opened the door to his chamber.

Miserable, she ran back to her improvised studio, grabbing her tote, intent on getting to her waiting livery car. In the dark back seat, she crumpled into sobs because she feared she was going to lose even this little boy. She refused to lose anyone ever again, never never again. The only solution, to care for nothing, for nobody, only for inanimate objects. Yes, that would be best. She deserved to be alone because she had been bad and wrong and exile held out the only hope. So, she couldn't approach anyone, certainly not a man; she never would have a child of her own and would always be alone.

FOUR

The next morning Jenna opened a bottle of fizzy water, gulping at it, and then splashed her face with a wet palm. She held in her hand today's *New York Times*, a publication she had banished from her life because she feared what it said about anyone from her past. Worse yet, she might have had to read something by Inti, but now she hunted for his byline. Just as soon as she got back from this little adventure of hers with Tasha, she planned to set up a date with him. As she paged through the whole newspaper, she could not help noticing the tone, so different from European papers, talk in and around and about money on page after page, as if a colossal money fest had erupted. It seemed that every story was about money. Wealth had broken out for her too, but here all talk spun in a carousel around it. She herself had so much, and if only she could take pleasure in her money instead of hiding away her bank statements and investment papers in a pile under her bed, she could become once more like her American compatriots, enthusiastically rich. At last, she found what she'd been looking for: "By Inti Weill" attached to "Gas Stove Linked to Explosion in the Bronx." She would leave a message for him when she got back from Chicago.

In a daze, Jenna rested her head on the seat as they crawled up the FDR toward the Triborough Bridge on the way to LaGuardia. She really had no plan as to what she would say to Tasha, so to cheer herself up she conjured up past visions of herself and Inti making love, wonderful images really, so different from Vince, less fraught, just fun and enjoyable. With Vince every caress brought her to the fire. She should dive back into it, she thought. Little Slutbag, that's what Granny would have called her, but in point of fact, she had other, more serious concerns. She had already broken her word not to contact people from the past and was shortly to talk to the very person the lawyers must fear most, next to herself. At this point, though, they could come after her anyway, so she might do as she wanted, no? In a moment of bravado, she vowed to see Inti as soon as she got back from this strictly forbidden visit to the other "other" woman.

Chicago in February was a city in frozen lockdown. Anything that hadn't been shuttered properly was buried in snow or blown into the distance by the wind. Jenna had very bad memories of snow in Ohio, mainly of cars sliding off the interstate into the median, almost comically side by side. Now she faced those memories head on. In her cab on the way to the restaurant Tasha's assistant had specified, she clutched her heavy coat around her, but when she got out, the wind howled down the sidewalk, hard enough practically to blow her into the side of a building. She was so nervous she pushed her hat down on her head so it wouldn't fly off, wrapping her scarf tightly around her neck. Would Tasha recognize her? Of course, Jenna remembered well the beautiful girl with high cheekbones, long caramel-colored hair, and a face so distinctive that it was difficult to look away from her, but maybe she too had changed her appearance. At least from her own research, that hadn't happened; Tasha lived a public life, CEO of a foundation to help children, quite visible. Perhaps too Jenna's own memories might have grown fuzzy and more romantic over time, but she would never forget the look on Tasha's face as she stood over her dead lover.

The restaurant was a noisy sports bar, and she couldn't quite figure out why Tasha had wanted to meet there. It would be too loud to talk. When first Jenna entered she was so nervous she just swiveled her head around wildly, wondering where among the beer drinkers and blaring television sets, she might see her former friend. At last, she spotted a bobbling head of that extraordinary hair still in the same style her Tasha had worn it in New York. Jenna waved, but the woman just stared at her. And so she hurried over, almost too nervous to look her in the eye because she saw only incomprehension. The woman didn't recognize her. "It's me, Tasha."

"You're Cate Myatt now?"

"Yes."

"I can't believe it. Where did that girl Jenna go?"

Jenna pulled out a chair and sat down, shaking out her hair, and pulling off her coat. "She's still here, but buried beneath her own lies and money."

"Good god, you look completely European."

"In most respects I am."

Jenna could smell that same floral perfume and admire the woman's strong figure and demeanor just as she had when they worked together in the Hull empire. Tasha ordered burgers and fries for them, along with two beers. "Very American," she said, and then the two sat there for some time in the lunchtime noise and hilarity.

Finally Jenna looked up and into the eyes of her one-time friend, a woman she hadn't seen in five years. Neither spoke until at last Jenna said in a low voice, as Tasha leaned forward to hear, "Why? Why all of it? I still don't understand, and I go over and over in my mind what happened. Why me and not you? Was it your race? Was that it? They didn't want people to think he was sleeping with someone black?" Such being the world of *NewsLink*, she had never directly mentioned her race to Tasha, as if it were too much a statement of the obvious and offensive in ways she couldn't quite figure out but could feel.

"Race played a role, I think, looking back," Tasha spoke carefully. "But that wasn't all that was in play. My life was complicated then."

"And it's not now?" Jenna felt a sort of heat go up through her.

"It's always complicated, though I try hard to simplify."

"Anything around that family would have been horrendous."

"Horrific and fascinating. Worth every moment, ultimately. I was in love and trying to deal with that. I had never been in love before."

"Ah, there's that. He was an extraordinary man, at least to me, but then I was basically a kid. I think I loved him myself." Unsure how much further to go, she refused to say that she herself was also sleeping with the man. "You were friends with Mrs. Hull, at least it seemed that way. Do you ever talk to her? "

"I don't see her anymore, I don't know her. She hates me, anyway."

"Wait, why? She didn't know you were sleeping with him, did she?"

Almost as if afraid to listen, Tasha bowed her head down into her hands. Jenna reached out and held those hands for a moment. "With people like that," Tasha finally said, "there's no way to get around their will. They'll grind you. I watched him do it time and again. He always got what he wanted. Weirdly enough, she's just like him."

"I'm amazed you understood as much about them as you did." But Jenna still felt mystified, yet wary of finding out even more.

They talked on into the afternoon as the restaurant emptied out, and when Jenna could listen with attention, she tried to understand something of the swirl of events she'd unwittingly been part of. According to Tasha, the family wanted urgently to protect Hull's children, and had it been a black woman, the press would have become even more salacious and insinuating and have asked all kinds of questions that would have dug up further, deeper family secrets. Nevertheless, Jenna still found her account questionable. "This is the modern age, Tasha. Race really doesn't mean what it once did."

"For you, not for them."

Jenna didn't buy it, she felt let down, but she couldn't get any more information from the woman, who seemed her senior by approximately one hundred years. Was race alone the mighty engine of her downfall? The only person she could ever ask, Sabine Hull, was strictly forbidden to her, but what an amazing hospital-unveiling-personal-life story meeting that would make, and she shuddered at the thought. The Frenchwoman so proud, and the recently minted Cate Myatt, Jenna who once was, the thoroughly bad young woman who had taken unimaginable amounts of money from the family, talking together over the past.

They emerged into a night of cold and wind and grasped each other arm in arm. These shared secrets involved them in a cloud of mystery and suspicion. "Do you think you would be helping people now, so much, if this hadn't happened?" Jenna asked.

"Not at all. I'd be back in publicity. Thank god it did happen. It got me away from a world that was killing me. I hate how I behaved in that city."

As a result of this meeting, once more on a plane that bucked mightily through wind and snow, Jenna leaned back, holding a glass of Champagne, and contemplated her own life. For one thing, she no longer had such mortal fear of flying, other fears having nudged that particular phobia out. But more important, where during the last few years she had thought her new profession too decadent and rarified to mean anything other than that wealthy people got their paintings fixed, she now saw it as a gift. Some of these works would find their way into museums where everybody could see them. That these *objets* should look right, perfect, just as they had hundreds of years before, was her job. Some of the paintings she had loved, others she had thought flawed, and others awful or even fake, but still she could invest her own small self into the painter's work on the canvas. It was a privileged role, allowing her to go into the distant mind and soul of an artist out there in the ether.

As her plane began its rocky descent into LaGuardia, a landing that recalled to mind her terrible trip to Wyoming with Vince, his face flooded in upon her again, that wonderful face, though cruel, a sharp smile, a hard word for everyone, but a big, warm hand that held on strong. All she and Tasha really shared was that connection, so they would probably never see each other again. These perilous intimacies meant too much, and to make things worse, she was in a fright about her schedule, whether she could get the painting into shape for its unveiling four days hence, whether she could see Inti, and how she could find out more about Sabine Hull. In the blessed safety of the back seat of yet another livery car, she emailed Inti on her new Blackberry and left him a message asking him to meet her for a drink.

Violations, violations, they were piling up. Did the

Hulls have hit men? Maybe one of those had killed Vincent. It's funny how being back in New York made her think of such conspiracies. She lay back against the warm, dark seat and began to doze, but moments later her magic little phone pinged, and up came the name of Rudolph Hayes. "Yes? Hello," she spoke into its small black shape, still unused to it, a bit like an obnoxious toy.

"I don't mean to alarm you, but we have a situation here that, unforeseen as it is, could cause problems."

Clouded air descended around her. "A situation?" Had he found out about Chicago two seconds after she hit the ground? If so, what a marvel of scrutiny.

"I was against your coming back here, even for a week, but Sabine Hull insisted on it, and now she wants to see you."

"Why me?"

"Obviously she has questions about that night and Vincent's death. Frankly, Miss McCann, she's gone rogue. Normally she's under my control, but with time things didn't add up for her, so here we are. Or maybe Tasha told her something."

Jenna shrank at the name of the woman she had just seen, but she certainly wasn't going to tell him anything about the visit. "I'll just listen. Maybe she wants to vent."

"Frenchwomen don't vent." The lawyer fell silent, and it seemed to Jenna that for once in this strange odyssey, she held the upper hand, and of course she did, now that she could reveal their lies regarding the death of an eminent man.

"You're just going to have to trust me."

"Ha!" Then he paused. "She's lost her mind. It's this painting she's so fixated on. It isn't even worth that much, and it certainly doesn't suit a bunch of sick children. She wants to set up the meeting, so wait to hear from her."

FIVE

nti Weill had remained single and had naturally joined the ranks of the wired, hardwired, wireless, and otherwise obsessed with small screens. He hadn't expected to encounter Jenna again, certainly not in New York, so when he saw her email, for a moment he considered ignoring her, but then he thought of his old coyote piece that had netted his long dreamed of offer from the *Times*, knowing full well that the photos had sealed the deal. He was grateful to her. Ever since 2001, just after the World Trade Center came down, he vowed never to leave the city and to toil honestly and thankfully at zoning and harbor problems, Staten Island discontents, and the sins of councilmen in every borough. Even now, four years since he had last seen her, he still thought of Jenna often, and cherished, in some odd way, the mental picture of her in monkish labor over a minute corner of a canvas from the eighteenth century, even if it might have been stolen. So when he read her email, having just emerged from an interview with the mayor at City Hall, he went straight to the press room, unable to stop himself from some hasty research on the whole Hull business and Jenna's possible role in it.

A flood of articles detailed the man's embarrassing death, with numerous photos of Jenna, round of face, wide-eyed, smiling like a girl fresh out of college, with those silly owl glasses, objects he had never seen before or since. He hadn't ever tried to contact her after their little French tryst, because he didn't want to tempt himself to lust after both her and a major story, each at the same time, and he had seen no future in it. Now, not sure what to do with this emailed invitation in hand, he felt the landscape shift, remembering in spite of himself her soft thighs and almost volcanic sexuality. Since that romantic interlude in France, Inti had had several involvements, one with an embassy staffer in London, another with a medical student in Washington DC, both of which had come with a lot of heat and frustration—not to mention travel—both now over.

Jenna had invited him to the King Cole bar at the St. Regis, a place he, now a genuine New Yorker, associated with non-serious drinkers who wanted to impress other people, so he determined to meet up with her there and drag her to his favorite watering hole, a cigar bar on Mercer Street that required membership of a sort, but anyone with one hundred and fifty dollars to blow on smokes could join. These included an unlikely crowd of lawyers, disreputable Russians, a few in the garment trade, and the extremely fashionable young, who drank martinis with one hand and twiddled their cell phones with the other. The older folks usually smoked and talked in deep-set velvet chairs, while the young circulated, trolling for the new and the now. For some reason it reminded him of France, just that level of menace behind the levity.

Having to rush out his copy on the latest doings in Albany, at six o'clock he stopped to buy a necktie at Sulka, a place he loved for its associations with Clark Gable in *The Hucksters*. The actor had purchased a "sincere" tie to get ahead in advertising. Inti flicked through the line of hundred-dollar neckwear, noting the incredible tie inflation at work since the 1930s and finally settled on a blue one, blue the color of empathy, yes, sincere, heart-felt. At this moment—one that he experienced as solemn—he didn't know whether he would say anything to Jenna at all about the continuing Hull mystery. It might tempt him too much. No wonder she lived in hotels.

For her part, Jenna sat waiting with a kind of patient hysteria as she sipped water at the bar. She didn't want to get too loaded before she saw him again. Why did she feel so completely different in New York? Not at home at all, but glamorous, ready for anything, hot with anticipation. She tugged on the straps of her green jersey dress. Was it just the city, or being in her own country at last? Or was it sheer exhaustion from yesterday's events? Amid all this, it would be interesting and fine and seriously dangerous to talk to Inti, worse yet to any journalist.

Their greetings over, quick and fierce with anxiety for both, Jenna and Inti sat opposite each other at a low round table for two. She felt guilty, appalled at herself for getting in touch with him. Now he seemed quieter, older to her, less jolly, and kept looking around at the other drinkers, afraid, it seemed, to look at her. She registered Inti's fine looks, the strong jaw and the curly dark hair. He had filled out, and his shoulders looked bigger, more assertive, which he proved by dragging her out of that posh place shortly after they finished their first drink. In the cab, while the driver engaged in the frantic forward motion only sometimes possible in the city, Inti put his hand over hers, causing her to cry out to the cabbie, "Slow down, will you sir? We're not in a hurry." She saw him smile at her fears, and he clasped her hand even harder as she looked over at him gratefully. New York drivers seemed even worse to her than the Italians.

"Do you want a cocktail?" the young waiter asked at the very moment Jenna and Inti had seated themselves in the smoky, fuzzy atmosphere of the Mercer Street so-called Cigar Club.

"Definitely," Inti said. "Scotch, single malt, neat. You choose one for me."

"Certainly, sir."

Jenna stared at the wine list, so long and complex. She had grown used to the vino ordinario of the Italian countryside, and nothing else seemed as delicious to her. "Anything red and dry," she sighed. "I'm spoiled by where I live."

"Yes, you're Italian now, but here we drink Scotch."

"I'm an aspiring Italian. I want that level of joy. Scotch is fine, but only for New York." Yes, and Scotch had been Vincent's drink of choice. She surveyed the Village hipsters, of all ages really, upscale people, full of something that looked like joy, or maybe they just wanted to make noise. The madness of contacting Inti came upon her like a swift punch, and she pondered how fast she could get out of the room.

"I was surprised to hear from you." He too looked about at the crowd. "I had no expectations."

"That's always best, I think." Jenna seemed distracted, and indeed she was. The room, the people, perilously close to the life she had once lived here. After all, New York was a small town, and every street corner presented the prospect of running into someone she had once known. Where were Vera and Allyson? Had they ever tried to get in touch with her? She frowned into her drink as she thought of them.

"Share the worry, beauty."

"Thinking of my old roommates. Vera, an aspiring interior designer, was dating this horrible man named Ed Delong. I wonder what happened to her?"

"Easy to find out these days. The world is at my fingertips." He pulled out his very small laptop, which he carried always, and tapped in her roommate's name. Within moments he found an article about her, dated six months previously.

"Who would write about Vera, I mean, unless she got famous or something?"

"'Vera Delong was involved in an altercation at the Brooklyn home of herself and her husband, Edward, who was the apparent victim of a stabbing. Mrs. Delong claimed her husband had come at her with a fork, and she repelled his attack with a paring knife. Both parties were taken to the hospital and pronounced safe, but drunk.'" This tidbit cheered her immensely. Vera and Ed had been destined for something awful, and sharing their gruesome little story with Inti made her feel more intimate with the town in which she found herself. She tipped her drink glass at him and saluted. In a further search, he announced that Allyson had indeed married her sportswriter chap and resided now in Great Neck. "See, I can find out anything."

"I certainly hope not," she said, but she laughed. They talked of her work on the Bélange painting, of its prospects in terms of not falling off the canvas, and then suddenly Jenna found herself confiding in him about Amon, the whole story, his paint set, the awful nurses, his harried mother. Now she wondered where he was and what was happening.

"You wear a lab coat when you work, don't you?" he asked.

"Of course."

"Just pretend you're a doctor and go looking for him. Only a few people know who you are around there, it sounds like. If you added a stethoscope, that would be perfect."

"Oh my god, I could never do anything like that. I hate to lie."

"Ah," Inti breathed out quietly. He felt like a prosecutor sitting across from a guilty woman.

Immediately she read his thoughts and agreed with every last one of them. Jenna stared about the smoky room, probably the last place one could smoke in New York, indoors anyway. It reminded her of home. Yes, she did now have a home, and it wasn't here. And then, in a strange moment, while stealing a glance at Inti as he tapped on his cell phone, she understood that he had figured out elements of her story. The one cardinal stipulation in her contract was about to be violated because she was going to talk to him. "You know everything, don't you?"

Inti looked up and frowned. "Not everything, but I can piece it together pretty much."

"Can you keep quiet about it?"

It would be a major tale, this one. Proliferating gossip, the fiery engine of twenty-first century journalism and even the *Times,* which called every miscreant Mr. or Ms. even while they headed to the slammer, would jump all over it. It would be huge, and for a moment Inti contemplated the abyss. "I promise not to do anything I don't tell you about."

"That doesn't seem reassuring."

"I'm not just some loathsome careerist journo, you know. I could have pursued it already. I could have outed you after France."

"But you didn't."

"No."

"Will you promise not to pursue it?"

Inti smiled at her and raised his eyebrows. "I don't know. Maybe you can figure how to persuade me not to."

"What about the count and his paintings? Were they the stolen ones?"

"The one your Monsieur Legard worked on was, but we could never find the Fragonard, so the whole thing got dropped. Too French, too much competing news."

"Thank god. I would have died if anything bad happened to my lovely maître."

Taking another sip of the mouth-burning Scotch, she spied a woman staring at her from across the smoky room. Jenna squinted, trying to look at her without being obvious. Did she know her or did the woman recognize her from former years? A staffer at the magazine maybe.

Inti drank in silence, provoked by the tiresome fact of the rich, older man, something that rankled. How had such an inappropriate person become the chosen love object of one very desirable female? He disliked the idea that women could overlook any physical problems, any deficit in looks, anything at all really, for money, pure and simple. What other attractions could a fifty-nine-year-old married man have had for such a young woman?

"You don't like me any more, is that it?" she said, with some prescience.

"Of course I like you. I'm here, aren't I?

"Barely."

He bent forward now to signal his full attention. "Let's go dancing."

"Yes. I want to get out of here." She looked back at the staring woman who turned away suddenly.

They went off to a Russian nightclub nearby, one of Inti's favorites. He turned out to be a very good man in the tight hold of a waltz and even more agile at some impossible Russian folk dance called the Kalinka. She loved the way he moved his body and remembered more vividly with each movement the wonderful times they had had in bed. Despite her fright at how much he knew, she vowed that she would not let this opportunity get by her, even if she had to drag him to her hotel. But he had other ideas. No longer merely a drudge with a backpack and laptop, he now had an apartment on the Upper West Side, and though slightly embarrassed about his semi-fashionable address, he was quite proud that he had furnished the place and made it look presentable, if somewhat generic. The only personal note: the photos he had taken in France, where he had a picture of the count's wine cave, next to it an Amish buggy pictured in upstate New York, and even one of Jenna's photographs of the coyotes in Rye. Jenna stared up at that one for a moment, until he handed her a cognac. His apartment had a clean, uncluttered feeling, as if he could handle silence and simplicity, and she surveyed it carefully. She sat down on the suede couch, nervous once again as Inti worked away in the kitchen. At last he emerged with a plate of olives and cheese, and as soon as he set it down before her, she reached over and kissed him. He pulled back. "Where are you staying?"

"The Lowell."

"Very fancy. But then you're an expert on hotels." As he spoke he could feel the liquor roiling his brain.

"I'm just staying there a few more days for this project. It's temporary."

"More days, more nights, who cares? Let's do it, what do you say?" He suddenly felt drunk and insulting.

"What do you want me to do?" She taunted him, feeling soiled in his eyes, as if she had done something very dirty. Of course she had, so it seemed right that he treated her like a whore. "Tell me in detail, so I'll know how to make you scream."

"You already did that in France."

"I've forgotten, though, so many lovers, so much time. I can't hang on to everything."

"You're hot." He shook his head and mocked her.

"I'm just acting out what you're thinking."

"How do you know what I'm thinking?"

"I can read minds . . . I can read futures." Jenna stood up and swirled her red cashmere shawl around her neck, grabbing her coat. "And I can let myself out."

"No." Inti stood up, but she was already through the door.

SIX

The next morning, racing to get to the hospital, Jenna hiked all the way, almost running, sweating, covered in too much clothing. Only one more day before the unveiling of *Diver*, which event she had been commanded not to attend. In fact, the powers-that-be had instructed her to return to Italy immediately after talking with Mrs. Hull. Anyway, after violating her contract so many times already, she figured maybe getting out of Dodge was a seriously good idea. Who cared what Inti thought? So what if he blew open her whole story?

And then another, happier idea occurred to her. Now she had some power over them. She could sue them all, right? Or they'd get prosecuted for something, though she couldn't quite figure out for what. Lying to paramedics? Still, she was no longer their little slut, and she hadn't killed the man. All this led her to plan whatever she wanted, if just for the next forty-eight hours. First thing, she had to hunt up Amon.

She went to her studio to put on her lab coat as Inti had suggested and brushed her hair. Should she actually pretend to be a doctor? No, of course not. Everyone on the floor knew her, and even with a stethoscope she would look ridiculous. She decided to brazen it out and made her way to Amon's room, not at all difficult, where she found a curtain drawn against the little glass window. She turned the door handle, but it was locked. Looking around, she tapped on the glass. No one answered, but before she could try again, a nurse she didn't recognize strode by her, observing her movements.

Jenna backed away, authoritatively she thought, however the nurse stopped. "Looking for something?"

"I'm looking for a patient, Amon Walters." Jenna knew she shouldn't say more, but she stumbled on. "He was here a couple of days ago, but now I can't find him."

"He's in the ICU. You can check there, Doctor."

Jenna flew down the steps, passing by a stunned orderly and a woman in a headscarf. The Intensive Care Unit was possessed of a fearful quiet, and Jenna slowed down instantly, trying to blend in. How to find him without blowing the fact that she shouldn't be there at all? She straightened up, aping the studied confidence of the physician, even if she was unprepared to claim such status, but before she had to do too much posturing, Amon's mother appeared around a corner bearing a pillow and a magazine.

"Cate," she cried and came up and hugged her. "I'm glad to see you."

"How is Amon? I've been so worried."

"He's so sick, just very very groggy, but they don't let him feel any more pain."

"Oh my god. Will he pull through?" She clasped onto Lori's sleeve. "Will he live?"

"Oh yes, don't panic. This is normal. He had the kidney transplant yesterday. It's good news, good news at last." Lori pulled her down the hall, and Jenna followed her into a dimly lit room. It was early morning, but the blinds were closed and the room cool, only the machines creating a whir of white noise. Lori still held her hand, and the two approached the bed. The little boy seemed small and incredibly black against the white sheets, but he breathed on his own and was hooked up to only one

IV. He opened his eyes when they approached, and Jenna sat down on the bed next to him. He smiled slightly.

"I'm forty-seven," he said in a low voice.

Jenna touched his hand. "You don't look that old to me."

"He has the kidney of a forty-seven year old woman, that's what he means," Lori said.

"Then you'll always be a good, grown-up boy," Jenna sighed. Amon giggled but then grimaced in pain. "Now, now, don't laugh at anything I say." Again he smiled and turned away slightly like the flirtatious little thing he was.

Lori and Jenna left the room together, the big woman's arm around her shoulder. It had been a long time since anything that familial had happened to her, and she felt as if she might cry. "He got the kidney of a woman killed in a car crash. They told me all about it."

"Oh my goodness. That's wonderful, it's fantastic, I mean I'm sorry for the woman, but so glad for you. Do you want me to stay here a while?"

"We'll probably move to another room soon."

"I'll go back to my studio. The painting I supposedly fixed is to be unveiled tomorrow. I'll find you later."

Back in her workroom, Jenna stared at the Bélange, and from some recent research she had learned it would fetch at least a million dollars at auction, only theoretically though, because right now it was worthless. It hadn't truly stabilized, and she decided to try some quick over-painting to get the images to look finished for the next afternoon's public event. Starting at the nape of the girl's neck, she picked out a pink and a light umber so sumptuous that the colors reminded her of the late Italian Renaissance. She dabbed the brush into the paint and then, with tiny strokes, quickly layered in lines of pigment. The neck softened and turned rosy as she worked and before long almost glowed in front of her. Jenna stood back, pausing to admire her work. She had done something Monsieur Legard would not have liked, altering the colors, but what else could she do? In any case the changes probably wouldn't last.

The odious lawyer called her to reiterate that no one wanted her at the hospital unveiling of the restored painting, no doubt a subdued affair in any case, but she would hear from Mrs. Hull. And then, as she worked away feverishly into the early evening, the Cavanaugh woman popped her head into the room and handed her a note without saying a word. Once again she held a heavy, ivory-colored envelope, on the front of which her name appeared in swooping black letters almost like calligraphy, similar to the note she had received in Italy. She looked up at the waiting woman, who said, "I know, from another era."

"Another time altogether."

She tore open the heavy envelope quickly. "We need to see each other. Come to the unveiling," and it was signed "Sabine Hull." The woman's cell phone number was listed at the bottom of the single page. "I'm to attend the unveiling." The curator just threw out her hands in resignation at the constant changes going on around this event and backed out of the room.

Jenna sighed at this new, heavy commanding note, and almost felt relieved when she heard her cell phone ring. Inti's voice crackled in her ear, "I'm sorry. Can I see you?"

"It's late, I can't, just got a note about something important. I need to go back to my hotel and contemplate."

"Contemplate with me." He promised to come to her.

"No."

"I'm coming over to the Lowell anyway."

Jenna sank down in a velvet chair in the lobby, defeated, nevertheless hungry. She waited less than ten minutes, and when he appeared, she moved to kiss him on the cheek, an unexpected intimacy that Inti took well, if awkwardly. Still, they went out the heavy doors arm in arm, and the concierge smiled after them. At last, some little sign of normalcy in the life of this comely young woman.

The nearby bistro Drago felt dark and fervently active on this Thursday night, and Jenna found herself activated out of her trance and into energy. She looked closely at Inti while he related several of his latest newspaper pieces, trying to hear above the din, responding in ways she had never done before. She saw him as a man of action and good cheer, mysteriously tranquil while she fretted over every little thing. That he knew the "real" story, or at least a good chunk of it, made him all the more attractive, and perversely, the more he talked of his journalistic exploits, the more excited, the less suspicious she got. His true interests remained regional, heavily New York, and so for him what she'd been through might seem like ancient history. The liquor, yes, more of it, the heat of the room, the festive atmosphere, it all loosened her tongue, and at last she said, "You really want to know everything, don't you?"

"You mean I don't already?"

"I've been keeping the secret for so long, I'm not sure I would actually know what to say."

But talk about it she did, starting with the moment she entered the Hull building, snuck upstairs, and placed herself under Vincent, not leaving out the fact of the very real affair with her boss. Unburdened by this relatively free talk, nevertheless she wanted to take it all back as she watched Inti's face. Whatever curiosity he might have had about the titan fell away the closer he got to the revelations of her feelings, because he sensed real passion, maybe even something like love. "I shouldn't have asked." He gathered up the bill and paid it without looking at her.

"But I'm so glad you did. Don't you see, you could never endure not knowing anything. It's like a bomb under the table."

"Or right on the top."

Outside, muffled up as they were, she took his arm and walked him some way down the street. "You did ask. . . ."

"I did, but now I'm kind of horrified. The family and all, and my friends in the press chasing you around."

"It was a long time ago. I didn't know what I was doing."

Inti studied her a moment. "There's a public lens out there, and it focuses for a moment on somebody or other, hot like a magnifying glass in the sun, and what that focus does is blow up, make gigantic, any faults or history of that person. It's entirely distorting and ultimately false. Simple things that happened to you appear sinister, and everything you are or ever did is spun into a web that makes whatever story they want to tell seem true. It happens over and over again. What surprises me is that my cohorts didn't follow you all the way to Europe. Like dogs, half of them are in heat, the other half chasing after their own ass end." But then he looked down, ashamed at the amount of following he himself had done.

"So you understand. Though I was found underneath him, I hadn't actually had sex with him—not that night." She felt herself go red and blank at what she did not say.

"I can accept that," Inti said, breaking through his own confusion. He pulled his thick wool scarf up around his neck and looked toward the street.

"You know, I can walk to my hotel. It's only a few blocks."

"I'll walk with you, then go over to the West Side."

"No, just go on your own. I'm exhausted, and the air will clear my head."

"I'm coming with you!" They walked without saying anything at all and parted awkwardly at the Lowell's front door, one reaching for the other, both just touching with a brief kiss.

Once upstairs, seated on her sumptuous bed, Jenna started channel flipping. War, fire, flood, apple peeling devices, a nice-looking dress for $49.99, men in suits selling coins, a vampire sucking a little blood in his off-time, what a riot of images, none of them comforting. She found a resting point at a cooking show, noting the huge portions the chef touted. As for the formidable Mrs. Hull, she wouldn't respond to the invitation until tomorrow. What would they do together, have coffee? The Upper East Side must be her stomping grounds, every little joint known to her, unless she just glided about in her chauffeur driven car and didn't really see anything out of the darkened windows, ordering in food whenever the chef had his day off. If they went somewhere together, hounds with big imaginations could be anywhere, maybe even Rudolph Hayes himself, waving papers and subpoenas. Once her mind cleared, she realized he had to act in secret, with stealth, he had no other choice, so she was safe from him, at least for the moment.

SEVEN

That Friday Jenna dressed with particular care in a somber black suit with a small sprig of lily-of-the-valley entwined in a buttonhole, appropriate for the ceremony to unveil what was supposed to be the newly rehabilitated Bélange. Would Sabine Hull preside over the affair? Would there be press? Surely not. This was all happening in private, especially since sick children were present in the building. She looked around but saw only one man with a camera, and he stood next to Mrs. Cavanaugh, presumably doing publicity for the hospital. Jenna wondered what in god's name the curator would say about the work, since it might look even wetter now, and she had no idea how long her quick fixes would hold. Worse yet, after this grotesque affair ended, what would Mrs. Hull do? Berate her no doubt for sleeping with her husband and then being so stupid as to be found *in flagrante* on the floor with him. How much of the truth did this woman know? The lie must continue, and the poor woman must hate her still, no way at all to placate her. Jenna so disliked being hated, a dreadful failing that had led her into misery trying to win over a number of disturbed people.

Normally, she should have delighted at this display of her work as she had been in the past, both in Italy and in France, but now, as she entered the festively done-up library she felt giddy with fear, sweating in her clothes. To make matters worse, Amon sat in his wheelchair, his mother by his side, and they waved and cheered her on as she entered the room. Doctors and nurses stood by solemnly, and there, in among them, reigned Mrs. Hull, looking much the same as she had five years before, in a flowery dress with a short black jacket buttoned tight at the waist. It was the curator who announced the repair of the Bélange and introduced "Ms. Cate Myatt" to all assembled as the "master hand" to whom they owed the painting's restored beauty.

Jenna smiled and waved at everyone politely, afraid to look at the Hull woman, but at least no sniper trained an eye her way right at that moment. Up went the curtain, and behold, for all to see was Marc Bélange's newly fixed *Diver*, shimmering in its sumptuous beauty. Jenna had a moment to see the work whole and new. Even in its damaged state, the victim of inherent vice, it had about it still the erotic charge she felt that first time seeing it in Water Mill.

"It's beautiful," she heard Amon cry out, and everyone laughed, beginning to clap.

Apparently Mrs. Hull shied away from public display because she was not introduced, though she was well known to the staff, who, at the end of the brief ceremony, effusively greeted her. Jenna awaited whatever was to come. Just as she bent down to speak to Amon, she felt a strong hand on her arm. The gamine, handsome Mrs. Hull said in a low voice, "Come with me."

In spite of her new look, her European mien, her dark hair, nevertheless Jenna feared that the assembled guests would see the two of them side by side and recognize the players in what had been a major drama in the city. She glanced around in anxiety and hurried out with her. No doubt the context was so different that this could not possibly be, and besides, would any woman have appeared in public with the scandalous young slut who had killed her husband in the act of love?

They walked down the hall together, not speaking, until Sabine Hull pointed toward a door. "No one will bother us here." Inside, an alternate reality prevailed, one that involved air hockey, a ping-pong table, video games, pinball machines, an adolescent's paradise. Jenna didn't know what to do, but Mrs. Hull sat down on the curved leather couch and pointed to a spot next to her. Having settled herself at a distance, Jenna finally got up the courage to look at her. The same sharp jaw line and soft hair, the same willowy frame, the fashionable clothes, older, but not by much. Did she have a lover, a boyfriend? Surely yes, Jenna hoped. "I'm glad we're finally meeting," Sabine Hull said at last, breaking through the dense, complicated air around them.

"Oh, I am too," Jenna interrupted, but then caught herself. "It's been so long." When she thought of how long, she couldn't go on, because she'd been paid for all of it.

"Too long. We should have talked when it first happened, but I had no idea what to say and was too shocked and horrified to get in touch with you."

A teenage boy with his leg in a cast popped his head in the door, and Mrs. Hull rang out in her finely tuned accent, "Come back later, young man."

They waited again in silence. "I'm so sorry about everything," but Jenna really wanted to find out how much she knew.

"It was a difficult situation. My husband was a complex man, brilliant, terrible, impossible to live with, but I loved him, and how he died came as a great shock."

"Yes, it would have been terrible, and my own part in it—"

"I know about your part. It was obvious, no?"

Was it? She had helped the man by helping his family, at least so she'd been told. "It looked bad. I was so ashamed. I still am."

"Miss McCann, you still are a Miss, right?" Jenna nodded her head. "You must give me credit for knowing what was going on. Initially it was not you under the body of my husband."

The ghost within these words crossed over them through the air. One absolute demand in her agreement had been not to reveal the truth to any living human being, because all family members could never know who had occupied that compromised position. Yet this woman claimed to know everything. Was she lying? Was she trying to get some admission out of her?

"I'm under an obligation to say only certain things."

"I know. I created the document you signed." Sabine Hull poked at her thick gold watch, frowned, and began to wind it.

What had she just said? Jenna felt dizzy, but after steadying herself, she rose to pour the two of them coffee from the carafe in the corner. It looked particularly bitter and black; nevertheless, when she handed the cup to her, Mrs. Hull seemed grateful.

"I was certainly aware that my husband had made love several times to Tasha."

Carefully Jenna sat down again on the couch. "I thought that was the whole reason I was there, to deflect you from knowing about her."

Mrs. Hull smiled wearily. "That is how the matter was meant to appear."

"You mean it wasn't true?"

"They had slept together that night, or he was in the act of doing so." The self-contained woman struggled with her words. "But the reasons, the motives may not have been clear."

"Motives?"

"I had asked her to do that."

Jenna momentarily forgot where she was. She looked around at the gleaming toys and games that encircled them. "I don't understand."

"I wanted Tasha to seduce my husband." The woman before her sipped on the brutal coffee.

"Why would you do that?"

"We needed to protect ourselves from him. He suspected us, and it was driving him crazy. In fact he had had a nervous breakdown of sorts, at least insofar as someone that far gone could go any more nuts."

"Us?" Jenna felt like choking.

"Tasha and myself. So she offered to engineer a seduction that would throw him off entirely. He would think she had an interest in *him*, rather than in me. You see, she and I had been involved, off and on, for over a year. Then he died in her arms. Sort of poetic, that, but she panicked."

"I was just there as the public face . . . someone to take the fall?"

"Exactly. We needed no more press scrutiny—there had been some of that already, and it frightened both of us, especially because of the children. Vince would, I think, have tried to kill me if he'd known the truth, but once he was dead, there was still the family and the public."

"You're not serious."

"He had ways of killing that wouldn't have involved guns, although he certainly had plenty of those. Something much more lethal: shame, disgrace, violent rejection, public humiliation. He would have thought of terrible acts, though I've often wondered how far he would have gone, given our girls. If he had known for sure that I was having an affair with a woman, I can't even imagine the steps he would have taken, so we agreed that Tasha should seduce him. She did—not very difficult, it turned out. That threw him off the scent."

"I always thought it involved her race, wanting to hide that."

"Not only her race but much, much more. His wife was having an affair with a black lesbian—he of the great mind, great ego, great body, too, if truth be told, and wealth beyond all imagining. You served a useful purpose, to deflect and distract. And, of course we knew he was sleeping with you at the time."

"How did you find out about that?"

"The Water Mill housekeeper is a very good friend of mine."

Jenna felt her face go red. "That time at the hotel when you were crying, was that about Tasha?"

"I was crying because I thought she had been unfaithful to me."

Jenna tried to stand up but couldn't and sat back down again, leaning in toward the other woman, trying not to yell in this most quiet of places. "Why now? Why are you telling me all this? It makes the whole thing even more horrible. You ruined my life, you and your goddamned sweetheart."

"Really? All that money, all that time and freedom? You were nobody and nothing."

"I was a young girl, enchanted by my job and the remarkable world I'd landed in. I was even enchanted by *him*. You used me and then forced me out of the country."

"Did you really think all that sex and good fun came to you for free? Besides, it could just as well have been you underneath him anyway. He was on the way out, so to speak, but with whom? We could have held a lottery."

"I suppose that's a comfort to you, isn't it? That I was guilty and might as well be punished, even if it was for the wrong crime."

"There was something more threatening, more uncontrollable, and it made you the ideal choice."

Jenna looked down at her expensive shoes, bought and paid for, and now perhaps she would find out how.

"Have you never guessed?"

Jenna looked away, trying to focus on another childish drawing on the wall over Sabine Hull's shoulder.

"He was in love with you. After all the partying, the travel, the rampant philandering, the lies—all that meant little to me because it was nothing to him. Then he fell in love with you. I didn't have to tell you, ever, but I thought perhaps it would help you to know." Sabine Hull looked down, pulling a cigarette out of her bag and lighting up, despite where they were. "Jorge knew it too."

Jenna stared at the pinball machines and the funny faces drawn on the walls to amuse the children, and now she felt empty, shattered, as if she'd been punched, but also suddenly filled with compassion for Vincent Hull, the real broken-hearted lover in all this. She stood up, gathering her coat and scarf. "Of course you had to tell me, because that's how heartless you are. I must have been the only one to have any feeling at all for him," she muttered and scrambled out the door, running down the hall, out the front door into a howling wind that almost knocked her down.

EIGHT

The next day, though she was scheduled to leave on the night flight to Rome, Jenna stayed in bed and drank tea and ate toast, treating herself like the victim of a horrid disease that could only be cured by hiding under the covers. In love with her? Vincent Hull was in love with her? So much so that it threatened his world? She looked back now on her recent talk with Jorge and wondered if he had been trying to tell her this too. She wanted to take comfort from it, be glad of it, but she could only wonder and grieve in confusion.

Drawn out of this funk by a ringing phone, she picked up. "We're going back to Ohio right away, Cate, so if you want to say goodbye to Amon, now is the time." Dragging herself out of bed, she took a shower and washed her hair, staring at herself in the mirror, convinced she had aged forty years. She looked the same, just dark circles under her eyes, but she felt as if she almost didn't want to live in the world that had opened before her. She could feel its weight right there upon her chest, a weight of knowledge so intense she couldn't even fathom how it had gotten there. Rousing herself, though, she sat down and wrote a very large check to Amon and slipped it into a hotel envelope.

At the hospital, she started to breathe again and even raced up the steps to the second floor, finding her way to room 207. Just in time, it turned out, because Lori had two bags in hand, while little Amon occupied a wheelchair once again. "Oh there you are," the boy said. "We couldn't figure out where you had gone to."

Jenna grabbed one of the suitcases, giving the boy a kiss on the cheek at the same time. "I'm so sorry, I had an illness in the family, something like that anyway." She handed Lori the envelope.

"What's this?" Lori glanced at her.

"Open it when you get home. It'll be more of a surprise then."

Amon tugged on her sleeve. "We asked the nurse to give you something I made for you. I was afraid you wouldn't come. She has it, and you have to go back and get it."

"I will, I will, but I should have a present for you."

"We didn't know we were leaving today. It's all a bit of a shock. They seem to be throwing us out." As usual Lori looked as if she'd been caught in a windstorm. A nurse strode up behind them and began pushing the wheelchair toward the elevator. The three of them had that strange, empty feeling that resulted from having spent too much time in the hospital dead zone.

"I'll miss you," Jenna said. She thought she might start to cry, but to stop herself she bent down and kissed the top of the boy's head. He looked up and put both his warm arms around her, and she held on, feeling his whole little body nestled against her. He dropped one arm and whipped a cell phone out of his pocket.

"You can call me any time. I have a camera on my computer at home. You can watch me on video."

"I'm going to do that."

She lingered as the two climbed into a cab and stared at the snowflakes beginning to fall, and then she walked slowly back upstairs. At the nurse's station on the second floor she stopped and waited while they ignored her, until at last one of them responded to her request for help.

"Yes, there is something, let's see . . . Vonda, where is the picture for Ms. Myatt? Wait, here it is." She pulled a smallish canvas up off the floor.

Amon had painted in oils a portrait of himself sitting before the canvas, viewed from behind, brush in hand. Over his shoulder a woman looked on, but turned away slightly toward the window, staring at the buildings outside, rendered like walls blocking the view. Jenna was that woman, her hair a little too brown, the chin a bit lopsided, but herself nonetheless. Some have skill as technicians, some have art, and then there are some who can see, and Amon could see. He could see *her*, at least. She turned the painting over and on the back saw that he had written in bold slashes of red paint, "My Friend Cate."

Jenna ran down the hall, trying to stifle her sobs but not really doing so. Then she hid her face in her hands, and several people reached out sympathetically to her, thinking she mourned a sick child. At last she reached the library, where the Bélange hung right alongside the other masterpieces. The room was empty, and now Jenna stared at the incredibly vivid picture of that young woman holding her wet hair behind her head, up to her breasts in the shimmering blue and white water. Up to her breasts.

In later years she could not remember how she got back to the hotel, only that it was through falling snow. Rushing to get her things packed and take her leave, she propped Amon's painting on a chair in the lobby, but not before she paid her grotesquely huge bill. Hotel living, such as it was, no longer suited her at all, and she longed for her own place in Italy, for her friends, but above all for the vision she had had of her life before these awful women had taken her in hand. Jenna had resisted the urge to call Tasha and confirm all that Mrs. Hull had said. She didn't need to confirm it; she knew it was true. It made brutal sense, but why hadn't she asked more questions at the time of Hull's death? Obviously, youth and panic and a dead man on the floor. She saw now that they were the desperate ones, so frenzied to hide their affair that they picked her, an easy target, a sympathetic victim, easy to lie to. But they were jealous too. Incredibly they saw her as a bigger threat than anyone else around them, so why not destroy her life and her reputation? It was the perfect revenge. Whatever this all meant, it was time to leave New York and go home. She had such a place there, not ideal, certainly, but a place where people liked her, even loved her, for real.

What to do about Inti? He had been leaving her messages, most of which she had left unanswered. She wanted to see him, but after these latest revelations, she felt even more secretive. The hypocrisy of these people, the lies— they would do anything. And now she possessed what they had feared revealing for years. Maybe they'd have her killed. Oh god, she thought, I've gone mad, and isn't that exactly what they want?

Jenna had hours before she had to leave the city, but they seemed an eternity. Should she just drink herself into a stupor, trying to forget? That seemed like a bad idea. Vincent, Vincent, she kept calling out in her mind. Why had she not known? She should be happy he loved her, but she could not feel that at all. Even in the midst of her packing hysteria, still she had wanted to dress herself up for something, for anything, and she had chosen a dark-blue wraparound dress that flattered her figure and made her feel sexy. Sexy for what?

Her cell phone pinged. Inti. Oh the wretched persistence of the man. Their conversation was short, and she told him her time was limited but arranged to meet him at an Indian restaurant over on Park.

At Akhbar, she now told Inti the upshot of her relationship with the Hull family, specifically the fact that Tasha and Sabine Hull had been in love. He took a bite from his chicken korma and boti kabab, fascinated by the tale. He spotted it instantaneously as one that was worth money, and beyond that, awards, fame, and every other gift the profession had to offer. In this time of hysterical celebrity worship, it represented pay dirt of the most serious kind. He didn't know what he could or would do, but this secret inflamed him in a way he rarely felt, and as Jenna talked excitedly, sometimes enraged, other times mystified—she was nervous, he could tell—he wondered about the nature of his own loyalties. He wanted to reassure her, but he wasn't sure he could. Yet it was grotesque to think of revealing everything, because this girl, this woman, had revealed it all to him without a care, without an inkling that he could betray her. The two of them seemed to sink under a wave of New York nausea, and so as she talked on, he resolved to get her out of the place and back to his apartment.

"I'm going, I'm going." She struggled once again into her coat. He held her tight as they emerged into the heavily falling snow. "*Andiamoci.*" She kissed him on the cheek. "I'm Italian now. I'm also slightly drunk."

So far she hadn't mentioned leaving for the airport. What was a little plane ticket? A nothing in her ocean of money. She could rebook, she could toss it into the East River, or give it to the USO for a lonely serviceman wanting to get home. Seriously drunk, she tottered a bit and leaned on Inti's arm.

He took her back to his apartment, where she immediately suggested another drink. "Oh, let's just watch bad television or listen to music," he said.

"Yes!!" She sank down onto his couch, still in her

coat, but he lifted her up and took her to his bedroom, pulling off the coat, sliding off the dress, leaving her in her sexy black thong. There she rested, while he went back out and sprawled on the couch, head not clear enough to figure out the future.

In the very early hours of the morning, snow covered every street, every solitary tree, all parked cars. Jenna had gotten up early, head pounding, mouth dry. Out in the living room Inti slept, one arm curled beneath his head. He looked so innocent, so good, better than that whole gang she had encountered at *NewsLink.* Maybe she shouldn't leave at all, just make love to him until his head flew off, and he promised her the world. But no, that didn't seem possible. "They" would try to deport her again, though she wasn't so sure what they could do now that Mrs. Hull had violated the contract. Or would they claim she had demanded the meeting? Too much, all too much to think of with a hangover.

Snow the first day of March, how mystically appropriate. Cabs remained where they had stopped in the middle of the road, and a bus lay diagonally across 72nd Street, frozen into a mound of snow. All had closed down, the whole world of noise and motion that was normally Manhattan. Jenna sat at the window while her erstwhile lover slept soundly, hardly moving. Nothing moved outside either, and the fearsome silence took her back to that night almost five years before, when she had slid her body under the cold, dead frame of Vincent Hull, still hot at the center.

No chance of getting to the airport now.

THE END

ACKNOWLEDGMENTS

Profound thanks to:

My daughter, Vanessa Taylor, always my first and finest reader.

Elizabeth Trupin-Pulli, brilliant agent and wonderful friend.

Jesse Holcomb, adept at just about everything.

Elizabeth Kaye, a sharp-eyed editor and a terrific writer.

I am so grateful to the inspired women at She Writes Press and SparkPoint Studio: Brooke Warner, Samantha Strom, Cait Levin, Crystal Patriarche, Keely Platte, and Paige Herbert.

As always, for my two best friends, Dorothy Duff Brown and Diana Ketcham.

Finally, for Eileen and Marie Rooney, without whose inspiration there would be no book.

Author photo by Deborah Geffner

A.R. TAYLOR is an award-winning playwright, essayist, and fiction writer. Her debut novel, *Sex, Rain, and Cold Fusion*, won a Gold Medal for Best Regional Fiction at the Independent Publisher Book Awards 2015, was a USA Best Book Awards finalist, and was named one of the 12 Most Cinematic Indie Books of 2014 by *Kirkus Reviews*. She's been published in the *Los Angeles Times*, the *Southwest Review*, *Pedantic Monthly*, *The Cynic* online magazine, the *Berkeley Insider*, *So It Goes*—the Kurt Vonnegut Memorial Library Magazine on Humor, *Red Rock Review*, and *Rosebud*. In her past life, she was head writer on two Emmy-winning series for public television. She has performed at the Gotham Comedy Club in New York, Tongue & Groove in Hollywood, and Lit Crawl LA. You can find her video blog, *Trailing Edge: Ideas Whose Time Has Come and Gone* at her website, www.lonecamel.com.